## Praise for the Café Cinema Mystery Series

"Chock full of engaging characters and engrossing plot twists, this buzz-worthy cozy is the reel deal.
— Kathleen Valenti,
Agatha-Nominated Author of *Protocol*

"Charming doesn't begin to describe the wonderful debut novel in bestselling author Vickie Fee's new Café Cinema Series. From its quirky, small town setting to its delightful protagonist and gripping mystery, *My Fair Latte* is a book worthy of a cozy mystery Oscar!"
— Ellen Byron,
Agatha Award-Winning Author of *Mardi Gras Murder*

"Love coffee? Love classic films? Love charming small towns, memorable characters, and intriguing mysteries? Then you'll love *My Fair Latte*, the first Café Cinema Mystery, by Vickie Fee. She blends humor, suspense, and heart, swirls in a touch of romance, and sprinkles a dash of family drama to create a story as intricate as a cup of latte art."
— Alexia Gordon,
Lefty Award-Winning Author of *Murder in G Major*

"An old movie theater, a want-to-go-there tourist town, designer coffee, a plucky heroine, and a murder? Sign me up for Vickie Fee's *My Fair Latte* and please send more!"
— Barbara Ross,
Author of the Maine Clambake Mysteries

# MY FAIR LATTE

**The Café Cinema Mystery Series
by Vickie Fee**

MY FAIR LATTE (#1)

# MY FAIR LATTE

## A CAFÉ CINEMA MYSTERY

## Vickie Fee

HENERY PRESS

Copyright

MY FAIR LATTE
A Café Cinema Mystery
Part of the Henery Press Mystery Collection

First Edition | March 2020

Henery Press, LLC
www.henerypress.com

Trade Paperback ISBN-13: 978-1-63511-579-6
Digital epub ISBN-13: 978-1-63511-580-2
Kindle ISBN-13: 978-1-63511-581-9
Hardcover ISBN-13: 978-1-63511-582-6

Printed in the United States of America

*For Granddaddy Blair*
*who always drank coffee for breakfast, lunch, and dinner*

# ACKNOWLEDGMENTS

Thank you to Steven at the Delft Bistro for giving me a peek behind the marquee. Thanks to the baristas around town for answering my questions and letting me stare as they work. Thank you to my fab agent, Jessica Faust. Big thanks to the whole Henery Press team— Kendel Lynn, Christina Rogers, Art Molinares, and a special thanks to editor Maria Edwards. For their friendship and advice, thanks to my blog mates at Chicks on the Case—Lisa Mathews, Marla Cooper, Kellye Garrett, Cynthia Kuhn, Leslie Karst, Becky Clark, Kathleen Valenti, and a special thanks to Ellen Byron who was an early reader on this one. And much love to my husband, John, who keeps me going and cheers me across my deadlines.

# CHAPTER 1

I stepped out of my beat-up Honda and took a good look, scanning from sidewalk to sky. Broken lights circling the marquee, chipping paint on the glass block ticket booth, and a bullet-shaped tower with spire, all hinted at the theater's former glory. While it may have been a glamorous leading lady in its prime, the Star Movie Palace was now a faded beauty whose slip was showing from beneath its tattered couture.

Still gazing up, I felt a splat on my shoulder as a pigeon took flight from the roof. I took the unwelcome avian attention as a sign that maybe it was time to take a look inside. I reached in my pocket and pulled out a fast food place napkin leftover from lunch to wipe the pigeon droppings off my shoulder.

The key the attorney had given me didn't fit the padlock on the chain threaded through the shooting star door handles. I walked around to the back of the building looking for a way in. At the alley entrance, the key slipped easily into a windowless metal door. I gasped as the heavy door slammed behind me with a jarring thud and left me standing alone in a dark building. The smell of stale popcorn hung in the air. Using the flashlight on my cell phone, I fumbled into the lobby, where sunlight streamed in, revealing that the inside of the building was almost as shabby as the façade.

"*Eeew*, what the..." I muttered, my shoe pulling against something sticky.

Looking up, I spied a door labeled "Projection Room. Do Not Enter."

*I've always wondered what it looks like inside one of those.*

Guided by my dim light I carefully ascended the dark staircase to the projection room. Once inside, I heard unnerving scratching and squeaking noises.

"It's only a ghost," I whispered to myself.

Not that I believed in ghosts, but I preferred the image of being haunted by a kindly spirit to the thought of being trapped in a dark building with a colony of mice.

I was standing beside a projector, looking down at the auditorium through the little window when a voice behind me bellowed, "Who are you and how did you get in here?"

Goose pimples raced up my arms as I spun around to see a shadowy figure in the doorway. It was no kindly spirit. It was a flesh-and-blood man, shining a light much brighter than a cell phone into my face.

"I'm the owner of this theater," I said, my voice quavering. I lifted my hand to shade my eyes from the interrogator's spotlight. "Who are you?"

"Leon Baxter owned this theater," the voice continued to bark at me from the shadows.

"My name is Halley Greer. Uncle Leon left the theater to me. And could you *please* move that light out of my face."

"He never mentioned you to me," the raspy voice said as he lowered his flashlight a bit.

"Maybe not, but he mentioned me to his attorney—the one who gave me this key." I said, holding it up.

He flipped a switch and an overhead fixture flickered before illuminating the small room.

*Why didn't I think to try the light switch?*

When I'd recovered my sight from flashlight blindness, I saw a slim, hunch-shouldered man with wiry gray hair who didn't look nearly as scary as he had sounded from behind the spotlight.

"I'm George Mayfield. If you're his niece, why weren't you at the funeral?"

"I'm his great-niece, and unfortunately, I didn't hear about his passing until *after* the funeral. Uncle Leon and my mother hadn't kept in touch in recent years." I didn't mention that my mother barely communicated with me, much less her late uncle.

"Is he buried nearby? I'd like to visit his grave."

"You can do that tomorrow. I'll take you, if you like. Have you checked into a hotel?"

"No. I was planning to stay in the apartment."

"Oh. Come on, I'll take you up."

"How did you know I was here?" I asked.

George flipped on lights as we walked.

"A neighboring business owner phoned and told me they'd seen someone wandering around the theater. I've been trying to keep an eye on the place since Leon's passing."

We continued down the hallway I'd first come through and up a staircase. The apartment door was unlocked.

"Is there a key to this?"

"I'm sure there is...somewhere. But Leon never locked it."

"I'm not sure I'm comfortable with that."

"Of course. I'll re-key the lock tomorrow and get a key and a spare made for you."

"Thanks," I said doubtfully.

I had no particular reason to trust this wild-haired stranger, except that he had known my uncle.

"If I'd known you were coming, I would've straightened up a bit. Leon never was much of a housekeeper." George opened a couple of windows a crack to let some air in.

A quick glance around the living room-kitchen combo confirmed that Uncle Leon was a slob, and that he most likely didn't have a female companion who spent time here. Even women who aren't much for housekeeping would generally draw the line at unsanitary.

"It's fine. I'm sure it's nothing a little soap and water can't fix."

A bit of bleach and air freshener couldn't hurt either, I thought.

After a quick look around we returned downstairs and I asked where I should park. George directed me to a reserved spot in the alley. He carried my suitcase up to the apartment, and then offered to buy me dinner. I protested briefly—and only half-heartedly. The thought of letting George pay for dinner hurt my pride a little. But my pride could afford the hit more than my wallet. The lawyer had given me the key and five hundred dollars in expense money to check out my inheritance. I had far less than that in my checking account in Nashville. Not to mention no job, no prospects, and a deadbeat former roommate who skipped out owing me two month's rent.


A faded welcome sign proclaimed that the tourist town of Utopia Springs, Arkansas had a population of 2,281. But its outdoor theater productions, concentration of funky art galleries, Victorian bed-and-breakfasts, and the natural beauty of the surrounding Ozarks brought in a half-million visitors a year, according to the sales pitch on the chamber of commerce web site. George played tour guide, pointing out restaurants and other businesses as we strolled down the sidewalk, streaked with late afternoon shadows. And I do mean *down*. We walked downhill, my calf muscles in braking mode, as a trolley filled with tourists chugged up the steep incline and passed us on the street. The group climbing up the hill toward us was easy enough to peg as a family on vacation. A woman in a straw hat, a man wearing Bermuda shorts and socks with sandals, and a sullen teen dressed all in black trailing behind his parents.

We passed a souvenir shop with t-shirts; a gift shop called Bell, Bath and Candle, with a display of wind chimes, handmade soaps, and candles in the window; and a bar called the Wooden Nickel Saloon, weaving our way through chattering tourists as they spilled out of shops and trudged past us. Tree-covered mountain peaks soared upward beyond the shops, making it seem the quaint town had been air-lifted in and dropped here.

We bypassed a diner and a pizza parlor as we made our way to the bottom of the hill, where George made a quick turn and walked through the front door of a small art gallery. The sign on the door read, "Mayfield's." Paintings, mostly of downtown Utopia Springs and landscapes of the Ozark Mountains, hung on the walls. Prints and postcards were also on display, along with a case of handmade silver and copper jewelry.

George locked the front door behind us.

"I hate it when Trudy leaves the shop wide open and unattended," he muttered.

"Is this your gallery, George?"

"Yep."

I followed as he walked into a back studio with clerestory windows. Propped on an easel was a half-finished painting of a chapel in the woods. Through the back door and up an outdoor staircase, he opened a door, unleashing the intoxicating aroma of garlic, onion, and basil.

"There are fancier places in town to eat, but you won't find spaghetti any better than Trudy's."

A gray-haired woman, who couldn't have been more than five feet tall or weighed much more than a hundred pounds, stood at a gas stove with her back to us, steam billowing around her.

"Have you brought company home for supper again

without giving me warning?"

She turned around and I could tell she was surprised to see me.

"I'm sorry, I don't want to impose," I said, embarrassed.

"No, no. Come on in and let me see you." Her kind hazel eyes looked me up and down before a broad smile crept across her face.

"You're younger and better looking than the characters George usually drags home for supper."

"Trudy, meet, er...sorry, I didn't get your name."

"Halley Greer," I said, extending my hand to shake hers.

"Nice to meet you," she said.

"She's Leon's great-niece and the new owner of the Star Movie Palace."

"That's wonderful!" Trudy exclaimed, clasping her hands. "I didn't know Leon had family. But I'm glad to know he did. Where are my manners? Please, sit down. Would you like a glass of wine?"

"That sounds awesome," I said. George and I sat down while Trudy performed a graceful figure eight move through the compact kitchen, collecting stemware and an open bottle of wine.

Placemats with a sunflower design adorned each of the four places at the turquoise blue table. After Trudy had poured wine for each of us, she lifted her glass and said, "Here's to family, and to absent friends."

I know a lot more about coffee than wine, but one sip told me this was a quality Chianti, not a cheap eight-dollar bottle, which was what my budget normally allowed.

"I'm delighted you're taking over the theater, Halley," Trudy said.

"Well, we still have to see about that. But I'm here to check into the possibility."

"What do you mean? If Leon left the theater to you, he obviously wanted you to have it. You're not just going to sell it for a quick buck, are you?" George said, arching his bushy eyebrows, which made him look both fierce and comical at the same time.

After a stunned moment, I said, "No one was more surprised than me to learn Uncle Leon had left me anything. I hadn't seen him in...years." I stopped short of saying how many years.

"Well, maybe you should've—" George started, but Trudy interrupted.

"George. This is a lot to take in. Inheriting a business, moving to a new city. Naturally, Halley needs time to think things through," Trudy said as she firmly massaged his shoulder.

"I s'pose so," he said, avoiding eye contact with me.

Part of me wanted to get up and leave. I didn't need a perfect stranger telling me what to do. But part of me, mostly my stomach, wanted some of that spaghetti.

Here's some bread to tide you over," Trudy said, placing a warm baguette on the table and pouring olive oil onto a plate for dipping. I moistened the edge of my bread in the olive oil and took a bite.

"Mmmm, this is delicious," I said with my mouth full.

"I can't take credit for making the bread. But we have a wonderful bakery in town, as well as a shop that sells the absolute best olive oils and specialty vinegars."

I and my grateful stomach decided to cut George some slack, since he'd been good friends with my uncle and was obviously still grieving.

"Tell me about the gallery, George. Are all the paintings out front yours?"

I had spotted his signature on a couple of pieces as we

walked through.

"Yes. I paint and Trudy makes the jewelry. She also teaches a yoga class three times a week."

"Tuesdays, Thursdays, and Saturdays," Trudy chimed in. "You're welcome to join us anytime. Strictly locals. There are pricey yoga classes that cater to tourists at the hotel spa, with lots of incense and flute music."

Trudy set down plates of spaghetti smothered with marinara sauce in front of us, before grating fresh parmesan on top and joining us at the table.

"So, Halley, what kind of work do you do, or were you doing before you came here?" George asked.

"I'm between gigs at the moment, but I'm a barista by trade."

"You mean you worked in a coffee shop?" George said.

Trudy shot him a sharp look, and by his pained expression I'm guessing she also gave him a swift kick in the shin.

"I believe baristas are trained experts in coffee, like sommeliers are trained experts in wine. Isn't that right, Halley?"

"In theory," I said, sheepishly. "In college, with a major in International Studies, I spent two semesters in Peru as an intern with a coffee company. I fell in love with everything about the coffee business."

I'd also fallen in love with the plantation owner's son, but didn't mention it.

"Dinner was wonderful," I said after gorging on pasta. "Thank you, Trudy. And thank you, George, for inviting me to enjoy your wife's cooking."

"I never said we were married."

"Oh, I'm sorry," I said, feeling my face flush.

"Don't pay any attention to him," Trudy said with a generous laugh as she swatted at George with her napkin. I've been shackled in holy wedlock to this old coot for more than twenty years."

George gave Trudy a pat on the behind as she stood and started clearing the table.

"Let me do the dishes, it's the least I can do," I said, picking up my plate as I stood.

"No, ma'am," she said, confiscating my plate. "You're company. Besides, I cook and George washes the dishes. That's our secret to a happy marriage."

Watching George slip on an apron made me smile.

"Then I guess I better head back. Thanks again."

"She plans to stay in Leon's apartment," George interjected.

"Oh, Halley, you can't sleep in that trash heap," Trudy said. "Please spend the night on our sofa. As Leon's oldest friends, the least we can do is show his heir a little Southern hospitality."

After I politely declined the offer, Trudy said firmly that she'd be by in the morning to help me clean up the apartment. Having seen the state of the place, I didn't decline *that* offer.

We exchanged phone numbers, Trudy insisting I call day or night if I needed anything. We said our goodnights and I started making my way back, forging up the steep hill we'd come down on our way to George and Trudy's place. The sun began to dip behind the mountains and a slight breeze stirred the sultry August air. As I walked past the bar I could hear off-key karaoke as some drunks belched out the chorus of Willie Nelson's "On the Road Again."

*Heir.* That's how Trudy had referred to me.

I suppose that's what I was, although I hadn't thought of myself in those terms. "Beneficiary" was the word the attorney had used. People joke about a rich uncle dying and leaving them a fortune. This rundown theater and trashed apartment wasn't exactly a fortune, but it was all Uncle Leon had. Why did he leave it to me—a great-niece he hadn't seen in twenty years?

# CHAPTER 2

Back at the apartment, a quick look in the bedroom convinced me that the mattress should be burned. The worn leather recliner in the main room seemed like the safest bet as a place to sleep for the night. I cleared off the pile of dirty laundry and empty beer cans and draped a beach towel from my suitcase over it.

After changing into my pajamas, I settled into the recliner with my robe as a blanket and turned off the table lamp. A streetlight cast a blue glow in the room. I'm not usually the jumpy type, but in a big, empty building by myself, knowing there was no lock on the apartment door, my eyes refused to close all the way. Through a fringe of lashes, I stared into the glassy eyes of a deer head mounted high on the wall.

Giving in to paranoia, I got up and pushed a stack of boxes against the front door and grabbed a golf club I'd seen leaned against a bookcase. With it propped beside the recliner, I climbed back into my makeshift bed and managed to close my very tired eyes, but still couldn't sleep. It didn't help that since I'd turned out the lights I could hear the same scratching and squeaking sounds I'd heard earlier.

"Kindly spirits," I whispered to myself.

I was nervously humming no tune in particular when I saw a whir of motion out of the corner of my eye. Something appeared to leap from behind the loveseat toward the dining table, making a hissing sound. I grabbed the golf club, sprang out of my chair, and knocked the lamp off the table as I switched it on.

Standing in the batter-up position, I stared into the bright green eyes of a calico cat, who stared back indifferently, sporting a black patch over one eye and a brown patch over the other.

The obviously well-fed cat jumped down from the table and walked purposefully to the kitchen before disappearing under the skirted microwave stand. I pulled back the fabric to see a full water bowl and an empty food bowl. A search through the cabinets turned up some cat food, which I shook into the bowl.

"How did you get in here?" I asked to no reply.

I looked behind a lumpy loveseat, which was under a window against an outside wall. A small swinging pet door exited to the fire escape.

*This must be Uncle Leon's cat.*

Although the apartment had a stale odor, it didn't smell of cat urine, which led me to believe the cat was housebroken. I knelt and held out my hand, not expecting much. But the kitty walked right up to me, and I scooped her into my arms without incurring any scratches.

"Tomorrow, I'll have to ask Trudy what your name is," I said, stroking her soft fur.

Back in the recliner, she seemed content to curl up on my legs, and I finally drifted off to sleep.


Sunlight slashing through the blinds woke me. My four-legged companion was gone.

Uncle Leon's coffeemaker, like everything else in the kitchen, would require a thorough scrub before use, and I wished I had packed my French press. I raked my fingers through unruly dark curls, pulled on yesterday's jeans and a fresh t-shirt, and smeared on some lipstick before slipping on my shoes. With cash and key tucked in my pocket, I headed out in search of coffee.

A place called The Muffin Man up the hill at the end of the block caught my attention. It seemed like a safe bet. As I opened the bakery door, I could smell deliciousness. Dough baking, sugary vapors, cinnamon, nutmeg—and coffee. The man behind the counter, the Muffin Man, I presume, had a pleasant face and the physique of the Pillsbury Doughboy. After I placed my order for a cinnamon roll and large coffee, I heard my name. When I turned, Trudy was standing behind me, her wild, steam-infused hair from last night pulled up into a tidy bun.

"I was on my way to your place and spotted you coming in here," she said. "That cinnamon roll smells enticing. After breakfast we can tackle cleaning."

*I wondered how long it had been since she'd seen Uncle Leon's apartment and if she realized a hazmat suit was in order.*

"That's sweet of you, Trudy. But you have a business to run, and you already made me a lovely dinner."

"Nonsense. I was cooking supper anyway. Besides, it's better for my and George's relationship if we don't spend too much time in the shop together."

Trudy and I collected our orders and sat by the door in bistro chairs with curlicue metal backs at one of the few empty tables in the place. A tall guy in khaki shorts, wearing a t-shirt stretched taut over rippling muscles, walked in and stared at me as he spoke to Trudy. After taking note of his baby blues and strong jawline, I looked over to Trudy.

"Hi, Nick. Please join us. I'd like you to meet Halley Greer."

"Hello," I said.

"Nice to meet you, Halley." He reached over to shake my hand as he took a seat across from me.

"Halley's the new owner of the theater. She's Leon's great-niece."

"Well, congrats," he said. "Do you plan to stay or sell?"

"Halley only just arrived, Nick," she said with the instructive glare of a kindergarten teacher.

"Oh, of course. I apologize. It's just...you look so young. What could you know about running a business?" he said, digging a deeper hole for himself with every word.

Despite the fact he was obviously a little dense, and lacking in social graces, even he realized he'd been offensive.

"I'm sorry. Let me start over. I'm Nick Raiford and I run Ozark Trail and Stream down the street, selling bikes, kayaks, rock-climbing, and camping gear and such. I'm also a kayaking and backpacking guide. If you decide you ever want to speak to me again, stop by. I'd be glad to talk to you about the local business and tourist trade," he said, getting up and slinking toward the counter. A few moments later, with a large coffee in hand, he shot me a smile and a weak wave as he left.

"Nick's not a smooth talker, but he's a nice guy once you get to know him," Trudy said, as if reading my thoughts.

"I'm sure he is."

I wasn't sure if I wanted to get to know him better or not, but I still enjoyed the view as he walked away.

Back at my apartment—*my* apartment. I'd only just arrived yesterday but was already thinking of this as my new home. Trudy and I made surprisingly quick work of making the place habitable, although I'd still have stacks of boxes to sort through.

After working at a frantic pace all morning, I felt worn out, while my co-cleaner, who I guessed to be about forty years my senior, wasn't even winded.

*Maybe I should sign up for her yoga class.*

"I have to get back to the gallery. George has a medical appointment. It's with an acupuncture therapist," she said in a near whisper. "But don't tell him I told you."

Trudy started to leave but stopped at the door and turned around. "I almost forgot. I've arranged a date for you for a late supper tomorrow night."

"Who with?" I asked, afraid she was scheming to push me into the arms of Nick from the bakery.

"Kendra Williams, who owns the escape rooms business across the street. She's a doll, and probably about your age. She'll phone you to arrange the details. I'll see you later. Oh, and here's a little something for you," she said, tossing me a baggie of homemade cookies.

I stretched my legs out on the faded green sofa and savored a couple of bites of a scrumptious oatmeal chocolate chip cookie. I'd been dying to look through some of Uncle Leon's personal papers, hoping to learn something about my benefactor who, despite the blood relation, was a stranger to me.

I sat down at the desk, opened the top drawer and leafed through business cards, sticks of gum, expired coupons— nothing personal. The drawer stuck as I tried to close it. When I pulled it out, something fell from the wooden slide underneath. A black and white photograph of Uncle Leon and his late wife. I had only vague memories of meeting him as a child and didn't recall seeing photos, since my mom was largely estranged from her relatives. But the family resemblance was undeniable. Uncle Leon favored my mom—and my brother, Josh. I brushed my fingers tenderly over the photo. Tears stung my eyes.

"That's enough of that," I said to myself. I put the photo in the drawer and wiped my eyes with the hem of my t-shirt.

As eager as I was to dig through Uncle Leon's personal effects, if I seriously wanted to take over the theater I needed to look at the financials. I grabbed a key ring lying on the desk and headed down to the business office just off the lobby. It turned out to be almost as big a mess as the apartment. The desk was piled with papers—and not in neat stacks. I tried the filing cabinet first, thinking there might be some semblance of order there. Thumbing through, I found a folder labeled "tax returns." The most recent return I saw was from three years ago, but that would at least give me an idea of the theater's revenue. It wasn't nearly as much money as I had hoped. I reminded myself that the building not only housed the business, but also provided me a home. I excavated papers on the desk and in the file cabinet for hours, sorting them into stacks, before dragging a pile of files upstairs with me.

I plodded up the steps to the apartment and discovered a key in the lock and another dangling from a string attached to it. Apparently, George had changed out the lock while I was gone.

I drank a beer I found in the fridge and polished off the rest of Trudy's cookies as I pored over papers, crunching numbers late into the night. I fell asleep in the recliner with my notebook computer on my lap and papers strewn about the floor.

I'm not sure when I had fallen asleep, but it was in the afternoon when I awoke. My feet were leaden as I got up to face the day—and the harsh financial realities that had come into focus in the wee hours of the morning.

The attorney who had sent me the key had asked me to call him in a day or two when I'd decided whether I wanted to keep the theater or put it up for sale. I desperately wanted to keep it, but I had no money to invest in fixing it up. I had no clue how to run a theater and no clear idea what my expenses or projected income would be. I could ask the lawyer if he had any suggestions, but didn't hold out much hope. No matter what happened I would *not* call my parents asking for money. Partly because I was too proud. And partly because I knew they wouldn't give it to me.

I steeled myself to call Mr. Hamish of Hamish, Davis, and Weltner.

His secretary seemed keen to put me right through.

"Hamish here."

"Mr. Hamish, this is Halley Greer, Leon Baxter's niece."

"Hello, Halley. So, what do you think of Utopia Springs?"

"It's charming, and the people I've met are very kind. And I love the old theater and wish I could make a go of it. I even have some ideas. But after looking over Uncle Leon's ledgers, not to mention my own bank account, I just don't see any way I can finance it. I guess I have to ask you to put the theater on the market for me."

I choked back tears, preferring not to have an emotional breakdown on the phone with an attorney I'd never met.

"Halley, I haven't seen your bank account, of course. And I don't know which of your uncle's ledgers you've been looking at. What I do see on the papers in front of me is a small trust fund that Leon set up in the event you decided to keep the theater. It's not a fortune, by any means. But if you're prudent, it should be enough to get the business up and running and tide you over for a bit until you can start showing a profit."

I suddenly forgot all about not wanting to get emotional on the phone with a stranger.

"Yes, yes...thank you, Mr. Hamish. And Uncle Leon, wherever you are, I LOVE YOU!" I said, punching my fist upward in jubilation. I realized the hand I had pumped over my head was the one holding the phone.

"Mr. Hamish, are you still there?" I asked sheepishly.

"I'm still here."

"Sorry. I got a little carried away."

"Understandable. But I need to advise you that there are guidelines for the administration of the trust fund. I'm not exactly handing you a blank check. And if you really want the theater to succeed, it's going to require hard work."

"That's fine. Just tell me what I need to do."

"My office is in Fayetteville, but I'll be passing through

Utopia Springs Friday on my way to a conference. I'd like you to put together an informal proposal outlining your plans for the theater. I'll meet you at the theater at, say, ten a.m.?"

"Perfect. I'll see you then. And thanks again, Mr. Hamish."

I stuffed the cell phone in my pocket and realized my hands were trembling. Owning a theater wasn't a dream I remembered ever having, but it felt like a dream coming true, nonetheless.

Uncle Leon's cat suddenly appeared and rubbed up against my leg. I realized I had forgotten to ask Trudy her name. I reached down and gathered her into my arms.

"Good news, kitty. Looks like I'll be able to continue feeding you. And myself."

# CHAPTER 3

My cell buzzed and a bolt of dread shot through me, half expecting it was Mr. Hamish calling back to say he'd made a mistake about the trust fund.

"Hello?" I answered nervously.

"Halley, hi! This is Kendra Williams. I own the escape rooms across the street. Trudy decided we should be friends," she said with a giggle.

"Oh, hi, Kendra. Trudy means well, but I don't want to impose. Not that I don't want us to get acquainted. Just, if this is a bad time..."

"No, tonight's great—if you don't mind eating a late supper. Tonight, and every weeknight except Monday, we close at eight. On weekends, we're open until ten. I'm afraid I'm not a good cook, like Trudy, but I have pizza delivery on speed dial. If you're game, come on over to my place around eight thirty."

"Okay, sounds good. Can I ask you a really random question? I forgot to ask Trudy. What is Uncle Leon's cat's name?" I asked as the kitty nuzzled my neck.

"A nicely filled out calico?"

"Yeah. Did he have more than one cat?"

"No. But a scrappy orange tabby has followed Eartha Kitty through the pet door more than once."

"*Eartha* Kitty?"

"Yeah, like the planet with an 'a' on the end. It's a play on the name of some singer from back in the day. Eartha Kitt. She played Catwoman on the old Batman TV show. You'll have to ask Trudy to explain it sometime. So, I'll see you at my place later tonight?"

"Yes. Wait. Where is your place?"

"I live above the shop, like you. Come around to the alley door."

Talking about dinner, especially a late one, inspired me to do some grocery shopping. The only things in Uncle Leon's fridge that didn't have to be thrown out were four six-packs of beer and an unopened jar of mustard. So I walked to the market a couple of blocks away.

Since my cooking skills were minimal, my grocery bags were filled with eggs, milk, cereal, bread, mayo, deli meats and salads, a couple of frozen dinners and ice cream. Oh, and cat food.

I made a sandwich for myself and got down to work on my business proposal for Mr. Hamish. After scribbling lots of notes, I got as far as realizing that I didn't know how to write a business proposal.

I noticed it was almost time to meet Kendra, so I freshened up and put on some lipstick before heading out.

On the walk over, I pondered whether it would seem inappropriate to run my business proposal by Kendra, since we'd never met. But I was dying to tell someone my ideas, and she did own a business in town. My game plan was to make polite small talk and hold off on talking business until after dinner.

I tugged on the back door to Hidden Clue Escape Rooms, and it opened.

"Kendra?" I called out with one foot over the threshold.

In a moment I heard a stampede of footsteps as she ran down from upstairs.

Kendra, a blonde who emitted positive energy like sunlight, was wearing jeans and a t-shirt with the same logo I'd seen on the front of the building.

We exchanged hellos and handshakes.

"I've never been to an escape room before. There was one in Nashville some of my friends went to, but I never got around to it."

"Would you like a peek at the new room I'm working on?"

I nodded and followed her down the hall and through a doorway into another time. My guess was the Victorian era.

"This room looks incredible," I said, my eyes scanning the room and taking in the green velvet curtains with gold cords adorning a wall. A brocade settee, parlor chairs, a roll-top desk holding important-looking papers, a skeleton key, and a safe in the corner. On a pedestal was a beautiful necklace laid out on velvet under glass.

"What year are we in here?"

"It's 1878. I'm laying out clues based on a real-life mystery of stolen jewels. Trudy made the necklace," she said as we walked over to take a closer look. "It's just paste, of course, but the faux ruby and rhinestones look the part of the priceless, stolen artifact in our story. And it's a treasure to me because it was made by a friend."

"It's gorgeous."

"I'm still planting clues and setting up puzzles. Teams working this room will have an hour to find the clues and solve the mystery. When they do, the room door will unlock."

"Kind of like walking through a mystery novel. That sounds like a lot of fun," I said.

"Once I get this room finished, hopefully in a few days, you can come over and play one of the rooms. We have two others set up already. Are you ready to eat?"

"I'm starved"

We went upstairs and Kendra held the door open as I walked into the apartment.

"Beer or wine, pepperoni or cheese pizza, or some of both?" she asked as soon as I'd stepped inside.

"I'll take a beer and start with cheese pizza."

"By the way, I'm so sorry about your uncle. Leon was a sweet man. He helped my brother and me with painting and such when we were getting the escape rooms ready to open. We'd be glad to return the favor by helping you out."

"Thank you. That's very generous."

She motioned for me to have a seat on the striped blue sofa. The side chairs were upholstered in denim and there were cheerful pops of red and orange in the throw pillows. I was a bit jealous of how cute and tidy Kendra's apartment was, but consoled myself that it was actually smaller than Uncle Leon's place.

"Your apartment looks great. Mine is currently decorated in dingy, old guy clutter."

"Don't worry, it's amazing what a little paint can do. It'll be great once you add your own touches."

"And get rid of the antlered deer head staring down at the recliner," I said.

"Yeah, I can see how that could be a little creepy."

Kendra handed me a beer and a big slice of pizza on a paper plate before picking up her own plate and beverage and plopping down at the other end of the sofa.

"Who else have you met here in town besides George and Trudy—and me?"

"That's it. Well, I briefly met Nick, who owns the outfitters store."

"Neanderthal Nick? He's okay if you go for that type. Do you?"

"It's been so long since I had a date, I don't know what my

type is. Trudy mentioned you have a brother."

"Yeah, Bart works at a bank in Fayetteville and helps me here a lot on weekends. He's really just working to get me established in a business of my own. I was a history major, with no inclination to teach. After grad school, I worked at two different museums, but got laid off from both because of budget cuts. And he's given up on me finding a man."

"What about Bart? Is he single?"

"No, he has a man. A keeper. But Simon travels a lot for his work, so Bart is available to help me out."

"Why do you say he's given up on you finding a man? You're pretty and nice."

"And boring. Honestly, my idea of a good time is staying home and reading or watching The History Channel. But there's still hope for *you*," she said, looking me over as if weighing my potential. "I need to introduce you to Joe Chang. He's great. And other than Nick, he's the only single male business owner in town under forty. His family owns the Jade Garden Chinese Restaurant. His older sister manages the Fayetteville location and he manages the one here in Utopia Springs, and their kid sister is in pharmacy school."

"If he's all that wonderful, why do you want to fix him up with me? Why not keep him for yourself?"

"He *is* great, but if Joe were interested in me, he would have made a move by now. We've developed more of a brother-sister connection. And I'm good with that. All I ask is once the two of you fall madly in love, you let me hang out with you now and then."

"Can I at least ask what Joe looks like?"

He's got this amazing head of jet black hair, so thick it looks like a comb could get stuck in it—although it's always neat. He has a cute boyish face, but with these soulful brown eyes," Kendra said with a faraway look.

"Let me get this straight. Joe has amazing hair and soulful eyes, but you two are just friends, right?" I asked, doubtfully.

"Yep. You two would make a cute couple. So now that I've worked out your love life, let me pry into your business affairs. Are you planning to keep the theater or sell? I have no filter, just tell me to butt out if I'm being nosey."

"Well, you are a little nosey for someone I just met. But I'd really like to talk it over with somebody.

"Shoot."

"I'd like to settle here and make a go of it with the theater. I've made a mess of it with pretty much everything else I've done. I'm twenty-eight, and I'm a broke, unemployed barista who's never really had a stable relationship. I interned with a coffee company in Peru for two semesters in college. I also fell in love with a plantation owner's son. That didn't go so well.

"Anyway, as much as I'd like to stay, after going through the records last night, it looked like I'd have to give up on the idea because I don't have any money to invest in fixing up the theater. But when I called the estate lawyer this morning, he told me there's a small trust fund that should be just enough to keep hope alive. Mr. Hamish, the lawyer, is coming through Utopia Springs on Friday and wants me to show him a proposal."

"*Ooh*, I've always fantasized about having a trust fund," Kendra said, dangling a half-eaten slice of pizza over her plate.

"It's not the kind of trust fund that finances the lifestyle of the rich and idle. In fact, the figure he gave me sounds more like a Christmas club fund than a trust fund. Not that I'm complaining."

It was obvious Kendra and I had moved beyond small talk, so I pulled the notes out of my pocket and laid them on my lap.

"There are lots of details, which can be tweaked and changed. But, big picture, I'd like to pretty up the interior a bit and re-open the movie palace as a theater showing classic films with a coffee and wine bar in the lobby instead of a popcorn stand."

"I think that's brilliant," Kendra said, a 100-watt smile lighting up her face.

"What's wrong," she asked with a worried look.

I've never had much of a poker face.

"I've got all these notes and ideas, but I don't know if Mr. Hamish will be impressed. I have no idea how to put together a business proposal. What if, you know, he's expecting to see actual numbers? Can you help me make this look good, at least on paper?"

"Hey, I'm the twice-fired history major, remember? I could e-mail it to my brother, the banker, if you'd like."

"I hate to ask him a favor before we've even met."

"You wouldn't be asking; I would. And trust me, you two are going to be fast friends—just like us."

"To new friends," I said, chinking my beer bottle against hers.

As I walked home I fell in step with a small group of tourists. I'm sure my buoyant steps and carefree smile would have led passersby to assume I was on vacation, as well. After coming in through the back door, I flipped on a couple of lights as I walked through to the lobby.

I stared dreamy-eyed at the drab walls and floors, envisioning exactly how I wanted everything to look once the renovations were complete. My mind's eye could see carpets and paint and fixtures and furniture. My reveries ended abruptly. I was startled when I turned and saw a man standing, staring blankly through the glass door, sinister shadows falling behind him. When our eyes met, he remained motionless, expressionless. The weight of his dead stare made me feel uneasy, even though I knew he couldn't gain entry through the chained door. I turned away. When I looked back, he was gone.

# CHAPTER 4

Wednesday morning, Kendra texted to let me know Bart was working up a business proposal for me to present to the attorney. She added that I shouldn't worry because her brother was "brilliant."

Anyone who can prepare a business proposal was brilliant in my book, and I figured whatever he did would be better than anything I could come up with. Still, I couldn't help but worry just a little.

To keep my mind off my worries, I set out exploring what I hoped would be my new hometown, with its quirky mix of funky little shops and galleries, historic stone buildings, and brightly painted Victorian houses.

My wallet could only afford window shopping, although I did spring for a couple of cat toys for Eartha. She was unimpressed.

Thursday morning I woke up with a stiff neck, I presumed from the way I'd slept in the recliner. I stretched and shuffled into the kitchen. I had scrubbed out Uncle Leon's coffee maker and tried making coffee in it once before tossing it in the trash.

Uncle Leon's free-spirited cat suddenly materialized. She walked past me and went straight to her bowl, which fortunately I had remembered to fill.

After her breakfast she walked over and brushed against my leg.

"So, Eartha, tell me, how do you think things will go with

the lawyer tomorrow? Will I get to stay here? You might not miss me if I had to leave, but I'd miss you. Would you even consider moving elsewhere with me?"

She put her tail in the air and walked away.

"Guess not."

I showered and dressed and stepped outside just after eight, almost running into Kendra, who looked like she was dying to tell me something.

"I've been dying to call you. I got notes back from Bart on your business proposal, but didn't know how early it was safe to call you."

"When you're doing me a favor you can call as early as you like. I can't thank you—and Bart—enough for helping me out here. I was just heading to The Muffin Man. Want to join me?"

"Sure. We don't open until ten. Hi, Zeke," she said as we entered the shop.

"Hi, Kendra," replied the smiling guy behind the counter whose name apparently was Zeke.

We got in line. I decided to try the shop's namesake muffins, since I'd had the cinnamon roll on my previous visit.

When we made it to the counter, Kendra said, "Have you met Halley yet?"

"Not formally. I saw you in here before with Trudy," he said looking to me.

"Halley is Leon Baxter's great-niece and the new owner of the Star Movie Palace," Kendra said.

"Wow, great to meet you, Halley. Glad we're going to be neighbors. I'm Zeke, a.k.a The Muffin Man."

"Nice to meet you, Zeke."

We paid for and collected our orders and sat down at the same table I'd shared with Trudy.

"I may technically be the owner of the theater, but we probably shouldn't introduce me that way until everything is settled with the attorney."

"No worries. I looked over Bart's proposal notes and it's going to knock the socks off Mr. Haywood."

"Hamish."

"Whatever. Here," she said, handing me her phone. "Type in your e-mail address so I can forward Bart's e-mail to you."

I complied.

"We can look over Bart's e-mail after you've had some coffee. Tell me what you've been up to since last I saw you."

I would've felt foolish telling her that I'd been spooked by a random tourist looking through the window and had a conversation with an indifferent cat, so I said, "Nothing much."

"Does Bart look like you?" I asked as I savored my cherry-almond muffin.

"Yeah, I guess so. Blond hair, blue eyes, big teeth. But I like to think I'm prettier."

After I'd finished my breakfast, I pulled up Bart's e-mail on my phone.

He zeroed in on the fact that, since movie theaters make their money from concessions, not ticket sales, having a coffee/wine bar instead of a typical concession stand would allow me to charge more—and therefore make more money. Bart even included estimates, which showed he had put some real effort and research into a proposal for someone he'd never met.

"Kendra, this is awesome. Bart is awesome. I'll never be able to thank you two enough. Now I'll be able to talk intelligently to Mr. Hamish and, fingers crossed, by tomorrow afternoon you can feel free to introduce me as the theater's new owner."

Kendra pounded her palms on the table excitedly before breaking into some kind of happy dance move from the waist up, jerking her shoulders and punching her fists in an almost rhythmic fashion.

I couldn't help laughing, and my new friend, who obviously doesn't take herself too seriously, laughed, too.

We walked out of the shop together laughing before I burst into tears.

"Hey, girl. Are those tears of joy?"

I nodded. "Mostly."

She put her hand on my shoulder.

"I'm okay, really," I said, tears streaming down my face.

"Let's go inside," she said as we reached the front of the theater.

I unlocked the door and we walked into the lobby.

"What's wrong?"

"Nothing's wrong. In fact, everything's wonderful. It's just, thinking about Bart and how great he is to put together this proposal for me, even though he's never met me just…just made me think of my own brother, Josh. I miss him a lot." I slid down the wall until my fanny landed on the floor.

"Aw, sweetie, I'm sorry. Where is he?"

"He passed away two years ago from cancer."

"I'm so sorry, Halley. Cancer sucks," she said, taking a seat on the floor beside me.

"By the time they diagnosed it, he only had a few months. He was three years younger than me and had just graduated from college with his whole life ahead of him. He was my best friend in the whole world and suddenly he was gone."

"I can't imagine how it would feel to lose Bart. He's older than me, eight years, and had always acted like a mother hen. Then after our parents died in a plane crash my freshman year in college, he smothered me with parental love and interference. And I don't know how I would've made it without him."

"I'm sorry about your folks, Kendra."

"Thanks. I was kind of messed up for a year or so, trying to wrap my head around being an orphan."

"Yeah, I took it hard, losing Josh. My parents were too lost in their own grief to help with mine, which is understandable. I spent last summer in Arizona with my grandmother, trying to pull myself together. You'd love her, she's a hoot. Lately, things hadn't been going so well for me. I'd lost my job, so inheriting the theater and moving here—this is just what I needed right now. It's great, but it's also kind of sad not being able to share it with Josh, you know?"

"Yeah, sweetie, I think I get it."

Mr. Hamish arrived promptly at ten Friday morning. I wowed him with my proposal, which was really Bart's proposal. In any case he was impressed—which meant I could gain access to the trust fund. He explained one important condition: expenditures over a certain amount had to be signed off on by both George and Trudy. He left a stack of papers with me about some estate stuff and continued on his way to his conference.

Tomorrow I'd need to talk to George and Trudy, but today there was a phone call I'd been needing to make.

"Hi, Grammy, you get my e-mail about moving to Arkansas?"

"I did. But I don't understand why you moved all the way out there to sleep in the balcony of a movie theater. You know you always have a place to stay with me here in Sun City, cupcake."

"I'm not sleeping in a balcony. There's an apartment above the theater. I have a place to live, and as soon as I get things in order, I'll have my very own business."

"Doing what?"

"Showing movies," I said, wondering if I needed to talk to Grammy's doctor about adjusting her meds.

"The theater will show classic films. Movies you'd enjoy. You'll have to come visit once I get settled. And instead of a typical popcorn and candy stand, I'll have a coffee and wine bar in the lobby."

"Are you sure you're ready to own a business, cupcake? What do you know about running a movie theater?"

"What I don't know I can learn. I love old movies. And I *do* know something about running a coffee bar. Wish me luck."

"I'll do better than that. I'll pray a rosary for you every night. Is there a Catholic church in that little town?"

"Yes. St. Cecilia's." I knew this because I'd driven past it on my way into town. The crucifix out front was a dead giveaway.

"St. Cecilia is the patron saint of musicians," she said. "Maybe the first movie you show should be a musical."

"Okay, I'll give it some thought. Love you, Grammy. Talk to you soon."

*Actually a musical wasn't a bad idea.*

# CHAPTER 5

Saturday, I had two items on my agenda: make an appointment with Mr. Carvello of Carvello's Winery to discuss selling his wine in the theater and broach the subject of the trust fund with George and Trudy. Trudy didn't worry me so much, but I was a little worried how George's eyebrows were going to react to my proposal.

After doing a bit of online research I discovered that, while there were three wineries in the area, Carvello's was the only one that made wines entirely with its own grapes. The other two vineyards had young vines and still bought most of their grapes from elsewhere. I e-mailed Rafe Carvello briefly telling him my plans for the theater, asking if we could talk about working together. Within thirty minutes, he had responded, inviting me to the winery on Sunday for a chat and a wine tasting. So far, so good.

Now to talk to George and Trudy. I picked up, then put back down the proposal I'd shown the lawyer. I hadn't written it anyway. Bart had. George and Trudy were veteran business owners in Utopia Springs, and I could learn a lot from them. The best approach was just to be honest—and humble—and ask for their help.

I hated to show up empty-handed—maybe it's a Southern thing. Since I'm hopeless in the kitchen with anything except coffee, I stopped by The Muffin Man and picked up some fresh-out-of-the-oven cinnamon rolls. They smelled so yummy it was all I could do not to take a bite out of one before I got to George and Trudy's.

The gallery opened at ten o'clock, and it was just after nine when I knocked on their door. Trudy looked happy to see me and George perked up when I set my offering of cinnamon rolls on the table in front of him. He plucked one out of the bag and took a bite.

"This is good. But you didn't have to bribe me. I've already promised Trudy I'll sign off on your trust fund expenditures—within reason," he said with an admonishing look.

"Oh, good," I said, slumping onto the dining chair across from George. "I'm relieved you already know about it."

"Mr. Hamish called," Trudy said. "Now tell us all about your plans."

The coffee and wine bar was a bit of a hard sell with George, at first.

"George, coffee is Halley's area of expertise, and an outlet for showcasing local wines in town seems like a good idea. More importantly, Bart the banker thinks the numbers add up. Don't be pigheaded," Trudy said.

"But it won't seem like Leon's place," he grumbled.

"It's *not* Leon's place anymore. And Leon would want us to support whatever helps Halley make it a success. You don't like people to know it, but you're just a sentimental old fool."

"Am not. I just really like popcorn and candy."

"We're going to sell a selection of traditional movie theater candies and snacks, like Raisinets and Jujubes and Cracker Jacks—for a touch of nostalgia. And, of course, we'll sell water and soft drinks for the kids, and adults who prefer it."

I was hesitant to bring up my meeting with Mr. Carvello, afraid George would offer to go with me. But since I didn't know anything about Mr. Carvello and could use some advice, I decided to risk it.

After telling them, George startled me by leaping out of his chair without a word. He grabbed a notepad and pen from a kitchen drawer, sat down at the table and began writing.

"You have to take charge with Rafe Carvello before he tries to steamroll over you in that very polite but insistent way of his. I'm writing down the general terms you should offer on the wine bar partnership. You type it up all pretty on your computer, print it out and stick it in an envelope. After all the polite small talk he'll insist on, hand this to him, say 'Thanks for the vino,' and walk away."

I started to say something, but George cut me off, "Trust me on this."

I looked over to Trudy, who nodded silently.

I had typed the terms that George had scribbled down for me and printed it out on the ancient printer in the theater office. After neatly folding and placing the paper in a business envelope, I tucked it in my purse and drove to my Sunday afternoon meeting with Rafe Carvello.

The view through my windshield was breathtaking and got more spectacular as the altitude rose, with towering oaks and limestone cliffs randomly jutting out to interrupt the lush green forests. But negotiating business deals wasn't really my area of expertise. The nerves in my stomach turned into altitude sickness as my little Honda struggled up the winding mountain roads. Around a curve the vista opened up to reveal a paved driveway with an arched sign that read "Carvello's Winery." I pulled up the long driveway and parked my old Honda behind a black BMW convertible in front of a palatial contemporary house that Mr. Carvello had referred to as "the villa."

A distinguished-looking white-haired man wearing a navy blue blazer with an artfully arranged handkerchief in the breast pocket walked out to greet me.

"You must be Halley," he said, grasping my right hand between both his hands. "My sincere condolences on the passing of your uncle. May he rest in peace. But I have to say I see no family resemblance—which is a compliment, by the way," he said with a hearty laugh.

We walked into the house through a room roughly as large as the Star Movie Palace lobby, with a stacked stone fireplace that dominated the double-height space. The glass wall across the back led to a patio, where I could see wine, glassware, and various cheeses laid out for a tasting. My mouth began to water.

A man in a blue button-down and khakis, who I presumed was the wine steward, was standing at a large teak table with his back to us.

"This is my son, Marco. May I present Miss Greer."

He turned toward us and I felt my breath catch. Marco Carvello was tall and tanned with dark wavy hair, and I guessed about ten years my senior. He was also much beefier, in a good way, than his slender dad.

"Hello," he said with a polite handshake and a lingering gaze.

"Please, call me Halley."

Marco opened the first bottle and poured a little into each of our glasses. His father explained a bit about the vintage, inviting me to swirl the wine in my glass and inhale the bouquet. After we had sipped he pointed out the woodsy undertones and citrus notes. I found myself making eye contact with Marco, who seemed only to take his dark brown eyes off me long enough to pour another variety of wine. He looked as delicious as the wine tasted, and despite my efforts to stay focused, I found myself drifting into a fantasy where I was stomping grapes in a vat with my bare feet, like in the classic *I Love Lucy* episode.

After the wine tasting, the senior Mr. Carvello excused

himself and left me alone with his son. Marco, who had said little in the presence of his talkative father, suddenly relaxed and chatted—and flirted—freely. Feeling a little flustered, I turned the conversation toward business.

"I think showcasing Carvello's wines at your theater is a superb idea, Halley."

"Perfect," I said, my voice cracking slightly. "And once we're up and running, maybe we could even schedule a wine tasting on occasion before a show, conducted by you or a member of your staff."

"I'd like that," Marco said. "Now it's just a matter of working out the financial arrangements and other details."

Before he could continue, I pulled the envelope out of my purse and handed it to him.

"Here's a proposal on those matters I've drawn up with my financial advisor. Look it over and get back to me with your thoughts. Thank you for the wine and hospitality and please give your father my best. I look forward to talking with you soon."

I started walking toward the exit. He seemed thrown off his guard and I was able to take the lead by presenting my proposal first—just like George had suggested.

When I reached the house Marco scrambled to open the door for me and I gave him my sweetest smile. He looked a bit sheepish as we said goodbye. And, maybe I flatter myself, but I thought he looked just a little impressed, as well. He called the next day, agreeing to the terms.

# CHAPTER 6

After an inspection determined the building was structurally sound, the next few weeks were a blur as I got the theater ready to open—with a lot of help from my new friends.

My vision was to give the Art Deco movie palace an appearance of its former glory—on a very limited budget. We put some things in storage in the hopes of doing a full restoration somewhere down the line. For the present we made mostly cosmetic, and cost-effective, fixes to put some shine on the place.

I scrubbed and scraped and painted. Kendra worked some of her set design magic, like she did in the escape rooms, including applying new gold fringe to camouflage the frayed edges of the velvet curtains on either side of the screen. George painted a gorgeous mural—inspired by the original faded and peeling one—on acid free boards mounted over the original artwork so as not to damage it. Kendra's museum conservation knowledge came in handy on this. And Trudy kept a close eye on the budget, haggling with electricians, plumbers, and suppliers. A cadre of volunteers, including Bart, Joe, and Nick, put in countless hours helping out. And George put me in touch with a theater owner in Fayetteville, who was an old friend of Uncle Leon's. He gave me advice and patiently answered all my nervous, newbie questions.

Ten days before the grand re-opening, I woke up early. The espresso machine and other fixtures for the coffee bar were scheduled to be delivered and it felt like things were finally coming together. I ran down the steps, my heart racing with excitement, walked into the lobby—and stopped dead in my tracks.

"What the..."

The back wall that I had stenciled with coffee terms, like "latte" and "espresso," and the brand new cabinets in the coffee bar had been spray-painted a lime green shade. Streaks dripped down from the scrawled words "Go home." I stared at the damage in disbelief. Then a wave of panic and nausea swept over me.

"The mural," I muttered as I ran into the auditorium. My feet stumbled across a streak of green spray paint running a crooked line down the length of the carpet in the center aisle and streaked across the screen, as well. But the mural panels George had installed were untouched.

Thank heavens, I thought as I crumpled into a seat.

I called George and Trudy on my cell phone, then dialed 911.

George arrived ahead of the police. He rattled off a string of profanities as he surveyed the damage vandals had inflicted on our hard work, then draped his arm around me as I sobbed on his shoulder.

"Good thing I took the scaffolding down last night," he said. "Otherwise, those thugs would've gone for the mural."

"We've already ordered carpeting to replace the aisle runner and it'll be a pain, but not too expensive to repaint and re-stencil the wall and cabinets," I said, trying to look for the positives. "You have any idea how expensive it'll be to replace the screen?"

"We won't have to replace it," he said calmly.

"You think the paint will come off without damaging the screen?" I asked.

"The paint's not on the screen. Bart and I stretched a thin film of protective plastic over it before we started renovations. Didn't you know?"

"No. But I love you—and Bart." I threw my arms around George, hysterically laughing and crying at the same time.

Of course, at that exact moment the cops arrived, having no trouble entering through the front door with the glass smashed out of it.

"I'm Officer Stone, are you the owner?" The petite cop's blonde hair was pulled back in a ponytail, and it looked like her face would break if she cracked a smile.

"Yes, I am. I'm Halley Greer. I'm Leon Baxter's—"

"Yeah, I know who you are. You're the niece no one had ever heard of until you inherited the theater. What seems to be the trouble?"

Since "the trouble" was so obvious, I was too shocked to respond for a moment. George jumped in.

"Vandals came in and wrecked the place last night after we've been working night and day the past few weeks to get the place fixed up and ready for the grand opening."

Without looking at the room, she took a pen and notepad out of her pocket. "Specifically, what was damaged?"

I waved toward the wall. "All this graffiti on the wall and cabinets, more on the carpet in the auditorium and across the movie screen," I said.

She glanced up briefly at the wall.

"What about the writing? What do you make of the words 'go home'?"

"I guess someone doesn't want me here," I said.

"Any idea who that might be? Do you have any enemies?"

"No and no."

"Are you residing in the upstairs apartment, Ms. Greer?"

"Yes, I am."

"Were you home last night and did you hear anything?"

"Yeah, I was home, but I didn't hear anything."

"Spray paint doesn't make much noise," George pointed out.

"Maybe not, but breaking out that glass would've made some noise."

Officer Stone did a quick walk-through of the lobby and auditorium taking a few notes.

"Do you have insurance, Ms. Greer?"

I looked to George. He shrugged.

"That's something I'll have to ask my attorney about," I said.

"Get me an estimate after the insurance appraiser has assessed the damage. I'll file a report," she said, heading toward the door.

"Wait, aren't you going to dust for fingerprints?"

"My guess is there are fingerprints on a can of green spray paint. Let me know if you find one," she said before leaving.

"Her name is Officer Susan Stone, but people call her Susie Stoneface. Behind her back, of course." George said.

"I call her 'no freaking help.' But why would anybody do this?" I asked, giving in to the tears again.

George, Trudy, Kendra and I worked long hours for the next ten days, along with a revolving crew of generous volunteers, to finish up the renovations—and redo the work that had been sabotaged.

I'd taken out an ad in the paper. But my most prominent advertisements were the posters out front beside the ticket booth, and the newly-relighted marquee listing our feature: *My Fair Lady*, and in smaller letters: coffee and wine bar.

The last thing I did the night before the grand opening was to hang large, simply-framed photos, black-and-white movie stills and publicity shots of glamorous movie stars drinking coffee. Peering over their coffee mugs were smiling images of Clark Gable, Lauren Bacall, Humphrey Bogart, and Rita Hayworth. And holding a paper coffee cup as she looked at jewelry through a window was Audrey Hepburn as Holly Golightly in *Breakfast at Tiffany's*.

I sighed as I admired the finished lobby. Most of the "wow" factor came from items accomplished with very little money. The second-hand chrome barstools that now looked shiny new. The basic bar base embellished with geometric wooden cutouts and spray-painted with high gloss paint to mimic finely lacquered furniture. Curved loveseats, oversized chairs, and ottomans sourced from a junk shop that had been reupholstered with an Art Deco sunburst design. The coffee terms Trudy and I had hand-stenciled behind the coffee bar. I stood with my back against the front doors as if I were a patron just entering. I surveyed the space, scanning from left to right, and then down at the carpet with its swirling dark blue design and large gold star, flanked by two smaller stars inlaid in the center of the lobby. The timeworn theater I'd walked into the day I arrived was gone and in its place stood a true Art Deco movie palace.

# CHAPTER 7

Opening night finally arrived and I was so nervous my hands were trembling.

Get a grip, I told myself. The last thing a coffee bar needs is a barista with unsteady hands. Looking around the lobby made me feel better. Trudy had dressed up as Eliza Doolittle—pre-makeover. And George, after some prodding, dressed as Professor Higgins. Since I was handling barista duty, I kept it simple with a white tuxedo shirt and black pants. And Marco Carvello himself was serving the wine, looking sharp in black shirt and pants with a black necktie.

Bart, who looked dashing in a tux and top hat, volunteered to work the ticket booth for opening night, and his partner, Simon, took over at the escape rooms to give Kendra the night off. Joe also took the night off, although he ran across the street a couple of times to check on things at the restaurant. Every time I caught sight of him his eyes were glued to Kendra, who was stunning. She had assumed a post-makeover Eliza Doolittle persona, with a black-and-white period dress that showed off her figure and a fabulous oversized hat. Handsome Joe's thick hair looked even thicker than usual. I'm guessing he used mousse. He was wearing a freshly-pressed dress shirt and tie— and a big smile. Operating the projector was a woman named Delores who George had dug up, telling me she'd been a movie projectionist back in the day. I didn't realize until I met her that he meant back in the day when most of the classic films were made. She had to be in her mid-eighties, but was spry and sharp as a tack. When she arrived for opening night wearing a gold lamé evening gown, I knew we had a winner.

There was a line extending halfway down the block when George unlocked the doors and let customers in at six sharp, opening an hour before the movie start time so people would have lots of time to purchase beverages. Trudy and Kendra worked the room, stirring excitement for the film—and talking up the coffee and wine selections on offer.

Despite my opening night jitters, pulling the perfect espresso shot and creating crowd-pleasing latte art, like hearts and leaves, with steamed milk were feats I could perform blindfolded. I expedited orders by writing customers' names on the disposable cups as they paid. I prepared the coffee orders and lined them up on the side bar for pick-up.

At twelve minutes to show time, Bart announced that champagne would be available for purchase during a thirty-minute intermission, halfway into the nearly three-hour movie.

Customers made their way to their seats and my veteran projectionist played a short cartoon feature to give everyone time to get settled.

As I heard the music for the opening credits start, I worried. Had I chosen the right film? I had taken Grammy's advice about showing a musical, and hoped St. Cecilia was smiling down on us.

I was wiping the counter when Trudy and Kendra walked up to the counter and interrupted my panic attack.

"Do y'all think I made the right choice? Maybe we should have run a screwball comedy for opening night?"

"Breathe in a cleansing breath and exhale slowly," Trudy said as she motioned upwards and demonstrated breathing, which was good because I'd suddenly forgotten how.

"Chill out. Things couldn't be going better. I heard a bunch of people talking about how much they were looking forward to the movie, and how awesome the theater looks," Kendra said.

Marco poured some champagne for us.

We chinked our champagne flutes. The bubbly must have tickled Kendra's nose because she let out two rapid-fire sneezes."

"Bless you," I said in unison with Trudy.

"Thank you," Kendra said, followed by a hiccup.

*Maybe I should keep tabs on her alcohol intake.*

Bart joined us. "We've got almost a sell-out crowd," he announced, beaming.

"Wow. Here, Bart, have some champagne," I said.

He lifted his glass and said, "Cheers to the new impresario of Utopia Springs."

I may have blushed just a little.

As soon as the intermission card went up on the screen, customers streamed into the lobby. I had pretty steady business with coffee orders, but Marco was definitely getting more customers—especially for the champagne.

Most people were making their way back into the theater when George stepped behind the bar and said he needed to have a word with me.

"We have a problem," George said in a hushed tone.

"What is it?"

"During intermission I did a walk-through of the auditorium to see if there were any spills that needed cleaning up. This one guy was asleep in his chair with his head tilted back. He didn't move, even when a couple of people crawled over him to get back to their seats, so I went to check on him, thinking he had passed out drunk. I shook him, and even gave him a discreet little slap, but he didn't respond."

"Should we call a doctor?"

"I'm afraid that won't help. He doesn't have a pulse."

# CHAPTER 8

I called 911 and George said he'd go back in the theater to discreetly make sure no one disturbed the bod—um, indisposed customer until the police arrived. I ran up to the projection room to explain our situation to Delores and tell her and not to start the film. To stall until the police arrived, I told a little white lie, and announced we were having some issues with the projector and asked customers for their patience.

Within minutes, one uniformed officer along with a plainclothes detective arrived, and an ambulance with flashing lights, but no sirens, pulled up behind them. The detective and one of the EMTs slipped into the auditorium. I told them George Mayfield could point out the deceased. After confirming the man was dead, the detective came back into the lobby.

"I'll go to the stage down front and make an announcement," he said. Then he instructed the uniformed officer: "You make sure no one leaves the building, and call for back-up. We'll need it to take statements."

The uniformed officer was Susie Stoneface, the one who had been remarkably unhelpful when I reported the green spray paint assault on the theater.

I stood in the back of the auditorium, waiting, as my nerves evolved into nausea. People turned and looked questioningly up at the projector window.

In a moment their heads turned to the stage.

"Ladies and gentlemen, may I have your attention, please.

I'm Detective Stedman with the Utopia Springs Police Department. I'm sorry to have to interrupt your movie, but unfortunately a member of the audience has died."

A wave of gasps rippled through the crowd.

"Most likely it was natural causes, but until we can establish what happened I need your cooperation. For the moment, I'd like everyone to stay in their seats, except for people in the last three rows on this side," he said motioning. "If folks in those rows would please make your way to the lobby, officers will begin taking statements. If any of you sitting elsewhere in the theater saw anything that struck you as unusual, please make your way to the lobby, as well. For the rest of you, we will be passing around clipboards to get your name and contact information. Thank you."

Additional cops soon arrived and snapped a few photos. The deceased, who had been loaded onto a gurney by the EMTs, was rolled out of the theater, covered by a sheet. They stopped in the lobby just before exiting through the front doors. I saw a gloved officer check the man's pockets, collecting a wallet and keys and other small items, and dropping them into a bag, before the paramedics took him out to the ambulance and presumably on to the morgue.

"Should we offer refunds since people didn't get to watch the second half?" I asked.

"If I may make a suggestion," Marco said. "Offer rain checks instead of refunds."

"Smart thinking," George said.

I walked over to the lobby seating area and loitered in Detective Stedman's peripheral vision. He finished his conversation and turned to me.

"What is it Ms. Greer?"

"Are the people in the theater free to leave after they've written their information on the clipboard?"

"Yes."

"Good."

"Why?" he asked.

"I'm going to announce that customers can pick up a rain check for a free show on their way out."

After I made the announcement I hurried back to the ticket booth and grabbed a roll of green tickets and took them to the bar.

"Here, everyone, take some of these and write 'ON' on them for 'opening night.' We're going to hand these out as rain checks to anyone who asks, along with our apologies."

People began leaving as the officers checked off their names on the list from each row. I'd guess less than half of the customers requested a rain check. But that's likely because the others weren't going to be in Utopia Springs for very long.

After the cops had finished with statements from anyone who had something to say, Officer Stone and another cop came over and asked Trudy and Kendra to come with them.

"Ms. Greer, do you have an office or someplace you and I can have a chat?" Detective Stedman asked.

"Sure, the office is right this way," I said.

"Mr. Mayfield and Mr. Carvello I'd like to talk with each of you next," he said.

Clearly George and Marco and I were getting special attention.

Inside the office, the detective sat down in my desk chair and invited me to take a seat in the smaller side chair. He obviously wanted to assume the superior position.

Does the name Vince Dalton ring any bells to you?"

"No, I don't remember anyone by that name. Why?"

He ignored my question and moved on.

He showed me a driver's license photo. "Ms. Greer, do you recall ever seeing the deceased before tonight?"

"No, but I haven't lived in Utopia Springs very long. And I've been spending almost all my time inside the theater the last few weeks getting things ready for opening night."

"Do you remember if he ordered any food or drink from the bar?"

"I don't recall serving him, but that doesn't mean I didn't. It was really busy."

"I see. Did anyone lodge a complaint with you tonight—about anything?"

"No. Wait, yes. One lady informed us that one of the stalls in the ladies' room was out of toilet paper. Trudy went in and refilled it."

"Did you have any more vandalism after the broken window and spray paint incident?"

"No. If we had, I would have reported it. Not that the police seemed very concerned the first time."

"I assure you the department is concerned about vandalism, thefts, or any crimes committed in Utopia Springs. There isn't always a lot we can do about it."

"Anything else you can think of you'd like to tell me, or that you should tell me, Ms. Greer?"

He stared at me as if he thought his eyes were lie detectors. I stared back as if I thought he was a jerk.

After a long moment I replied, "No."

"Ask George Mayfield to join me, please," he said, dismissing me.

I relayed the message to George. Officer Stoneface was interviewing Trudy, and another cop was talking to Kendra. Marco was behind the bar, cleaning up. Bart and Joe, who had already been interviewed, were handing out rain checks to the last of the customers.

Trudy finished her interview and joined me at the bar. A moment later, George walked back into the lobby, and Marco headed to the office for his interview.

When Kendra had finished her interview, she came over to me. Joe was just a few steps behind her.

"Halley, I know you're bummed out about opening night getting shut down. But none of the customers can blame you for some guy dying, even if it was inconvenient," Kendra said.

"Right," Joe chimed in. "And the good news is, most of the people were tourists who will be gone in a couple of days. Next weekend we'll have a whole new crop of tourists and they won't know anything about what happened tonight."

"Good point. Thanks."

Marco rejoined us at the bar, the detective strolled in behind him, flipping through his little notebook and scanning over his notes. He stopped beside the coffee bar.

"Goodnight. I'll be in touch if we have any more questions."

He and the other cops left, and I locked the door behind them. My shoulders slumped forward as I leaned my back against the door and let out an exasperated sigh.

"Hey, does anyone know if Delores is still upstairs?" I asked, worried what effect the stress of a dead customer might have on my elderly projectionist.

"No, she gave her statement and asked the detective if she could go ahead and leave," George said.

"Oh, thank goodness," I said.

I looked at my beautiful band of friends, feeling much gratitude. It had been a doozy of a night, and Delores was the only one getting paid.

"Guys, it turned out to be a rough night due to circumstances beyond our control. But y'all were amazing. Opening night, and with a big crowd, but everyone here played their parts beautifully. Thank you from the bottom of my heart. And Joe pointed out that by next weekend most of tonight's customers will have gone back to wherever they came from and we'll have a new crop of tourists with no knowledge of tonight's proceedings. It's getting late, why don't all of you go home and I'll finish cleaning up in the morning."

"Why don't we all stay and drink some of this champagne we didn't get to enjoy during intermission," Trudy said.

"I'll drink to that," Bart added as he grabbed a bottle and started filling flutes while Marco lined them up on the counter. They were plastic, disposable champagne flutes I'd purchased for opening night. But they were still festive, as well as practical.

We took our champagne and plopped down on the loveseats and plump chairs in the lounge area of the lobby.

"The detective asked if I remembered serving the dead guy, as if I could remember everyone who ordered tonight in a theater full of people," I said.

"I always remember people who spend a lot of money in the gallery. Their faces look like Benjamin Franklins to me," George said.

"Do you know if the dead guy was a local or a tourist?" I asked.

They collectively agreed they didn't recognize him.

"I don't remember seeing him. Probably a tourist," George said.

"Good," I said, heaving a short sigh of relief.

"Why is that good?" George asked.

"Since most people are killed by someone they know, it makes it less likely that it's foul play and less chance that the cops will suspect any of us," Kendra chimed in.

"She likes to watch those true crime shows on The History Channel," Bart explained.

"Most likely he just had a heart attack," George said. "We didn't hear or see anything weird happen in the theater, and I got up close and personal with the guy and didn't see any signs of injury."

"Wait. Kendra mentioned that most people are killed by someone they know. Even if he's a tourist, he could have been killed by his family or whoever he's traveling with," Bart pointed out.

"Why would you go on vacation with somebody you wanted to kill?" George said.

"Maybe they didn't want to kill him before they left on vacation," I offered. "We had some family road trips where I know my dad had to be having murderous thoughts, what with my mom's constant complaining."

"In this case, I think George is right. It was most likely a heart attack or aneurysm or something like that," Trudy said.

After a final toast to the continued success of the Star Movie Palace, Kendra and Bart left to help Simon close up at the escape rooms. Joe took off to check on closing at the restaurant, and Marco said his goodnights, as well.

"Halley, I know I gave you some flack about it, but you made a wise decision going with just the Saturday night opener and forgoing the Sunday matinee this first weekend," George said.

"Thanks, George. I wanted to have time to regroup and fix any problems or technical glitches we might encounter with the first run. I never imagined *this* kind of problem coming up."

"You handled everything like a pro," Trudy said, leaning over and wrapping an arm around my shoulder. "The coffee and wine service went smoothly. And it was a sharp public relations move to offer rain checks, even though events were clearly out of your control."

"Leon woulda been proud of you, kid," George said.

A couple of stray tears may have escaped despite my best efforts to hold them back.

# CHAPTER 9

Sunday morning, I got busy with the less than glamorous, but necessary job of cleaning the ladies' room of the Star Movie Palace. After wiping down the toilet seats and swishing the bowls with cleanser, I mopped my way out of the lavatory and sat down for a minute in the adjoining ladies' lounge, a throwback to a more glamorous era. The only thing this area required during renovations was to replace a cracked mirror and lay new carpet. The gold and cream vinyl upholstery on the padded high-back seats lining one side of the lounge was in near-mint condition. Opposite this seating area, a counter lined with lighted mirrors served as a perfect spot for women to check their hairdo and put on a fresh coat of lipstick. When the theater opened in the 1920s, no doubt the counter would have been stocked with Bakelite ashtrays.

I yawned. It had been a late night by the time the police finished questioning us and the ambulance had taken our recently deceased patron away. Maybe I should've accepted Kendra's or George and Trudy's offer to sleep on their sofa. But I certainly wasn't afraid to sleep in my own apartment because some guy had a heart attack in the theater.

I guess it was selfish of me, but it would've been nice if he had waited until he got home to drop dead. His untimely death had cast a pall on what had been shaping up to be a fabulous opening night for the Star Movie Palace. I figured I was entitled to treat myself to at least a modest pity party.

After cleaning the men's room—cleaning urinals was a new experience—and vacuuming the lobby, I walked to the deli down the street and purchased a club sandwich and a bottled water to go. On the way back to the theater, I passed a newspaper rack and noticed the word "theater" emblazoned on the front of the local paper. I dropped some of the change I'd just received at the deli in the coin slot and retrieved a copy of the Sunday edition of the *Utopia Springs Sentinel*—all eight pages of it.

The headline read, "Man Found Dead in Theater on Opening Night."

I wondered how they'd managed to get this story in the morning paper when it just happened last night. Apparently, a random death is stop-the-presses kind of news in Utopia Springs.

*Great. Just the kind of publicity I don't need.*

I was considering buying some ice cream for my newly-revived pity party when I spotted a photograph in the story.

It was a picture of the deceased, Vince Dalton. But it wasn't the tiny driver's license photo the detective had shown me, which like most DMV photos, looked nothing like him. I hadn't seen the victim last night, except when he was rolled through the lobby on a gurney with a sheet covering him.

However, I did recognize the picture on the front page of the newspaper. It was the same man I'd seen staring at me through the front doors earlier on the night the theater was vandalized.

I quickly read to the end of the not-so-well-written news story. They had buried the lead.

The last paragraph stated, "A source close to the investigation, on the condition of anonymity, told the *Sentinel* that police have reason to suspect the victim did not die of natural causes."

I dragged myself up to the apartment and stuck the club

sandwich in the fridge, having just lost my appetite and developed a headache in its place. I washed an aspirin down with the bottled water.

I read through the story again, thinking there must be some mistake. It implied he had been murdered, but no one could have killed a man in a crowded theater without being noticed. And George would've seen any obvious wounds. Maybe the newspaper reporter was just making up the anonymous source thing to spice up his Page One story. I was about to call George and ask him what he thought, when my phone rang. It was Sergeant somebody or other asking very nicely if I'd come down to the station to answer a few questions.

The polite invitation to the police station was the last cordial word I heard for the next three hours.

After they finally said I could leave, I walked home and went straight upstairs, grabbed a beer out of the refrigerator, collapsed in the recliner and gazed up at the deer head, who offered no comfort. I wished Eartha Kitty was around to cuddle, but her comings and goings were strictly on her own terms.

After a few swigs I checked my cell phone and listened to a voicemail from Trudy asking if I'd seen the newspaper.

Not only had I seen the story, I could already envision the front-page headline in tomorrow's edition. "Police zero in on new theater owner as prime murder suspect."

I called Trudy and told her I had just seen her missed call because I'd been at the police station being interrogated. Before I could say anything else she said, "Hold that thought. I'll be right over."

I thought it would be nice to offer Trudy something other than super cheap beer. So, I fished a corkscrew out of the kitchen drawer and opened a nice bottle of Carvello wine Marco had given me as a grand-opening gift. I retrieved a couple of wine glasses from the cabinet. Moments later, there was a tap at the door.

I offered Trudy a glass of wine, pouring one for myself as well.

She took a sip. "*Mmm*, I see we're drinking the good stuff. What's the occasion?"

We sat down at opposite ends of the sofa and turned slightly to face each other.

"I think not being locked up in jail after the grilling the cops gave me today is reason enough to celebrate for the moment."

"Oh, Halley, I'm sorry. The police really think foul play was involved in Vince Dalton's death?"

"Not only do they think he was murdered, I seem to be their number one suspect."

"They didn't actually say that, did they?"

"Everything but."

"Why on earth would they suspect you had anything to do with his death? You'd never even seen the man before."

"I know that's what I said last night, and I probably should've stuck to that story. When they showed me his driver's license, he didn't look familiar. But when I saw the photo in the newspaper this morning, I did remember seeing him once."

"When was that?"

"The same night the theater was vandalized. I was in the lobby after I got back from having dinner with Kendra. I looked up and saw him standing just inches from the front door staring blankly at me. It kind of creeped me out at the time, but I told myself I was being silly, that it was just some tourist trying to get a peek inside the theater."

"I don't see how the fact that you saw him once through a window gives you any connection to the victim," Trudy said.

"Because, as it turns out, Vince Dalton was the one who vandalized the theater."

"Why in the world would he do that? What reason could he

possibly have had?"

"Beats me, especially since he apparently wanted to be the new owner. According to the cops, he called Mr. Hamish just after Uncle Leon's death anxious to buy the theater. He was less than thrilled to find out Uncle Leon had an heir. They're convinced he approached me about buying the theater and when I turned him down he resorted to vandalism to frighten me away. Neat story, but not true. He never said a word to me."

"So, Vince Dalton must be the same guy who tried to buy the theater from Leon," Trudy said.

"Someone tried to buy the theater? When was this?"

"Just a few months ago. George told me about it, said Leon turned him down flat—and the man got pretty ugly about it. The same man, I'm assuming it was Dalton, also tried to buy the candle shop on your block. And the owner, Linda Halsey, seriously considered selling."

"Really? So, when he couldn't buy a big, old theater, he tried to buy a tiny candle shop instead? That seems odd."

"Yep."

We both paused, momentarily lost in our own thoughts, as we sipped Chardonnay.

"The cops think you knew somehow that Vince was the vandal and you decided to kill him—in your own theater on opening night? Wait...how do they know he was the vandal? And how was he killed anyway?"

"They didn't say. In fact, they didn't say a lot of things. Maybe they found some green spray paint at his place, I don't know. Since George didn't mention any obvious wounds, I'm guessing they think it was death was by poison. Presumably, I slipped something lethal into his coffee in front of an audience as I made and served espressos, lattes and cappuccinos to a lobby full of people."

"Now listen, sweetie. The cops may have grilled you to see if you knew more than you were saying, especially after you said you'd never seen him before, then changed your story. But that doesn't mean they think you actually killed the man. I think you're inferring more than you should."

"You weren't there. I thought they were going to lock me up at any moment. And they told me not to leave town without checking with them first. They seem to think I'll become a fugitive on the lam, like Humphrey Bogart in *Dark Passage*."

Despite wanting to put up a brave front, hot tears stung my eyes. Trudy reached over and grabbed my hand.

"Isn't that the movie where he had his face all bandaged up?"

I nodded.

"Just promise me you won't have plastic surgery to change your appearance like Bogie did in the movie. Your face is lovely just the way it is," she said, pushing my hair out of my eyes and brushing her fingers affectionately against my cheek. "Besides, as I recall it turned out Humphrey Bogart was innocent, too, wasn't he?"

I smiled and nodded. Thinking about Bogart's character's innocence made me feel better for some reason.

"Maybe you and George could suggest a defense attorney, just in case. The only lawyer I know is Mr. Hamish of Hamish, Davis, and Weltner. But since he handles estates, he probably doesn't try criminal cases. Maybe Davis or Weltner does?" I wondered aloud.

"I don't think we need to find you an attorney just yet. But I do think you should call Mr. Hamish in the morning. If Vince made an offer to buy the theater, either before or after you arrived in town, it seems to me he should have told you about it. You talk to Mr. Hamish, and George and I will see what we can find out about Vince Dalton. Knowledge is power."

Trudy got up to leave. "Why don't you come down and have

supper with us tonight? I've got a lovely pot roast in the oven."

The thought of Trudy's pot roast made my mouth water, but I didn't feel up to being sociable.

"Thank you, but I have some leftovers I should eat," I said, trying not to show my distaste for the soggy club sandwich in the fridge.

"Okay, sweetie," she said, giving me a hug, "but soon. You know we love having you visit."

After Trudy left, it occurred to me I was starving. I took the sandwich out and removed the meat and cheese, toasted two fresh slices of bread and reassembled the sandwich with a shot of mustard. Not too bad, I thought after taking a bite. I grabbed a cold beer and sat down at the table. Beer was one thing I wouldn't run out of soon. Uncle Leon had several cases stacked in the bedroom. My guess was he stocked up when it went on sale. I was dying to call Kendra and tell her everything, but weekends were her busiest time and the escape rooms were open until ten on Friday, Saturday and Sunday nights. The clock on the microwave told me it was five o'clock.

There was plenty of cleaning left to do downstairs, but I was tired after losing sleep last night and any reserve energy I possessed had been drained during the inquisition at the police station. Since there was no showing tonight I stretched out on the sofa and gave in to a nap. When I woke up later it felt like I'd slept for hours, but I discovered it was only a little after six. I decided to watch an old movie to boost my flagging spirits, wondering if people in prison get to watch television. After thumbing through my box of classic movies, I pulled out a DVD of *Dark Passage*, popped it in the player, and let the black-and-white movie images comfort me, as they had since I was a kid. Although, I was more into the antics of Abbott and Costello than the romance of Bogart and Bacall when I first fell in love with old movies.

I still had time to kill before the escape rooms closed and I could phone Kendra. Knowing I was currently Public Enemy Number One of the Utopia Springs Police Department was giving me the jitters. I needed to keep busy, so I got to work sorting through more of Uncle Leon's boxes of junk, something I'd gotten woefully behind on during the theater renovations.

I went in the bedroom and grabbed one of the boxes stacked in the corner. Another excursion into bits and pieces of Uncle Leon's life, what seemed like millions of sheets of paper and ephemeral—most of them useless. But I couldn't bring myself to just toss them wholesale into the dumpster, hoping to find something meaningful. I longed to get to know him in some small measure.

I came across a postcard from Las Vegas. Nothing was written on the back, and I wondered if he'd ever actually been there. I dumped everything else in the box into a trash bag, carried it down to the alley and tossed it into the big green dumpster. I jumped, startled as something brushed against my leg, but looking down, I was relieved to see it was Eartha, who looked up at me and meowed.

"About time you turned up. I know you and Uncle Leon had an open relationship where you came and went as you pleased. But I feel better when you stay home nights."

When I knelt down and petted her she climbed up on my knee. I cradled her in my arms and Eartha Kitty purred as I carried her inside with me.

As soon as we entered the apartment, Eartha leapt from my arms to check her food bowl, which was empty. She shot me a look of betrayal and sharply meowed her displeasure. I obeyed and filled her bowl.

With Eartha happy, or at least appeased, I restacked the boxes I'd taken down to sort through. The rest would have to wait for another day. Picking up a box to add back to the stack, I jostled the contents and spied a party hat inside with a confetti design printed on it and silly frills tumbling from the top of the cone. I tried to imagine Uncle Leon wearing it. For some reason, I was suddenly curious how it would look atop the deer head. I moved a dining chair over, climbed up and placed the party hat on the antlers, adjusting it to a jaunty angle. Stepping down and viewing it from the center of the room, I was pleased with the effect. He definitely looked less stern wearing the hat.

"Okay, you can stay," I said to my antlered companion. "I think I'll call you Derek."

Eartha, who had finished her dinner, padded over and leapt onto the back of the sofa. It could be my imagination, but she shot me a look like she thought I was crazy.

# CHAPTER 10

At 10:36 p.m. I called Kendra.

Before she could even say hello, I rattled off, "Kendra, I have so much to tell you. Can I come over and help you clean up? We can talk as we work."

"Sure. Come on over, we can talk while we *eat*. I just phoned and ordered a large mushroom pizza."

Pizza sounded good. It had been a while since my sandwich. Before walking over to Kendra's place I stopped by the theater snack bar and grabbed a box of M&M's and a box of Raisinets, thinking the least I could do was bring dessert. I tossed money for the candy on the shelf under the counter to remind me to pay for it later. I wanted to make sure I was straight-up business when it came to the business side of things.

Kendra was standing in the alley by the back door when I arrived. After we stepped inside she locked the door behind us.

"Won't you have to unlock in just a few minutes for the pizza delivery person?"

"Already delivered a couple of minutes ago. We've got fresh, hot pizza waiting for us upstairs, girl."

I felt way more excited about that than was seemly.

"I brought dessert," I said, pulling the candy boxes out of my pockets. "You can choose your fave, or we can split them."

"I'll take some of both. You can't go wrong with chocolate, and we can pretend the ones with raisins are healthy."

After we'd each scarfed down a slice of pizza, I filled Kendra in on my eventful, but not in a good way, day.

"Wow. So the dead guy is the one who stared at you through the window—and who spray-painted 'Go home' on your wall. Sounds like he had something personal against you, doesn't it?"

"Hey, you sound like the cops. Who's side are you on anyway?"

"You know I'm on your side. I'm just trying to look at this from the cops' point of view. Figure out what they're thinking. Mr. Dalton seems like a bundle of contradictions."

"How do you mean?" I asked.

"Well, he seemed eager to buy the theater, which is a huge space. But he also wanted to buy the very small candle shop. And if he wanted the theater, why would he trash it? Why didn't he just approach you and offer you a bunch of money? If I were him I'd figure your uncle was old and didn't want to sell, but you might be happy to swap it for cash."

"What do you mean 'happy to swap it for cash'? I don't want to sell the theater."

"I'm not saying you do, or did. But how was he to know? Seems like it would've been worth a shot if he really wanted to buy it. Wait. What if it's not about the theater? What if he just wants properties on your block? Maybe he's a developer."

"That's an intriguing possibility," I said as I nibbled on the crust. "And if he were a developer it could be that there's someone who was seriously opposed to his development—or maybe he had a falling out with his business partner. One of those people could have killed him. It would be nice if I could suggest suspects to the police other than me. How can we find out?" I said.

"I suppose we could start by checking with the planning commission to see if any proposed development plans have been submitted.

\*    \*    \*

I'd just gotten up Monday morning when Trudy phoned and asked me to meet her at the muffin shop for breakfast. Since the escape rooms were closed on Mondays, I called Kendra to see if she wanted to join us. I hurriedly dressed and tried to make my hair presentable. I gave up on the hair and put on a baseball cap. It featured the MGM logo, along with the movie studio's trademark lion. I'd found it among Uncle Leon's mountain of possessions. Snatched it out of a bag tagged for the charity thrift shop, in fact. I'd carted so many loads of donations to them it was embarrassing, so I had started storing some in the basement to space out my trips. I felt an obligation to guard Uncle Leon's reputation, not let word get out to everyone in town that he was a hoarder, even though he was—on a grand scale.

Trudy and I ordered Zeke's sinfully good cinnamon rolls along with some coffee and took a seat at a bistro table in the corner. I spotted Kendra as she came in and waved to her. She waved before going to the counter to order.

"What's up? Are you hiding from George?" I asked Trudy, quietly.

"No, whatever would give you that notion?" she said with a bemused expression.

"It's kind of early, I figured you'd have breakfast with your husband, that's all."

"It's not early for old folks like us, we've been up since five. And George usually meets some of his geezer friends for coffee on Monday mornings.

Kendra made her way to the table. After exchanging hellos, Trudy said, "The reason I called you this morning was I did a little asking around about Vince Dalton and found out he had been renting a cottage in town from my friend, Paula Turpin.

She said the cops searched his place yesterday and hauled off a bunch of boxes. When I inquired, she also said it would be okay for you to come by and take a look around his place, if you like. Kendra, I think it would be good if you could go with Halley. I'd go, but George is conducting a painting workshop, which means I have to mind the store."

"Sure, I'm game," Kendra said.

"Paula runs a little B&B and I think she serves breakfast to guests between seven and nine. So, you probably could drop by around nine thirty. I'll text you her address," Trudy said to me as she punched buttons on her phone.

"Did Paula tell you anything about Vince when you talked to her?" I asked.

"No, she didn't have time to talk right then and I didn't want George to know what we're up to just yet. He says the police are questioning everyone at this point so there's no reason to think they suspect you. He also said we should keep our noses out of it and let the police take care of finding a killer. He just doesn't want us to wander into danger—I don't want us to, either. If anything scary happens you call the cops right way, you hear? But I think you're safe talking to Paula and looking around Vince's place, since the cops have already finished going through it."

"Sounds like a plan," Kendra said.

"Good. But you gals be careful. And remember, we don't have to catch the killer, just come up with a suspect to make the police lose interest in you."

"Got it," I said.

Trudy started getting up to go. I almost choked trying to speak with a mouthful of hot coffee. I raised my hand, motioning for Trudy to wait.

"Hang on a sec," I said, and she planted herself firmly back in the chair.

"I wanted to ask you. Have you heard about any proposed development plans for downtown, specifically the block the theater's on?"

"No, why?"

"Kendra and I were talking, and we think it seems weird that Vince was interested in buying the theater and the candle shop—not exactly related businesses or even buildings of a similar size. Kendra suggested maybe Vince was some kind of developer, who just wanted the property."

"I'll ask George because if there was even a rumor of development, he'd know. I think it's extremely unlikely though. The city is super strict with developments in the downtown area. Plus, more than one building on that block is on the historic register, which means a developer would be very limited on what they could do to the buildings. Even if he could buy up all the buildings on the block, he wouldn't be able to tear them down or gut them," she said.

"Oh, that's a good point. I hadn't even thought about the registered buildings," Kendra said.

"And, just so y'all know, Paula's okay but she's a bit of an odd bird. Sometimes she's chatty and sometimes she's tight-lipped. Play it by ear and don't be too pushy. That's probably the best approach. I need to do a few things before the gallery opens, but call or stop by later and let me know how it goes."

"Will do—and thanks," I said.

Kendra and I lingered over another cup of coffee before heading to Paula's place.


Residential areas near the downtown district are made up largely of charming, colorfully painted Victorian houses, from mansions to tiny cottages. And nearly a hundred of them operate as bed and breakfasts.

Paula Turpin, fiftyish, her graying brunette hair pulled back in a French braid, opened the front door and stepped outside as we approached her lavender and gray Victorian with gingerbread trim. After introductions Paula sat down in a white-washed wicker chair on the side porch and invited Kendra and me to take a seat across from her in a wooden swing. The chain suspended from the purple ceiling squeaked as we sat down.

"As I told Trudy, the cops already searched Vince Dalton's rental and hauled some things off. So, I see no harm in letting you look through it. The police are supposed to let me know if they get in touch with Vince's mother or some other relative who might want to collect his belongings."

"How long had Vince been living here?" I asked.

"About a year, although he hadn't renewed his lease."

"They didn't mention in the paper. What did he do for a living?" Kendra asked.

"Not much, as far as I could tell. Spent a lot of time poring over books and papers. His desk was next to the window and I could see him there all hours, day and night. Thought maybe he was doing research for a book, but he never said so."

"Could he have been some kind of developer? Maybe looking over maps or blueprints. Did you ever see him with oversized papers, like an architect might have?" I asked.

Paula thought for a moment. "Not that I recall. Of course, I couldn't see everything he had spread out on the desk. But I don't see how he would've had money to invest in developing or building anything. He always paid, but he was late with his rent half the time."

Paula fidgeted with her rings and glanced at her watch a couple of times. Remembering Trudy's admonition not to be too pushy with odd bird Paula, I sensed it was time to move on.

"Well, we don't want to take up too much of your time. Could we take a look at his apartment now?" I said.

Paula nodded and started off across the yard. "This little cottage in the back was his. I rent rooms in the main house to overnight guests, but it's easier to rent my other properties out to long-term tenants. I've got two more long-term rentals down the street—a three-bedroom family home and a converted carriage house behind it."

The little frame house that had been Vince Dalton's had a sagging porch and could use a coat of paint, but it was still cute. Paula unlocked the front door and led us inside. It was a wreck. I wondered if the cops had left the mess, ransacking the place for evidence, or if they had found it in this condition.

"Pull the door closed when you leave. It will lock on its own," Paula said. We said thank yous to the back of her head as she turned quickly and left.

"Paula said he pored over lots of books, but I don't see any books here," Kendra said.

"The cops must've taken them. They may want to page through them looking for notes or underlined stuff," I speculated. "We're probably wasting our time. Anything of importance the police have probably already taken away."

"Let's look with open minds," ever-sunny Kendra said. "If nothing else, maybe we can get a sense or impression about Vince Dalton, what kind of person he was."

"You're right. We're here. We might as well make the most of it."

I dug through scraps of paper in the trash can and looked for indentations in the paper, hoping to find words left behind from the pages on top that had been carted away by the cops. After rubbing a pencil over the indentations on several blank pages, I revealed two words: ham and barber.

"Good news, Kendra, I think I've discovered that Vince ate a sandwich and got a haircut at some point."

Kendra had been thoughtfully eyeing some knickknacks on

a shelf, as well as making a careful examination of a lamp beside the table.

"So does the historian/former museum worker think any of this stuff is valuable?" I asked hopefully.

"Not really. I was looking at the lamp because there's a burn mark. I wondered if someone had tried to electrocute Vince before they poisoned him, or however they killed him. More likely, it's just faulty wiring. But this is interesting," she said turning her attention to a man's ratty old boot, sitting on the shelf.

"Yeah, everything else on the shelf looks like a keepsake or at least decorative item," I said. "Why display one beat up boot? Or maybe the cops found it in the closet and just happened to leave it on the shelf."

"The boot could be worth something, if the other half of the pair was here. I've looked through the house and didn't see it. I'm pretty sure it's Civil War era, possibly a Confederate soldier's boot. But I'm no expert. Hand me that pencil and a piece of paper, please."

Kendra placed the paper I handed her against the boot and rubbed the pencil across to make an impression. Then she held the piece of paper up to the light.

"What do you see?" she asked me.

"Looks like there are a lot of cracks in the old leather to me."

"Look right here at this darker mark," she said, pointing it out with the pencil tip.

I squinted and examined the mark.

"It looks kind of like an anchor, I guess. Wait, an anchor! Does that mean this boot was worn by someone in the Confederate Navy?" I asked, excited by the possibility that we were looking at a piece of history, valuable or not.

"No. I think we may be looking at a map. And if it is, it

could be what got Vince killed," she said in a near whisper.

I stared at her in disbelief and was about to explode with a hundred questions. But before I could ask one, she said quietly, "Let's not talk about this here."

Kendra took several shots of the boot from different angles with her cell phone and we left, making sure to pull the door shut behind us.

# CHAPTER 11

I drove back to the theater and parked in the alley, and we hurried up to my apartment. I was dying to hear what Kendra wouldn't tell me at the cottage.

I grabbed a couple of beers out of the fridge.

"A little early for beer, isn't it?" Kendra said.

"I don't have any Cokes, and the only food I have in the house is a bag of pretzels. Do you want a glass of water instead?"

"No, I'll take a beer with the pretzels. The escape rooms are closed today, so I can live on the edge."

"Okay, now tell me how this old, raggedy boot is a map and how it could've gotten Vince Dalton killed."

"Did you notice, if you looked at Vince's decorating style as a whole, it kind of had a Wild West vibe?" Kendra said.

"No. When I looked at his place as a whole, it had a complete mess look, kind of like Uncle Leon's place the first time I saw it. But now that you mention it, there was a cowboy hat and a little stagecoach statue—and that boot. By the way, can we get back to the boot now?"

"I'm getting there. The hat and the stagecoach stuff reminded me of some research I did on outlaws almost two years ago when I first moved to Utopia Springs that I thought about using for an escape room theme. But I got distracted by a jewel robbery—the one Trudy made the necklace for—and never got back to it.

"The Jesse James gang spent some time in this area. When

it comes to Jesse James, there's a lot of legend and not much substantiated history, which is probably why I lost interest. I'm into actual history. Anyway, Jesse and Frank's step-grandparents owned a house about fifteen miles from Utopia Springs. It's still standing; I've driven past it. And there are hundreds of stories about the James gang hiding buried treasure in or near caverns, mostly in Oklahoma and Kansas, but also in the Ozark Mountains in Missouri and maybe even on the Arkansas side of the Ozarks, close to here.

"Wherever they supposedly had buried treasure, Jesse James and his gang carved symbols on nearby cliffs and cavern walls to mark the spot. And one of the symbols that repeatedly shows up is two facing, interlocking 'Js,' which look like..."

"An anchor!" I said, a lightbulb finally going off in my head.

"There are also a lot of stories about how Jesse once carved a treasure map into his boot and left it with his mother for safekeeping."

"Are you saying that old boot may have actually belonged to Jesse James?"

"I very much doubt it," Kendra said. "In fact, the more closely I look at the boot the more I wonder if it's actually a reproduction. You know, like something Civil War reenactors might wear."

I felt deflated.

"I don't get it. If it's not a treasure map from Jesse James then why is it worth anything and why would somebody possibly kill Vince over it?"

"It may not be real, but Vince—and others—could have believed it was authentic. Let's look at what we know about Vince Dalton. A: he was trying to buy buildings on your block in downtown, but it's unlikely it was for any kind of development. B: he had a fascination with the Wild West and possessed a boot he may have believed was a treasure map. And he was poring over maps and books. And C: there are caverns and tunnels under the city, on the very block where you live. They even give tours about underground Utopia Springs," she said.

"Vince Dalton thinks, or thought, there's buried treasure under the theater and other businesses?"

"It would explain why he was so desperate to buy buildings he couldn't tear down or substantially change. But he still would have needed a partner—someone with money. He could barely pay his rent, according to Paula. Exploring and excavating under the buildings without causing them to collapse would probably take a lot of expertise—and some expensive equipment. And why should the partner share the loot with Vince once he's learned everything Vince knows?"

"Wow."

I leaned back and took a swig of Uncle Leon's Red Stone beer, a bargain basement brand that I'd actually developed a taste for. Although it might be partly sentimental on my part. And partly practical, since there was so much of it on hand.

"Okay, so I'll do a little research on the buried treasure lore at the library, museum, and hall of records. If Vince was digging and asking questions there, his partner—or killer—may have been looking for that information, too. I'll see what I can find," Kendra said.

She took a swig of beer and grimaced.

"We should buy you some decent beer. Something that normal people can drink," she said. Obviously Kendra hadn't developed a taste for the cheap brand the way I had.

Kendra looked up at the deer head on the wall that stared down at the recliner.

"I see you never got around to taking that thing down. I've got some drywall board and spackle and such at my place. If you have time this afternoon we could take the deer head down and patch the wall. Then in a day or two you could paint."

"I know I had said I wanted to get rid of him. But I've decided to keep Derek."

"Derek? You've actually named a deer head hanging on your wall? I'm concerned you may be spending too much time alone."

"Don't be silly. It's just, after I put the party hat on him he started to grow on me. I figure I can put twinkling lights on the antlers at Christmas and festoon them with red, white, and blue streamers for the Fourth of July. Besides, I don't plan to keep much of Uncle Leon's décor—obviously—but I have a feeling this deer meant something to him," I said, gazing up at Derek with affection.

"Alright then, Derek stays."

Kendra ate a few more pretzels and downed the last of her beer with a frown before starting toward the door. "I should work on a few things in the escape rooms. And it just so happens, tonight is the quarterly meeting of the local history society. I'll see if I can find out anything on the sly there, as well. Before the history society thing, I'm meeting Joe for an early dinner at Jade Garden. You want to join us?"

"No, but thanks. I halfway promised Trudy I'd have supper with her and George tonight."

"Okay, give them my best. So long, Halley. See ya, Derek."

I hadn't actually promised Trudy I'd take advantage of her standing invitation to mooch dinner off her and George. But I did want to fill her in on what Kendra and I had discovered. And I didn't want to be a third wheel with Joe and Kendra, who are obviously crazy about each other—even if neither of them seems to realize it.

I called Trudy, saying I'd like to come by later and tell her about our trip to Vince's cottage. Thankfully, and predictably, she invited me to stay for supper, sparing me the embarrassment of inviting myself—and also sparing myself a trip to the market for some groceries.

I finally got down to work cleaning the auditorium and quickly came to the realization that cleaning up sticky stuff was going to be a part of my life from now on. But I figured it was a small price to pay in exchange for owning my own business in a charming town.

The fact that the main entrance to Trudy and George's apartment was through the kitchen, meant it pretty much always smelled delicious when I walked in. And since I was usually hungry when I visited, this was a good thing.

Trudy was fussing over something on the stove when I tapped on the door and let myself in. She made unnecessary apologies. "I hope you don't mind leftover pot roast."

"Are you kidding? Pot roast is one of those foods that's always better the next day."

She put a lid on the pot she was tending, poured us two glasses of wine and motioned for me to join her at the kitchen table.

"Where's George? Can we talk freely?" I asked in a hushed voice.

"He was taking a shower; he'll be here in a minute. But you don't need to worry about him overhearing. We had a little talk and I told him since you're a suspect we are going to do some snooping whether he likes it or not, and it would be more helpful to you and better for our marriage if he's not an old grouch about it," she said as she raised her wine glass and clinked it against mine.

The chinking of glasses must've been George's cue to enter.

"Hi, Halley," he said. He walked to the table, stood between my chair on the end and Trudy's beside me and laid a hand on my left shoulder and one on Trudy's right shoulder. "Did you and Kendra find anything interesting at Vince Dalton's place?

"Sit down, hon, I'll get you some wine," Trudy said.

Trudy started to rise, but George gently pushed down on her shoulder. "You stay put. I'll get it."

George filled a glass and set the wine bottle on the table as he sat down, facing me.

I told them all about Kendra's buried treasure theory.

"I think the idea that the boot belonged to Jesse James is a bunch of hooey," George said.

"Kendra doesn't think it's actually Jesse James's boot. Just that Vince could have believed it was," I said.

"If he shared his ideas about where some alleged Jesse James loot might be buried, it could've gotten him killed. People have certainly killed for less. And people who dig for treasure aren't necessarily inclined to share. Just think about all the old-time gold prospectors who knocked someone off over a claim. But I think it's time you told Halley about that *other* possible motive," Trudy said giving George an instructive look.

"Yeah, well, assuming Dalton was the man who approached Leon about buying the theater—which seems a safe bet since we know he approached Hamish about buying it after his death—Dalton didn't exactly take no for an answer when Leon refused to sell. He resorted to blackmail, trying to strong-arm Leon into selling," George said.

"Really? What was he blackmailing Uncle Leon about?"

George shook his head. "I don't know. Honestly, Leon didn't tell me. He said it wasn't anything illegal, just something Dalton thought would be embarrassing if word got out. But Leon told me he wasn't a blushing schoolboy and he didn't care if Dalton took an ad out in the newspaper, he wouldn't pay that...so-and-so one red cent."

"Should we tell the police?" I asked.

"We thought about that. But, honestly, hon, it would just make things look worse for you. Like Vince was threatening to sully your great-uncle's memory. Plus, we don't have any proof or even know what it was about. But there's more. Leon may not have been the only business owner Vince tried to blackmail," Trudy said, turning to George.

"She didn't come out and tell us, but after talking it over this morning, Trudy and I believe Dalton likely played at blackmail with Linda, the candle shop owner, too, after he offered her a fair price for the shop and she refused. Around the same time Leon told me about the blackmail attempt, Linda came to Trudy and me confidentially and asked our advice about possibly selling her shop. We thought it was strange at the time that she seemed so conflicted about whether to sell or not, since she told us she couldn't imagine doing anything else.

"Do you think Linda may have killed Vince?" I asked.

"No, I don't," George said. "The one thing we know for certain is that Leon didn't kill the blackmailing son of a…But I'm almost as sure that Linda didn't kill him either."

"I can't see Linda as a killer either," Trudy said. "But, George, I don't know why it didn't occur to me earlier, but if Vince was interested in buildings on that block, he likely approached other business owners, too, like maybe the owner of the Wooden Nickel Saloon."

"Could be," George said, stroking his chin. "We know Dalton was playing at blackmail, at least with Leon and maybe with Linda, too. If anyone in town has skeletons in his closet my money is on saloon proprietor Trey Tilby. I'll see if I can quietly find out if there's any real dirt on that sleazy wannabe cowboy."

"Great. Meanwhile, I think Halley and I should drop by the candle shop and have a friendly chat with Linda to find out if Vince was the one who tried to buy her shop. If so, maybe she can give us some insight into what Vince was really after, and if he tried anything else with her—like blackmail.

"At the very least, she would be in a position to tell us if the cops know about the blackmail. If they found evidence at his place that he was blackmailing Linda, I feel certain the detective would have had a chat with her about it by now."

"I've got a question," George said.

"What's that?" Trudy asked.

"Is it time for supper? I'm starved."

"Oh, I think everything's about ready. You really worked up an appetite today trying to teach amateurs how to paint?"

"I depleted all my reserves being nice to people who have no talent but think they do. It wore me out."

"Poor baby, I know how much effort it takes for you to be nice to people," Trudy said with a laugh.

Trudy set heaping bowls of mashed potatoes, gravy, and baby carrots, along with the roast platter on the table. We helped ourselves, passing the dishes family style, and I savored every bite of the melt-in-your-mouth tender pot roast. This was exactly the kind of comfort food I'd been craving without even realizing it. But if I kept eating like this on a regular basis I was going to have to do more than scrub sticky stuff off the floor for exercise.

George filled us in on the demanding and not-so talented students at his painting workshop. Sounded like he'd had a pretty rough day—at least to hear him tell it.

"Can I ask you two something?" I said.

I must've sounded more dramatic than I intended because George and Trudy both gave me their full attention, stopping their forks midway between their plates and mouths.

"Are Kendra and Joe the only people in town who don't know they're in love? She never stops talking about him. And opening night, Joe couldn't keep his eyes off her."

"Kendra *was* absolutely gorgeous in that Eliza Doolittle-inspired dress. They obviously have feelings for each other. I think they just haven't figured out exactly what those feelings are yet. It's a little complicated," Trudy said.

"Nothing complicated about it," George said. "If Joe had a lick of sense he would have already—what is it the kids say?—put a ring on it."

"I'm not sure that's what the kids say," Trudy said, rolling her eyes. "But it *is* complicated. Her parents died in a plane crash just after she started college. Bart, who's several years older and very protective, didn't want her to worry about anything after their folks died. So he and Simon babied her, paid all the bills, basically took care of everything through college and grad school. Kendra is just now really out on her own, albeit still partly subsidized by Bart. Not that there's anything wrong with family support. I think she's just never thought a lot about the future."

"I see. Kendra had basically told me all that, I just didn't put it together. What about Joe? Couldn't he take the lead?"

"Joe's parents are immigrants and they have some pretty traditional ideas about the kind of girl Joe should marry," Trudy said.

"How could they not like Kendra? She's one of the sweetest people I've ever met."

"It's not that they dislike her. It's just..." Trudy paused.

"She's not Chinese," George interjected.

"Oh," I said.

"I don't think Joe would let his parents arrange a marriage for him. But it's always nice to have your family's support, especially if you work together every day. And it might help things along if Kendra was a little more encouraging," Trudy said.

"Basically, they're both waiting for the other one to take the first step, which means they're standing still on the dance floor," George said as he spooned more mashed potatoes onto his plate and ladled gravy over them.

When Trudy transferred a plate of oatmeal raisin cookies

from the counter to the table I somehow managed to limit myself to just one. My self-control may have gotten a little boost from the fact that I was already stuffed.

"This is so good, Trudy," I said with my mouth full. "Which reminds me of an idea I've been wanting to run by you two.

"Let's hear it," George said as he placed a stack of three cookies on the edge of his plate.

"I think I already mentioned that I'd like to try opening the coffee bar for two or three hours in the mornings. I mean, coffee *is* what I know. It would draw people into the theater, and hopefully once they've had a look around they'll come back for the movies."

"I think that's a splendid idea," Trudy said.

George nodded.

"Since showcasing wine from Carvello's on movie night was a hit, I wonder if I could get some of the restaurants and bakeries in town to let me showcase their sweets one morning a week at the coffee bar. You know, muffins from The Muffin Man one morning, pastries from another eatery on a different morning. I could display a sign on the counter with the name of the featured bakery or restaurant and even put out their business cards or flyers. And we could split the money we take in. I wouldn't really be pulling business away from them since I'd just be offering coffee and a very limited, rotating selection of pastries. Do y'all think any of the bakers might be interested? And who should I ask?"

George brushed crumbs off his mouth with his napkin, which led me to believe he had something to say.

"I think that's a good idea. Hit up The Muffin Man, Donut Dealer, and Our Daley Bread bakery, for sure."

"I agree. You might add Tudor House Restaurant to your list. They serve breakfast and their scones are to die for."

"If you talk to Edgar at Tudor House, take Trudy with you.

He's always had a soft spot for her," George said. He batted his eyelashes at Trudy in a mock flirtation, and she rolled her eyes in response.

*They're pretty cute sometimes.*

"George, are you maybe a little jealous?" I said, teasing him.

"No, I'm not jealous. But, I'm not blind either."

"I'd be glad to go with you to talk to Edgar, or any of the other bakers if you'd like," Trudy said.

"Thanks. You're so good to me. I think I can handle Zeke at The Muffin Man on my own, but I'd appreciate some moral support with the others."

Trudy was scheduled to teach her yoga class tomorrow and had a custom jewelry order to finish, as well, so we made arrangements to get together on Wednesday to approach local bakers—and to stop by the candle shop to see what we could find out from Linda.

# CHAPTER 12

Tuesday dawned a beautiful day. I opened all the window blinds to let the glorious sunlight stream in. And I felt rested for a change. My sleep had been less than optimal the first few nights after Vince's death scene on opening night. But last night, I had the benefit of a big meal in my stomach, and Eartha Kitty slept curled up on my lap. As usual, she was gone when I awoke.

*Wonder if I snore?*

Kendra called just before Hidden Clue Escape Rooms' ten o'clock opening time.

"Hey, I can only talk for a minute, but I spoke to Edgar, the president of the historical society, after the meeting last night. He hinted he might know about someone researching Jesse James treasure and parlayed that into having coffee with me. Sadly, he seems to think it's a date. It's not. Anyway, I'm meeting him at The Muffin Man Wednesday morning, so we'll see."

"Wait, Edgar? Is this the same Edgar that owns the Tudor House Inn and Restaurant?

"Yeah, why?"

I started laughing.

"What's so funny?"

"It's just Edgar is trying to con you into a date, and he has the hots for Trudy—or at least George thinks so. He must be quite a character. He likes his women young—and also very mature."

"Honestly, I think he'd settle for breathing, and even that might be ambitious on his part," Kendra said.

"Don't put yourself in harm's way just for a little information."

"Edgar's not dangerous, just odd. He acts chivalrous and puts on a phony British accent. And he mostly wears tweed. Besides, I think I'll be safe enough at the muffin shop. I'll let you know what I find out."

"Thanks, I can't wait to hear what you discover. And, long story, but Trudy and I are talking to Linda at the candle shop tomorrow and I may have some info to share with you, too."

Rested and excited by the possibilities, I got busy cleaning some nooks and crannies in the theater that I'd missed earlier, then ran the vacuum and cleaned the bathroom in the apartment. I practiced my sales pitch aloud as I cleaned. Then I tried to make myself look presentable, and hopefully capable and reliable as well, before marching purposefully down the block to The Muffin Man. The morning rush was over, and I had the perfect opportunity to order a cinnamon roll and tell Zeke, the owner, my idea as he rang me up. Much to my delight—and relief—he said yes.

Feeling empowered after my triumph at the muffin shop, I walked back to the apartment and steeled myself to make a phone call I'd been putting off for way too long. I'd only talked to my dad, and said a quick hello to my mom, once since moving to Utopia Springs. And I didn't exactly mention that my address had changed. I called my dad's cell phone, figuring I'd start with him and work my way up to talking to Mom.

"Hi, Dad."

"Halley, how's my girl? Is everything okay?"

It's telling of my relationship with my parents that when I call they assume something must be wrong.

"Everything's great, Dad. How are things there?"

"Beautiful as always. We live in the sunshine state, after all."

Something to that effect was always my dad's reply. Taking early retirement just over a year ago, moving to Florida and playing golf most days definitely agreed with my dad. Not sure it was my mom's dream retirement, but then I have no idea what her dream retirement would be.

"Dad, I've got some big news."

"Well, let's hear it."

I sucked in a deep breath.

"I've moved to Utopia Springs, Arkansas. Uncle Leon passed away recently and left his second-run movie theater to me. I just reopened it as a classic film theater with a coffee and wine bar. Opening night made a big splash and has the whole town talking," I said, which was completely true, if slightly misleading.

There was an uncomfortable moment of silence on the other end of the line.

"That's wonderful, sweetheart. If that's what you want."

"It is what I want. It's beautiful here. The people are nice. And the business allows me to indulge two of my favorite things—old movies and coffee."

"Then, I'm really happy for you, Halley."

"If you could pass the phone to mom, I guess I should tell her the good news, too."

"Of course. But listen, sweetheart. Don't be disappointed if your mom doesn't seem excited about your news. It's just..."

"I know. I never do anything to please her."

"That's not it. The thing is, your mom had kind of a complicated history with her family, especially Uncle Leon. That's all."

I heard him call out to my mom in the next room. "Honey, Halley's on the phone," and a beat later, "Here's your mom."

I shared the news with my mother. I couldn't actually hear her clenching her teeth, a habit of hers, but I could tell they were clenched by how tight her words came out.

"Halley, you're a grown woman, and goodness knows you'd never ask for my advice. But Leon Baxter never thought of anyone but himself. Sell that theater, take the money and move as far away from there as you can. And you can think of him however you like, but please don't refer to him as 'Uncle Leon' to me."

"Mom, whatever happened with your family, with Uncle— with Leon, maybe you could try to move past it now. He's gone."

"I can't forgive him for what he did to our family, to my dad. It broke my mother's heart. Death doesn't absolve people of their wrongdoing." She started choking up.

"Mom, please..."

"Halley, it's Dad. Your mom passed the phone back to me."

"Why can't she just be happy for me?"

"Sweetheart, it's not you. I told you, it's a complicated family thing. Good luck with the theater. I better go check on your mom. Love you."

I sank into the recliner sulking for a moment, my lip stuck out like a pouty two-year-old. I decided to go in the kitchen to distract myself with cooking or cleaning. But the dishes were all washed up and the only things in the fridge were beer, eggs, mayo and mustard. I popped open a beer and set about making deviled eggs while I cried.

My lunch of deviled eggs did little to console me.

The phone in my pocket buzzed. It was Trudy.

"I'm on your block, passing through on an errand. Okay if I drop by?"

"Of course, I'll let you in through the front door."

I jogged down the steps and sprinted through the lobby. I peered out the front door and in a minute Trudy came into view.

"Hey, young lady," she said as she stepped inside. "I have some very serious business to discuss with you." She gave me a schoolteacher look that typically meant you're getting sent to the principal's office.

"Oh," I said, feeling a surge of nerves.

"Don't look so worried, it's not *that* serious," she said with her trademark laugh. "I just think it's about time you met my and George's elite social circle—the Arts and Old Farts Bowling League. It's artists and some other business owners, mostly geezers like us. Did you know that Utopia Springs has more artists per capita than Paris?"

"Really?"

"I don't know. I just made that up, but we have a lot. Over a hundred full-time artists live here, last I heard. Anyway, the other old farts are jealous that we haven't introduced you to them. We meet once a month at the bowling alley, and tonight's the night. You'd lower the average age of our group by a good twenty years. Please come and let George and me show you off," she said with pleading eyes.

"I'd be delighted to meet your friends. But...I can't bowl."

"Don't worry, neither can I. Most of the men and a couple of the women bowl, while the rest of us mostly sit in the snack bar, drinking beer and gossiping. But tonight will be a little different. It's our league's annual bowling tournament. So, us non-bowlers will be cheering on our favorite team, which for you and me will be George's team—or else he'll get cranky. Winners get a cheap plastic trophy and bragging rights, which they take very seriously. Please say you'll come."

"Wouldn't miss it."

"Yay, go team!" Trudy said rolling, then raising her arms in a cheerleader move. "Okay, hon. I'll see you tonight about seven-thirtyish?"

"I'll be there."

After I'd let her out and locked the door behind her, I realized I was smiling. Trudy had acted like I was doing her a favor, but truth was, getting invited to bowling night so she and George could show me off to their friends had lifted my spirits.

I arrived at the bowling alley at the edge of the main shopping district a little after seven thirty as Trudy had instructed. It wasn't hard to find with its animated neon sign of bowling pins falling down.

The league had the lanes at one end, near the snack bar, staked out. I spotted George, wearing a Hawaiian shirt, setting a bowling bag down at his lane. He'd brought his own bowling ball. Trudy waved me over to the snack bar, where she was bunched with a group of four or five ladies.

I said "Hi, Trudy" as I walked up, and they opened space in the huddle for me to join the circle. There were hellos and introductions all around.

"George is cute in his Hawaiian shirt," I said.

"That's his lucky bowling shirt," Trudy said. "But he doesn't bowl any better when he wears it."

"Why is it lucky then?" I asked.

"He wore it on our honeymoon," she said with a knowing smile, eliciting "oohs" and "I heard thats" from the group.

"Hon, we're gonna toss back a couple of quick beers. Once they get going, we'll stand behind our team and yell a couple of sis-boom-bahs to show our enthusiasm," said a woman with a raspy, deadpan voice who'd been introduced to me as Phyllis.

Claire, a bubbly woman wearing a vintage cheerleading uniform said, "Halley, I think it would really rouse our team if you shake your pom poms."

I wasn't sure how to respond to that. Claire turned around for a moment, reaching into a bag, before handing me a set of actual pom poms.

"Claire is captain of our cheerleading squad," Trudy said, suppressing a giggle. "She and her husband own the stained glass studio near us."

"That's my Arnie over there in the orthopedic bowling shoes," Claire said, pointing out a man on George's team before sitting down next to Phyllis at one of the tables.

A woman whose name I didn't quite catch returned from the snack counter with a basket of nachos, which she set down next to Claire. She pushed an adjoining table up against it and scooted chairs over to accommodate our little group.

"I'll get us some beers," Trudy said, touching my arm. "Red Stone for you, right?"

I nodded and pulled some cash out of my jeans pocket, but she waved it away.

I sat down next to the nachos lady.

"So sorry about your uncle, Halley. It's sad Leon's not here for the tournament. First time in ages," she said, before moving on to other subjects.

Trudy returned with our beers. There were four teams of four playing in the tournament. They passed around sheets and seemed to be going over rules or procedures for an inordinate amount of time before they started actually bowling.

When it was our team's turn, Claire leapt up and grabbed my hand. Trudy hurried to join us and Phyllis trailed along behind. We lined up behind the bowlers and Claire reached down and vigorously patted Arnie's shoulders.

George was first up. He steadied the ball, did a hopscotch-like move on the approach. He leaned forward, kicking his right leg behind him as he released the ball. He knocked down all the pins, except one. But he picked up the spare.

Claire jumped up and down, Trudy yelled, "That's how you do it!" and I called out, "Yay, George!" as I timidly waved my pom poms.

George glanced up at us with an appreciative nod as he went back to his seat, but I could tell he was keeping his head in the game.

We rejoined the group in the snack bar. The bowling alley echoed with laughter and the clatter of pins getting knocked down. In between snippets of gossip about people I didn't know and digging into my background—Where was I from? Had I ever been married?—they shared some stories about Uncle Leon. How he loved fishing almost as much as he loved telling exaggerated fishing tales. How Eartha Kitty had leapt through the apartment window from the fire escape into his arms—and his heart. And how he never talked about his service in Vietnam but quietly slipped a few bucks to any veteran down on his luck, along with never charging them for a movie ticket.

In a bit, Trudy touched my arm and cocked her head, indicating I should follow her. We grabbed a couple more beers and sat down at a table for two.

"Hon, Leon is on everyone's mind tonight because this is our first tournament since his passing. I hope all the talk about him isn't upsetting to you."

"No, just the opposite. I really would like to know more about Uncle Leon, but I haven't wanted to ask you and George too many questions because I know y'all were good friends. I don't want to make you feel sad."

"Aw, Halley, I'm sorry. I'll be glad to reminisce about your uncle, but you're right that George may not be ready to stroll down memory lane just yet. I can tell you one thing about Leon—and I hate to speak ill of the dead—but the man was a lousy bowler. George is a serious competitor, so it tells you something about how fond George and the other guys were of Leon that they kept him on their team."

I looked over at George in his lucky Hawaiian shirt and

Arnie in his orthopedic bowling shoes with feelings of affection and gratitude.

"Oh, Trudy. George is up," I said, hurrying over for cheerleading duty. Trudy came with me and Claire, of course, was already in place. I'd mislaid my poms but pumped my fist and yelled, "Go, George."

He did his fancy footwork move, ending with the right leg extended back, and scored a strike. We clapped and cheered loudly. Claire was so excited she nearly knocked me over.

George's team won the tournament, apparently for the first time ever. After they shook hands with all the bowlers on the other teams and collected their awards, George held his tiny plastic trophy aloft and said, "This one's for Leon," which elicited a big wave of applause, along with a few tears.

# CHAPTER 13

Wednesday morning, I picked up a couple of cinnamon rolls from The Muffin Man and brought them back to the coffee bar to have for breakfast with Trudy. When she arrived at nine thirty I solicited an order from her for a vanilla shot latte and a cinnamon roll, the confection du jour, as a trial run for the coffee bar's new morning hours starting tomorrow. I showed off the signs I had designed, printed and laminated of the places I hoped would let me feature their specialties at the coffee bar. I was counting on the power of positive thinking by printing them ahead of time. Then I ran my sales pitch by her—the one I'd used successfully at The Muffin Man.

"I think that pitch is just about bulletproof. But keep in mind we'll need to indulge in a little small talk first. You can't go straight for the sale, you have to ease into it. This is the South, after all. And when we get to Tudor House Restaurant, let me handle Edgar. He's putty in my hands. George wasn't too far off on that one," she said with a laugh.

I didn't have the heart to tell Trudy that Edgar had cheated on her this morning by having coffee with Kendra at eight thirty. *Wonder how that went?*

We set out for our sales calls a little after ten, hoping to catch the owners after their morning rush.

Turned out the Donut Dealer was putty in *my* hands, or at least he was onboard with letting me showcase his doughnuts one morning a week.

"I think it's a great idea. My doughnuts are superb," owner Adam Caine said, raising his fingers to his lips in a chef's kiss. "My location is not the best in town, so hopefully some new customers will discover my doughnuts through you—as long as you're flexible about the selection I give you."

"Of course. Besides, it's a good idea to mix it up and showcase a variety of choices. I'll be open for two to three hours Tuesday through Friday mornings. Do you have a preference as to which day?"

I could make this offer because Zeke at The Muffin Man had said he was flexible about his day.

"If it's available, I'll take Wednesday. It's usually a slower day."

He decided to provide a dozen each week to start, saying we could adjust according to sales.

After we'd left Donut Dealer, Trudy said, "You're good at this, Halley. Maybe you should've gone into sales as a career."

"I *have* gone into sales. I'm selling coffee, doughnuts, wine, candy, and movie tickets—so far."

We shared a giggle and I entered Our Daley Bread Bakery with a big smile. But owner/manager Gisele Daley quickly wiped the smile off my face. After some awkward chit chat, the dour baker reacted to my sales pitch, which had worked brilliantly up to now, like I was trying to snatch her hot cross buns.

Trudy came to my rescue and Gisele finally agreed to think it over for a week or two and perhaps talk to Adam the Donut Dealer and Zeke the Muffin Man to see how it was going for them.

"That could've gone better," I said as we left, feeling deflated.

"Don't let crabby Gisele bring you down, kid. It wasn't a firm no. Besides, I'm sure we'll have better luck with Edgar. Putty," she whispered, rubbing her hands together.

We entered Tudor House Restaurant and Edgar hurried over to welcome us. I'd never met him but easily recognized him, based on Kendra's description. Even so, he wasn't quite what I expected. He was dressed like a country squire with a tweed jacket, brown boots, and a rose boutonniere on his lapel. He greeted us with a broad gap-tooth grin and a posh English accent.

"Hello, Trudy, always a pleasure to see you," he said, giving her a gentlemanly hug.

"Halley, this is our dear friend, Edgar Wentworth. Edgar, this is Halley Greer, Leon's great-niece."

I extended my hand and he gave me a gentle, but lingering, handshake.

"Halley, my sincere condolences on the loss of your great uncle, but we're delighted to have you join our little community."

"Thank you, Edgar. I love the restaurant's décor. I'm sorry I haven't had a chance to visit before now. We were so busy getting the theater ready for the opening."

"Please, please. No apologies. I'm delighted you're here now. What can I do for you, lovely ladies? Would you like brunch or tea?"

"We'd love some tea—and some of your delicious orange scones. And Edgar, if you have time to join us for a few minutes, we have a little proposition for you," Trudy said, batting her eyelashes exactly like George had demonstrated at dinner the other night. I managed to suppress a smirk, just barely.

"Well, now. I love being propositioned by beautiful women," he said, beaming. "You just make yourselves comfortable in that corner booth and I'll be with you shortly.

"You're a brazen hussy," I whispered to Trudy, who shot me a sly grin. We scooted into the booth next to each other, leaving the seat across from us for Edgar.

The Tudor House Restaurant was a warm and inviting space with soaring pitched gables, half-timbered walls, a huge brick fireplace, and banks of windows admitting generous sunlight. Dark-stained woodwork and medieval style tapestries completed the look.

"How many rooms does the Tudor House Inn have?" I asked.

"I'd guess about thirty or forty," Trudy said.

The waitress brought over a pot of hot water, teacups and a variety of teas. Trudy selected Earl Grey and I settled on Darjeeling. A few minutes later Edgar joined us, carrying a tray of scones, along with clotted cream and jam.

Trudy was right. The scones were to die for. She was also right that Edgar was putty in her hands. I was able to concentrate fully on my scones because I barely got a word in as Trudy and Edgar endeavored to out flirt each other. I didn't peek under the table to confirm it, but I had the distinct impression they were playing footsies. It was a little weird, but all perfectly harmless, and we left with a commitment from Edgar for scones on Fridays.

Fortified by tea and jam-laden scones, Trudy and I headed over to the candle shop to have a little chat with Linda.

When we entered Bell, Bath and Candle we were greeted by the aroma of scented candles and the gentle tinkling of windchimes. New Age music played softly in the background. As we passed a display of handmade soy candles an ample figure swathed in flowing fabrics hurried toward us.

"Greetings, gentle spirits. Hello, Trudy, wonderful to see you. Namaste," she said, bringing her palms together and bowing her head slightly.

Trudy returned the greeting.

"Linda, have you met Halley yet? She's Leon's great niece."

"Not formally. We exchanged quick hellos the night of the

theater's opening as I was waiting for my glass of wine. Halley, I'd like to try some of your coffee sometime, but I have to end my caffeine consumption by noon or it disrupts my circadian rhythm."

"I understand completely," I said.

"Actually, starting tomorrow Halley will be opening the coffee bar on Tuesday through Friday mornings from eight to ten thirty. If you have a chance, stop by for a cup before you open the shop."

"I'll be sure to do that. And Halley, I'm so sorry about your great uncle. Leon was a dear man and he is missed."

"Thank you."

"Linda, we plan to do a bit of shopping while we're here, but we actually have an ulterior motive," Trudy said.

"Oh." Linda raised her eyebrows.

"The terrible business with that man dying on the theater's opening night was bad enough. Now, the police have decided it's probably murder, and they seem to be eyeing Halley as a suspect—which is completely ridiculous, of course."

"Oh, my, why ever would they suggest such a thing?"

"Well, you know he offered to buy the theater from Leon, like he offered to buy your shop. And—" Trudy paused scanning the room to make sure no one else was around. "—we can't be sure, but we think Vince also tried to pressure Leon with a bit of blackmail, as well."

"No, I didn't know, but I'm not surprised. I hate to speak ill of the dead, but Vince Dalton was not a nice man. Did he try to continue his blackmail game with Halley?" she said, looking me up and down.

"No," I said. "In fact he never even approached me about buying the theater. But the cops seem disinclined to believe me because it turns out Vince was the one who vandalized the theater and nearly delayed the grand opening. They think that suggests it was personal."

"Mind you, it's not common knowledge that he was the vandal, so please keep that quiet for now," Trudy said.

"Of course, you have my word."

"Linda, I realize this is a delicate matter and I don't won't to impose on our friendship, but since Halley is in a tough spot, I was wondering if you could tell us—in complete confidence, of course—did Vince Dalton try to pressure or blackmail you when you refused to sell the shop?"

Linda's sunny yellow aura turned gray around the edges. She exhaled a deep breath and said, "Yes, he did—twice. Mind you, it wasn't about anything criminal, just something foolish I had done years ago that would have been quite embarrassing for me if it became public. However, I couldn't bring myself to sell my shop. I trusted my friends, like you and George, to stand beside me even through humiliation, and firmly told him no. When I refused to sell, Vince tried to make alternate blackmail arrangements with me, which I won't go into, but which I also refused. I held my breath waiting for him to go public with the embarrassing information he had on me, but he never did."

Linda's cheerful countenance returned, and she reached out and clasped one of my hands and one of Trudy's.

"Thank you. It feels good to release the negative energy I've held bottled up inside me for months."

"That's wonderful Linda. Thank you. And you can absolutely trust our discretion," Trudy said. "If the police had found any blackmail evidence among Vince's belongings I'm sure they would have questioned you about it. They haven't, have they?"

"No, and that thought had crossed my mind. I also wondered if I have an obligation to tell them about it, what with his death being a murder investigation now. But, while he threatened blackmail on two different matters, he never went through with it, and he had ample time before he died. The way I see it Vince was a bully, but not exactly a blackmailer. All talk, if you will."

"I see what you're saying," Trudy said. "Can you tell us anything else about Vince, like did he ever mention a business partner? And did he tell you what his plans for the shop were if you had sold it to him?"

"He never mentioned a partner, but he did tell me it was a cash offer. Of course, he never showed me any proof of that. And he didn't say what he wanted to do with the shop—I had a hard time envisioning him selling soaps and candles. But now that you mention it, there was something odd. He honestly seemed more interested in the basement, and there's nothing special down there."

"Really? That does seem a little odd," Trudy said after she and I exchanged a discreet glance.

The tinkle of windchimes signaled someone had entered the store.

"Would you mind if we took a quick peek in the basement while you tend to your customer?"

"I guess not," she said with a curious look and directed us to an unlocked door beyond a curtain.

We flipped on a light switch before descending the creaky wooden stairs. I coughed after inhaling the dank air mingled with scented soaps and candles. It was aroma therapy, but not in a good way. The dimly lit basement had a few boxes of unopened inventory near the stairs. Against one wall, empty boxes had been collapsed and neatly stacked, along with some pallets, and in a far corner was a pile of stored items that had been there for so long it was covered with a veil of cobwebs.

"What are we looking for?" I asked.

"I don't know, I guess whatever it was that caught Vince's attention. I'm just hoping we'll know it when we see it," Trudy said.

Three walls had obviously been covered in plaster at some point, there were still bits clinging to the masonry. The third wall, along the side facing the street, was plaster free.

"That's interesting," Trudy said as she pulled keys from her purse and flipped on the small flashlight attached to the keychain.

"What is?"

"This wall looks to have been built later," she said, shining the flashlight at chips in the mortar and examining the wall closely. "No use. I can't see anything."

Just then, the door at the top of the stair opened and Linda *yoo-hooed* to us.

"Are you two okay down there?"

"Yes, Linda, we're just heading up."

Once we'd rejoined her upstairs, Trudy asked, "Do you know if your shop has a sidewalk tunnel?"

"One of the people who conducts those underground tours told me he thinks there might be. But it's not listed on the property records and there's no lavender glass in front of the shop. Do you think that's what Vince was looking for?"

"I have no idea," Trudy said. "It just struck me that the front wall doesn't have any bits of plaster like the other walls. Made me wonder if it was added later. Oh well, thanks for letting us look around."

"It was so nice to meet you, Linda. Hope I see more of you now that we're neighbors, and I'll be back to look at windchimes. I think that would make a great gift for my Grammy's birthday."

"Lovely. Drop in anytime. And I'll try to make it by the theater for a cup of coffee."

I hit my head on some dangling windchimes near the exit.

Trudy and I walked the short distance down the block to

the theater, wordlessly dodging our way through a steady stream of pedestrians. Once we were inside the lobby, I turned to Trudy and fired questions at her with machine gun speed.

"What do you think about Linda's take on Vince as simply an aspiring blackmailer? And what was that all about in the basement? What is a sidewalk tunnel?"

"Whoa, hang on. To answer all those questions I think I'll need some coffee."

"Coming right up. A latte with a vanilla shot?"

"Perfect."

I got busy behind the counter and Trudy pulled up a barstool.

"Linda has a point about Vince not exactly blackmailing her. At any rate, it would be up to her to tell the police. We have nothing to show them. If we said Vince tried to blackmail Linda, she could just deny it."

"I guess. So what about these tunnels?" I asked.

"You've heard of the underground tours they do downtown, right?"

"Yeah, but I don't really know anything about it."

"Okay, so there are springs here, you've seen signs around town about those, like the one in the pocket park, right?"

I nodded.

"The first businesses in town were built to accommodate people who started coming here because they believed those waters had medicinal properties. People who drank from and bathed in the springs claimed to have been healed of everything from heart disease to hot flashes. Those first businesses were built near the springs, which were also near a creek. Problem was, it was low-lying land and the creek had a habit of overflowing after a big rain and flooding the buildings.

"So in the late 1800s, the city devised a scheme to fill in and build up the land. Many existing stores built another story on top of the street level floor of their business. The second floor became the main entrance after the ground was raised. The way I understand it, a retaining wall was built along the street at where it met the sidewalk. In the basements of a couple of buildings in town they still have the original storefront windows that look out across the old sidewalk at the retaining wall. Over the years, most of these got altered and closed up. The spaces between the storefront and the retaining wall are referred to as 'sidewalk tunnels.'"

"Wow. I can't believe I haven't heard about this before. I need to take the underground tour."

"Well, don't get your hopes up too much. As I said, most of those original storefronts have been covered over and most entrances to the old tunnels have been sealed up, some of them have collapsed. You don't actually get to go into any tunnels for safety reasons, I believe. But you get a peek into a couple of old sidewalk tunnels, plus some interesting history."

I handed Trudy her latte.

"How do you pour swirls of milk on top and make it look so pretty. I'm sure if I did that it would look like a blob. What's your secret?"

"The trick is not to over steam the milk. If you get it too frothy, it won't create a sharp image. But don't tell anyone I told you."

"I'll keep it under my hat, kid."

"What's that about the lavender glass?" I've seen a couple of those purple insets in the sidewalks.

"There aren't many of those left, but they were originally installed to allow sunlight to filter through to the sidewalk tunnels. By the way, hon, your coffee's not only pretty it tastes wonderful. No wonder you're a pro."

"Thanks, I'm glad you like it. The history about the tunnels is cool, but how does it help us?"

"Maybe Vince was able to see something through the cracked mortar that I couldn't. Or maybe he has a map that shows a sidewalk tunnel on the other side of that front wall. It fits with Kendra's buried treasure theory, and I couldn't see any other reason he would have been fascinated by Linda's basement."

"Yeah, unless he likes the aroma of *eau de* stinky. I haven't looked all that closely at the theater basement as I've been hauling boxes of Uncle Leon's junk down for storage. You want to go down and take a look around?"

"Some other time. I've got to get back to the shop before George starts thinking I've run off with Edgar. He was sulking because you and I were going to Tudor House to talk to him. But I think it's good for our marriage to let George feel jealous every now and then," she said with a laugh.

# CHAPTER 14

Upstairs, I continued the seemingly endless chore of clearing out boxes. I was sorely tempted to just take a quick peek in each box before trashing it, but reminded myself there could be something important, a letter or photo that might reveal something about my great uncle, or possibly even something that could shed light on the murder victim who had threatened him with blackmail.

Eartha Kitty joined me. Normally she'd just sit in one of the empty, or nearly empty, boxes. Or on top of my clean laundry—a favorite spot. But at the moment she was pawing and mewing at a box in the middle of a stack. I figured it was worth a look, so I moved the boxes and pulled that one out. I sat on the sofa, cross-legged with the box beside me, pulled out a stack of papers and laid it on my lap. Eartha promptly jumped into the box and settled in, peering over the edge at me.

First stack, second stack—nothing. I gently lifted the cat to reach another stack of papers. Underneath I discovered the reason, I think, Eartha was drawn to this particular box. A solitary tennis shoe that reeked. I retrieved it and tossed it on the floor. Eartha jumped down and nestled her head against the shoe. Apparently it smelled like Uncle Leon to her.

"You miss him, don't you, girl?" I said, reaching down and stroking between her ears.

The new stack of stuff on my lap smelled a bit like old feet and included a photo album. I started paging through. There were some pictures of buildings around town. There were several photos of birds. Obviously, he had been something of a bird watcher. There was a nice picture of George and Trudy I set aside thinking they might like to have it. As I flipped the pages, some of the pictures shifted, and I could see there were pictures stuffed behind other photos. I fished them out and found more pictures of birds, a cute picture of Eartha and...What?

There was a faded Polaroid photo. I held the picture up to get a closer look. It was Uncle Leon and my grandfather, his brother. Their long hair and wardrobe told me it was the 1960s. So did the date stamp on the bottom of the picture: Aug. 6, 1968. I noticed a smiling little girl, peeking around my granddaddy's leg. Upon closer inspection, I realized it was my mom.

What had Uncle Leon done to my grandfather that had made her hold a grudge against him for so long? In the photo, Granddaddy and Uncle Leon looked so happy. After staring at the photo for a couple of minutes, it yielded no answers and I tucked it into the desk drawer.

I flopped down on the sofa and pulled up the photos on my cell phone. I scrolled through to a photo of Josh. It was the last picture I ever took of him. I should've had him smooth down his unruly hair and tuck in his shirt. But then I thought, no. I liked it better this way. It looked just like him. I touched my index finger to the image of his face. I missed him so much it hurt. I swallowed hard and then brought up my Grammy's number on the phone.

"Hi cupcake. How did your opening night go?"

"A man died," I blurted out before proceeding to let all my woes tumble out to the one person in the world I knew truly loved me no matter what. I ended my tearful unburdening by telling her about my conversation with Mom.

"Gram, why can my own mother not stand me? She'll

hardly talk to me since Josh died. Does she blame me somehow? And why does she hate Uncle Leon?"

"My, my, that's a lot of questions. I'll start with the one about Uncle Leon. The answer is I don't know. Other than her mother and father, she never liked to talk about her family, so I didn't push. I'm just the mother-in-law, you know. Now concerning you, I can tell you that while she may have a hard time showing it sometimes, your mom does love you very much. And I don't think she blames you or anyone, other than maybe herself, for Josh's death. Like she should've known something was wrong sooner."

"After he died, I tried to call and visit them more often, but it felt like Mom didn't want me around."

"Sweetie, you and Josh were so close, it's hard for your mother. She can't look at you without thinking of him. Do you understand what I mean?"

"I guess. But what am I supposed to do?"

"You just have to give your mom time. Josh's loss is still an open wound for her—and your dad. But for what it's worth, you've always got me out here in Sun City."

"It's worth the world, Grammy. Thanks for listening to me whine."

"Call anytime, cupcake."


Kendra had called and invited me over for dinner at her place. I headed over about eight thirty. I was dying to tell her about our little chat with Linda, and I was curious to hear how her "date" with Edgar had gone. She had said she'd leave the back door unlocked for me. I let myself in and locked the deadbolt on the metal door behind me before jogging up to her apartment.

"Knock, knock," I said, tapping on the door, which was slightly ajar.

"Hey, come on in. I hope you didn't have your heart set on pizza, we've got Chinese take-out from Jade Garden on tonight's menu instead."

"Sounds—and smells—good to me," I said, inhaling an aromatic medley of garlic, ginger, and soy sauce.

We usually sat on the sofa with our pizza slices on paper plates. But Kendra had set places at the table with real plates and paper napkins, so I took a seat in one of the dining chairs.

"We've got Kung Pao chicken, Moo Goo Gai Pan and spring rolls—and rice, of course. Help yourself. I kind of doubled up on chicken. I guess I should have gotten something like Moo Shu Pork to mix it up. But I'm just a chicken kind of gal," she said with a broad smile.

"No complaints here."

Kendra tucked into her dinner, expertly lifting bites to her mouth with chopsticks. I made a couple of clumsy attempts before reaching for a fork.

"I've never been very handy with chopsticks."

"I wasn't either until Joe showed me the trick to it. Most people hold the sticks in the middle. Here, hold them up higher, about a third of the way from the top," she said as she demonstrated.

I gave it another shot, doing as she showed me. Still clumsy, but a little less so.

"I think maybe I could get the hang of this with a little practice."

"How did it go with getting local bakeries to let you sell their sweets at the coffee bar?" Kendra asked.

"Pretty good. The Muffin Man, Donut Dealer and Tudor House are on board. Gisele at our Daley Bread didn't say yes, but she didn't say no. She didn't say much. She mostly eyed me with indifference, or maybe it was indigestion. Anyway, Trudy thinks she'll come around."

"That's great."

"By the way, I got to meet Edgar. Trudy and I chatted with him over tea and scones. He wasn't exactly what I had expected. I'd imagined him looking more like a butler for some reason. How did your meeting go? Did he have any useful information?"

"Yes and no."

"He did say Vince had expressed an interest in local history, especially concerning the tunnels."

"The sidewalk tunnels? Trudy explained to me what those are."

I told Kendra about my and Trudy's excursion to Bell, Bath and Candle's basement.

"Wow, that's cool. Actually I think Vince's interest in the sidewalk tunnels would only have been as they connected to other tunnels. The earliest tunnels were constructed in a failed effort to divert the creek that kept overflowing and flooding the town. Those tunnels were built years before the sidewalk tunnels and would be the ones possibly leading to natural caverns."

"Which is the most likely location of any buried treasure, if I'm following you," I said.

"Right. But I was also interested in whether Vince had a partner, so I asked Edgar if anyone else had shown an interest in the tunnels or treasure lore lately. He was cagey about answering those questions. I mentioned how I'd read different but persistent stories about Jessie James hideouts and how he even purportedly drew a treasure map on a boot. I was baiting him a bit, trying to gauge his reaction."

"And?"

"He went very quiet. And Edgar is *not* the quiet type."

"You're right. He struck me as the extremely chatty type," I said.

"I had the feeling there was something, or someone, he

wasn't telling me about," she said, stabbing another bite of Moo Goo Gai Pan with her chopsticks.

"Well, Linda, the owner of the candle shop, was much more chatty and forthcoming with Trudy and me than Edgar was with you. Turns out Vince was not only a vandal, but a blackmailer, too."

"Whaaaa?" Kendra said with her mouth agape.

I filled her in on what Linda had told us about Vince threatening her with blackmail, and I told her what George had said about Vince attempting blackmail against Uncle Leon, as well."

"Wow. Has Linda told the cops? Should we tell the cops?" Kendra said.

"We asked Linda about that. She said she refused to give into his blackmail, twice apparently, and he never went public with the information he had on her. She thinks that makes him not-so-much a blackmailer as just a creep. She kind of has a point. Trudy and I talked about it and we don't really have anything to take to the police.

"Good point," she said.

"These spring rolls are really good," I said, dipping the end of my roll in a bit of duck sauce.

"Yeah, they're my fave," Kendra said. "I'm beat," she said, leaning back in her chair. "I discovered after my last group that one of the young kids had sticky hands, and he managed to get sticky stuff all over the jewelry heist room. I think I got most of it off the table, desk and case. He even left his sticky paw prints on the wall. I managed to scrub it off, along with some of the paint. I pinned the curtain over a bit to cover it. But when we're closed on Monday, I'll need to do some touch up."

"I had to scrub sticky stuff off the floor in the theater. It's a glamorous life, huh? Not that I'm complaining," I said.

"Me either. Not much, at least. I'll stop by the library before the escape rooms open one morning and check in with the reference librarian. See if anyone's been researching hidden treasure or Jesse James lately," Kendra said.

"Sounds good. Here, let's see what our fortunes say," I said, peeling the plastic wrap off one of the fortune cookies on the table.

"Mine says, 'You will take a short trip with a tall man,'" I said.

"Oh, I like that one. Wonder who the tall, handsome guy is?" Kendra teased.

"Unfortunately, it didn't mention anything about handsome. What does yours say?"

She read it silently and smiled. "Maybe this is a good omen. It says, 'You will need a map for your journey.' Maybe it's a treasure map."

Kendra yawned.

"I need to leave and let you get to bed. Thanks for dinner—and the company. Trudy, and probably George, too, are coming by for opening day of the morning coffee bar experiment at the theater. Why don't you drop by? Having you all there will steady my nerves, and we can chat about our investigations."

"I'll be there."

I left Kendra's place, but didn't much feel like going home. It was a quarter to eleven and there were lots of people still walking around downtown, so I decided to stop at the Wooden Nickel for a drink. I'd yet to meet Trey Tilby, the saloon owner, and hoped perhaps I could casually charm a little information out of him. I was curious to get a look at him after hearing George's description.

Those wandering the street were mostly couples, many of them window-shopping outside the closed shops. I expected a similar crowd inside the saloon, but I was wrong. Other than one couple and three college-aged girls sitting in a booth laughing, I think I was the only woman in the place. Still, everyone looked harmless enough. I didn't expect any brawls to break out.

Toward the back of the bar a man with a shiny shirt splayed open to reveal a large medallion nestled in his abundant chest hair had taken the jukebox hostage. He had an obvious fondness for disco and fancied himself John Travolta's character in *Saturday Night Fever*. Judging by their laughter and the fact that they let him continue playing musical selections from the seventies, the twenty-something-year-old guys hanging out in his vicinity were enjoying his antics.

Two guys were tending bar, but I was able to quickly deduce which one was Trey. I took a seat at the end of the bar closest to where he was serving a customer. The saloon's proprietor, dressed in jeans and a half-unbuttoned shirt topped by a leather vest, took payment from the customer and walked over to me.

"Hello, darlin', what can I do for you?"

"I'll take a Red Stone beer."

I reached for cash in my pocket, but he waved his hand and said, "First one's on the house."

"By the way, I don't believe we've met, but I'm Halley Greer, owner of the—"

He cut me off.

"Oh, darlin', I know who you are. I'm Trey. I hope we're going to become good friends," he said, extending his hand for a handshake. I hesitated before placing my hand in his. He grabbed my hand firmly and lifted it to his lips giving it a slobbery kiss. I forced a small smile onto my face.

The young, wild-eyed guy working behind the bar took a few steps in our direction before leaning around to look at me.

"Ooh, Trey, aren't you the smooth operator."

"Pay no mind to doofus here. He's a little slow-witted. I hired him out of pity," he said with a disquieting sneer leveled at his employee.

Doofus had a hangdog look as he turned and shuffled to the other end of the bar. Trey popped open my beer then popped one open for himself. He clinked his bottle against mine before I'd even picked it up and said, "Here's to new friends."

The disco standard by the Bee Gees playing on the jukebox was followed by that classic from the Commodores, "Brick House," which put a spring in Trey's step—and a gyration of his pelvis, as well. My head may have been bouncing to the tune as well, since disco was my mom's favorite oldies music when I was a kid. Suddenly, Trey set the cocktail shaker down on the bar, faced me and traced an imaginary hourglass figure with his hands.

"Thirty-six, twenty-four, thirty-six. Ow, what a winning hand," he crooned. He punctuated his little performance by firing at me with a thumb-and-index-finger gun, followed by a wink."

I tried to smile. The top number was definitely a generous assessment of my stats. I was strangely torn between feeling flattered and being creeped out. But leaning toward creeped out.

I had a growing feeling of indigestion and wondered how fast I could down my beer and make my escape. About then, Nick Raiford, who apparently had just entered the bar, walked up beside me.

"Hi, Halley. Sorry I'm late, I got delayed closing up. Trey, can you get me a matching beer? How 'bout you, are you ready for another?"

Part of me resented Nick thinking that I was a damsel in need of rescuing. But my distressed stomach felt relieved all the same.

"No, I'm good. Just started this one. Shall we move to a booth?" I said nodding toward a line of booths against the wall and as far away from the bar as possible.

Trey scowled as he handed Nick a beer. His drink wasn't on the house.

We sat down across from each other in the booth.

"Are you waiting for Kendra to meet you?" Nick said.

"No, I just had supper with her, but she was beat. I hadn't been inside the saloon yet and thought I'd pop in for a quick drink."

Not sure why I felt I needed to explain to Nick, since I barely knew him. Although he was nice enough to help out during renovations, an effort for which he'd only received random offerings of pizza and beer I provided for the volunteers.

"All the businesses in town seem so family-friendly, I guess I just assumed..." I trailed off, feeling embarrassed.

"Early in the evening it's mostly couples and some old guys in here, and single women singing karaoke, but later on it can sometimes turn into a frat house, I'm afraid. When you want to go out for drinks, I'd suggest the hotel bar as a much nicer place to go. And Trey has a reputation for being a wolf with the single ladies."

"What about you, what's your reputation with the single ladies?"

After a pause, he said, "I think I probably have a reputation for being a jock, you know, kind of a clod with the ladies."

He blushed, which was totally cute.

"You don't seem like a clod."

"You haven't known me very long."

Nick made me laugh, telling me about a heavyset customer who got stuck in a kayak he was considering buying.

"I was trying to act cool like, 'No, worries, happens all the time.' But I was seriously beginning to wonder how I was going to dislodge him from the kayak. We got way more hands on than I normally would with a stranger, with me working my hands down under his butt and him wrapping his arms around my waist, but I finally managed to get him unstuck."

He waved at the bar, signaling we'd like another round. Doofus brought over our beers.

"I'm glad I ran into you," Nick said. "I've been meaning to drop by and see you, but I knew you were busy with the opening and everything. Sorry I wasn't able to make it on opening night. I was playing guide to a group of backpackers. And I was very sorry to hear about the death. Was it really a murder, or was the guy at the *Sentinel* just trying to sell papers?"

"I don't know if it's official, like with autopsy reports. But the cops think it was murder, and the detective has been eyeballing me as a suspect."

"What? That's crazy, you've only been in town a few weeks."

"Did you know the dead guy?" I asked.

"No. The photo in the paper looked familiar, so I guess I'd seen him around."

"Apparently, he'd been trying to buy some of the businesses downtown. He or his partner never approached you?" I was fishing. I watched his face, trying to figure out if he knew more than he was telling me.

"No, nobody's offered to buy my place. But I wouldn't sell anyway. This is what I want to do. And besides, I doubt anyone would be interested in buying if they looked over my sales figures," he said with a smile that showed off his dimples.

When my second bottle was empty, I told him I should be going.

"Yeah, it's getting late," he said with a sexy grin, reaching over and touching my hand. "I'd like to take you home."

I jerked my hand away.

"Running into me in a bar and buying me a drink does not make this a date, Nick Raiford," I said, feeling my face flush.

"Halley, wait. I just meant I'd walk you to your door. Nothing more. Honest."

Maybe I'm gullible, but I believed him. We left together and walked up the block to the theater. I stopped at the front door instead of going around to the alley entrance, saying goodnight and thanking him for the drink with a sideways glance. I wanted to make it absolutely clear there would be no goodnight kiss.

# CHAPTER 15

About seven Thursday morning, I walked down to The Muffin Man, hoping he'd have a dozen muffins or cinnamon rolls boxed up and ready to go. I worried for a moment because Zeke was busy handling orders for a pretty long line of customers. But he spotted me and motioned to the end of the counter.

"Halley, your order is good to go."

"Thanks, Zeke," I said as I picked up the box. From the heavenly aroma wafting up to my nostrils I could tell the box included at least a few of Zeke's magic cinnamon rolls. As I stepped onto the sidewalk with a smile my phone buzzed. I fished it out of my pocket and caller I.D. told me it was Marco. My smile got even bigger.

He asked if it would be okay to make a wine delivery at the theater around three thirty to replenish stock. He would be making the delivery himself. Why did that make me so happy?

The warm glow didn't last long. As I approached the theater, I spotted Detective Frank Stedman standing in front of the door like a blockade

"Hello, Detective."

"Ms. Greer, could I have a word?"

"If you don't mind talking while I get things up and running for customers," I said, pointing to the sign on the door about the morning coffee bar. "If you want me to come down to the station again, it will have to wait a couple of hours."

"We can talk here—for now," he said, noncommittally.

I unlocked the door and we entered. It wasn't time to open, but I left the door unlocked desperately hoping someone would wander in and interrupt my conversation with the detective.

"That smells good," he said, motioning to the box from Zeke's.

I set the box on the counter and flipped open the lid, letting all that enticing deliciousness waft toward him. I spied a mix of muffins and cinnamon rolls.

"They're for sale."

"I'll pass."

He sat down on a bar stool at the counter and eyed me wordlessly for a long moment as I got busy prepping for service. Finally he spoke.

"I think we may have a problem, Ms. Greer."

I glanced up at him briefly, thinking how his monotone delivery reminded me of Sergeant Joe Friday from *Dragnet*, only with less enthusiasm. As he talked, I kept expecting him to yawn.

"It's come to my attention that you're inserting yourself into my murder investigation. Following after the police, questioning witnesses. What do you have to say for yourself?"

"I can assure you I haven't been following after you, Detective. I have no idea where you've been or who you've talked to. And I haven't been questioning witnesses, as you put it. Now that the grand opening's behind me I have been trying to get acquainted with some of the other business owners. Is that illegal?"

"Could be, if you're interfering in a criminal investigation. But my bigger concern right now is that you may have tampered with or removed physical evidence."

"What evidence?"

"It seems a certain item from the victim's cottage has gone missing. It's clearly visible in evidence photographs that were taken at the residence, and now it's gone. And according to his landlord, you and your pal Kendra Williams are the only people who had access to the scene. Paula Turpin said she let you two look around his place, at your request. Shortly after you left, she had the locks changed. There's no sign of forced entry and no one other than her has the new keys, and yet, an item has gone missing. How can you explain that?"

"I can't, but I can assure you that the only thing Kendra and I took was a look around. We left empty-handed."

"What were you looking for?"

"I don't know. I guess I just wanted a sense of who this man was who had vandalized the theater, even though he apparently had wanted to buy it at one point."

"Did you find anything?"

"Honestly, no, except that he was a slob. Unless the police were the ones who made such a mess of his place."

The detective remained expressionless. Apparently, he would neither confirm nor deny that the cops trashed Vince's place.

The front door opened. Trudy stepped inside, looked over at the bar and stopped in her tracks. "Is the coffee bar open for business?"

"Yes, it is. Come on in," I said with a smile, before turning to the detective and asking, "Is there anything else?"

"That'll do for now," he said quietly. "But if I catch you meddling in this investigation or if I find you removed so much as a cockroach from the victim's house, I will not hesitate to lock you up, Ms. Greer."

"Always a pleasure talking with you," I called after him. The image of a cockroach was unsettling. But as much as he ticked me off, I forced a smile as he left.

Trudy wiggled her fingers in a wave to Detective Stedman as she walked past him and took a seat at the counter.

"Where's George? I thought he was coming with you."

"He'll be along in a minute. He stopped to give directions to some confused-looking tourists. George is remarkably friendly and helpful for an old curmudgeon," Trudy said. "What did the detective want?"

"I'll tell you after George and Kendra get here."

I started making a latte for Trudy. In a moment George entered and held the door open for Kendra. She lit up as she waved and said hello. George almost smiled as he said, "Good morning."

I took their coffee orders.

"Help yourself to some muffins, on the house."

"I'll take a muffin, but we'll pay for it. After all, you're not getting them for free," Trudy said.

"I've been married long enough to know 'we'll pay for it' means I need to take out my wallet," George said with his usual charm, before adding, "Not that I'm complaining."

"Ooh, I'll take a muffin, too," Kendra said, using a napkin to pluck a blueberry muffin from the box. "Only, I'm okay with letting Halley treat."

Out of the corner of my eye I saw Trudy cut her eyes sharply to George. He saw it, too, and pulled some more cash out of his wallet.

"Breakfast is on me," he said.

"Detective Stedman was leaving as I came in," Trudy said. "Halley, now that the gang's all here, you want to tell us what that's about?"

"Apparently, he thinks I'm a thief as well as a murderer. He all but accused Kendra and me of stealing something from Vince Dalton's cottage."

"What does he think we pinched?" Kendra asked.

"Beats me. But Paula Turpin put us in the frame for the missing item and that seems good enough for the detective."

"Pinched? In the frame? You know you two don't talk like normal people your age, right? Y'all sound like a couple of gun molls out of an old movie or a reenactment on The History Channel. Maybe you should expand your television viewing to include some current pop culture and hang out more with people your own age," Trudy said.

"I like the way they talk. Makes me feel like the hip kid in the room," George said.

Kendra and I started giggling.

"I guess it's good that we can laugh on our way to prison," I said.

"What exactly did Stedman say?" George asked.

I filled them in on my little chat with the detective.

"Paula threw you and Kendra under the bus?" Trudy said.

"Totally," I said.

"That stinks," George said.

"Yeah, it's not like we're close, but I don't know why she'd go out of her way to incriminate Kendra or me."

"Wait just a minute. Didn't you say she changed the locks shortly after you and Kendra left?"

"Yeah."

"And the detective said there was no sign of forced entry?"

"Yep. Oh, I see where you're going with this. If we didn't take whatever it was, then most likely..."

"Paula did," Trudy and I both said in unison.

"I'm wondering what she took. And why did she take it then? She had plenty of opportunity to go through Vince's belongings before she let us in," Kendra said.

"I don't know, but I think Halley and I should ask her. We'll have the perfect opportunity today. She almost always comes to my Thursday afternoon yoga class."

"That sounds like a plan. I'm eager to hear what she has to say for herself," I said.

"I haven't been sitting on my thumbs while you gals have been out investigating," George said with the look of a kid who was picked last for the kickball team. "I just learned something about one of our suspects that could be important," he said.

He took a dramatic pause and Trudy looked like she was ready to smack him.

"Well?" she said.

"Trey Tilby inquired about renting some excavating equipment. Not like a backhoe to dig in open ground, but the kind of rig you'd use to carefully excavate under a building."

"When did he do this?" I asked.

"Not sure exactly when. A couple months ago, maybe. He never actually rented it, but he obviously had some project in mind."

"I wonder if he's wanting to dig under the bar or one of the other businesses on the block," Kendra offered.

"Either way, I don't think the excavation would be to expand the business operating space," George said. "Which gives credence to the idea that Tilby was involved with Dalton somehow—maybe even a business partner. Lusting after buried treasure seems completely in character for Tilby. And getting into a brawl wouldn't be exactly out of character for him either."

"Maybe he and Vince had a falling out," I proposed. "Good work, George."

After the creepy way Trey Tilby had come on to me last night, I found the idea of him as a murder suspect appealing. But I decided not to mention it to George.

"By the way, I filled Kendra in on our chat with Linda, but I keep thinking about her saying he blackmailed her twice. "Do you think he pressured her for sexual favors?" I asked, wide-eyed.

"You met Linda, right?"

"George, really," Trudy said, swatting at him.

He cleared his throat. "I think that's highly unlikely. But one kind of payment blackmailers have been known to accept in lieu of cash is information on a larger, richer target. Linda's grafted onto the gossip grapevine. Not much goes on in this town that she doesn't know about, so she could've provided him with blackmail info. Although, I think he would've demanded proof, not just hearsay, and I don't think that Linda would have had incriminating evidence on people just lying around," George said.

The front door opened and a lady in a light pink sweater peeked inside. "Is the coffee bar open yet?"

"Yes, ma'am. Come on in," I said.

"You're in the right place. Best coffee in town," Trudy said.

"I better get to work," Kendra said.

"Us, too," Trudy said, as they got up to leave in unison.

"Trudy, when and where should I meet you to chat with our favorite landlady?" I asked.

"A little before one. At the community center. Class wraps up around a quarter to one. You drop by and wait by the door. I'll stall her as the other students are leaving, then we'll corner her for a little chat," Trudy said, deviously arching an eyebrow.

It was by no means a deluge, but I had a steady trickle of customers all morning for which I was thankful. Right at ten thirty I was washing up, just about ready to lock the doors when I heard someone enter.

"Am I too late to get a cup of coffee? I hear yours is pretty good," he said.

"You're just in time, come on in."

I turned around to see a handsome, bearded face with a broad smile. But what really popped out at me was the Roman collar at the top of his black shirt.

"Mornin'," I said awkwardly.

The priest, who I guessed to be in his late thirties or early forties, walked up to the counter and extended his hand.

"Hi, you must be Halley. I'm Father Ben from St. Cecilia's. I've heard so much about you," he said. He hastened to add, "All good."

"Wow. Really?"

"I'll have a cappuccino and a muffin if you have any left."

"Coming right up. Oh, and you're in luck—last muffin," I said, pointing out the blueberry muffin sitting on its own in the corner of the tray.

"It would be a shame to let that go to waste. I'll take it," he said.

I placed the muffin on a paper plate and handed it to him, along with a napkin before starting on his cappuccino.

"Has word really gotten around town about me?" I asked, feeling slightly paranoid.

"Well, of course, everyone knows you are Leon's niece who inherited the theater. That's big news in a small community like ours. But the good things I mentioned I've heard from Kendra—and from your grandmother."

"My grandmother called you?" I said, almost spilling his coffee as I set it on the counter.

"She worries," he said kindly.

"Father, I apologize. I'll tell her not to bother you again."

"No, no. Please don't. She's lovely and we had a nice chat. I promised her I'd check in on you, which gave me the perfect excuse to come in for some coffee. I'd been wanting to meet you anyway."

"Since you couldn't exactly lie to her, I guess you had to admit you hadn't seen me at Mass?"

"Actually, I was kind of cagey about that. I'm good at keeping confidences—part of the job. And just so you know, Evelyn, I mean your grandmother, didn't tell me anything all that personal. Mostly that she worries about you being on your own in a new town, especially after having a man die in the theater on opening night. And she mentioned your parents aren't totally supportive of your new business venture here.

"Of course I'd love to see you at Mass, but I won't press you on that. I just want you to know I'm here if you want to talk about anything, or about nothing in particular. I'm a good listener."

"You're very kind. Thank you for listening to my grandmother's ramblings, and for checking on me. And for offering to listen to my woes. I've actually been very lucky. Some of Uncle Leon's friends have taken me under their wing, especially George and Trudy Mayfield."

"I'm glad to hear it. Good people. George can be a little prickly, but everyone knows his bark is worse than his bite. And Trudy is a peach—and a good cook, which you've no doubt already discovered."

"Yes," I said with a laugh. "I'm a frequent guest at their supper table. You said Kendra had mentioned me. I didn't know she attended St. Cecilia's."

"She comes to Mass on occasion, but she always helps us with set designs for our Christmas and Easter productions for the children's choir. Sounds like the two of you have become fast friends. I'm glad. You seem to be keeping very good company, Halley. I'll be sure to tell your grandmother the next time she calls."

"Are you sure you don't want me to call her off? I don't want her to be a pest."

"I'll be mad at you if you tell your grandmother not to call me anymore. I enjoy our little chats."

"You mean she's called more than once?"

He just smiled.

"I'll drop by for coffee again. And you know where to find me."

I walked him to the door.

"Father Ben, there is one thing you could do for me. Please light a candle and ask that the police are able to track down whoever killed Vince Dalton very soon. And tell Grammy hello when you talk to her."

"Will do."

# CHAPTER 16

I ran upstairs to eat lunch and give some thought to the best way to approach the conversation with Paula "police informant" Turpin. When I walked into the apartment, Eartha was meowing loudly. She had dragged her empty bowl into the middle of the kitchen and was clearly lodging a complaint.

"I'm coming. You know I'd have dinner waiting for you if I had any idea when you were going to show up."

She turned her head away as if to show complete disinterest in what I had to say. She did, however, act interested when I filled her bowl. She ate while I topped off her water bowl.

I sat down in the recliner with pen and paper and the intention of making notes on what to say to Paula. A few minutes later the paper was still blank as I bit down on the pen cap.

Eartha finished her meal and walked slowly toward me. She licked her paw then stretched out near, but not touching, my feet.

"You're welcome," I said, reaching down and gently petting her.

After I'd made my way to the community center, I stood in the hall pretending to look at notices on the bulletin board as people, mostly women, streamed out of Trudy's class. Through the crack in the door I could see Trudy talking to Paula, who was rolling up her orange yoga mat. When the room had emptied, except for the two of them, I stepped in and closed the door behind me. Paula's healthy glow turned into nervously flushed cheeks.

"I'd better be going," she said.

"Don't rush off. I had an interesting conversation with Detective Stedman this morning. He somehow had the idea that Kendra and I had taken a certain item from Vince's cottage. Any idea what gave him that notion?"

Paula looked to her yoga instructor.

"I'd like to hear the answer to that one, myself," Trudy said.

"I didn't tell him I thought you two took anything. I just told him I didn't know who else could've had an opportunity, that's all."

"You had opportunity, Paula. In fact, if you did change the locks shortly after we left, and the detective said there was no sign of forced entry, that means you are the only one who had opportunity. What I don't understand is why did you wait until then? You could have easily gone through Vince's cottage and taken whatever you wanted before the cops came or just after they left. If you can help me to understand then I won't suggest you as the best suspect to Detective Stedman when I see him again."

After a flustered moment, Paula said, "Oh, okay. If it turns out to have any bearing on the investigation, I'll hand the dang boot over to the cops."

My eyes met Trudy's briefly. *The boot.*

"I watched you two through the window with a little help from my binoculars. I know Kendra has worked in some museums, dealing with antiques and valuables. When she took so much interest in that old boot, I thought it might be worth something, like maybe I could sell it online."

"Did you? Sell it, that is?"

"No. After I took it home I realized I had no idea what it was worth, or even how to describe it, so I showed it to Edgar

Wentworth with the historical society. He knows a good bit about collectibles—and, well, he's always had a little crush on me," she said, blushing as she cast her eyes down.

I bit my lip and managed not to giggle. Trudy didn't look amused.

"What did Edgar say?" I asked.

"He said he didn't know. But he took a few pictures with his phone and said he'd check on it for me."

Paula picked up her mat and tucked it under her arm.

"I hope you won't tell the police, but do whatever you think is right," she said. "I really do have to go now. I have guests arriving soon."

After Paula had gone, I stared at the ceiling trying to sort things out in my head.

"What are you thinking?" Trudy asked.

"I'm thinking that Kendra had a conversation with Edgar yesterday, subtly probing the subject of whether anyone had recently inquired about the Jesse James gang's exploits in and around Utopia Springs or about hidden treasure. He told her Vince had brought up the subject, but he neglected to mention the boot. What do you think?"

"I'm wondering how often she used those binoculars of hers to peer into Vince's window before she used them to spy on you and Kendra."

I may have gasped just a little.

"And if she could see into his window, then maybe he could see into hers, too," I posited.

"That's a good point. We know Vince was a blackmailer. Maybe he was blackmailing his landlady for free rent?"

"That could explain why she felt entitled to help herself to his valuables," I said.

Trudy gathered up extra yoga mats, flyers, a towel and a water bottle, and I helped her carry things out to her car.

Walking behind my friend who's about seventy years of age, I couldn't help but notice her fit figure and perfect posture.

"Trudy, you look amazing. Could I trade you coffee lessons or free movies for some yoga classes?"

"You don't have to trade me anything, but feel free to drop in on my classes anytime. Although, if you think you could show me how to make better coffee, George would be grateful."

"You're on. I'd better get back. Marco is coming by later to replenish my wine stock at the theater."

"Ah, Marco is *bene* handsome and charming, no?" she said in a bad Italian accent.

"Trudy, I'm trying to build a business. I'm not looking for a man, *capiche*?

"Honey, someone as young and pretty as you doesn't have to look for a man. He'll find you."

As she got into her car, she gave me a wink.

# CHAPTER 17

I was dying to tell Kendra that Paula had taken the notorious boot from Vince's place and shown it to Edgar, but it would have to wait. She had customers and I needed to get ready for a delivery. I walked briskly back to the theater. I wouldn't admit it to Trudy or Kendra, but I was jumpy just knowing that Marco was coming by. I should've spent the time rearranging the bar area and stocking cups and glasses for tonight's seven o'clock show. Instead I ran upstairs, put on makeup, fiddled with my uncooperative hair, and put on a skirt. I almost never wore a skirt. It occurred to me I was primping for a forty-year-old man.

*Pull yourself together, Halley.*

I ran through a litany of justifications in my head. *I need to make myself presentable before the show anyway. I'm not just the barista around here; I'm the owner. A higher standard for my appearance is in order.*

I completed my mini makeover and made it down to the bar at about 3:20. I hurriedly moved some things around behind the counter. Through the front windows I spotted a truck with lettering on the side that said "Carvello's Winery." I wiped my sweaty palms on the front of my skirt. I may have convinced myself earlier that I was primping for the customers, but I couldn't deny the butterflies that were taking flight in my stomach when I saw Marco pushing a handcart loaded with a couple of cases of wine.

I went over and held the door open for him.

"*Buongiorno*, Halley." He flashed a boyish smile and I may have blushed just a little.

"Hi, Marco. Come on through." I led the way to the bar and he set the cases on the counter.

"This should be enough to get you through the weekend shows. But if the customers consume all this, give me a call and we'll be happy to restock."

"That would be a nice problem to have. But I'm more worried about no one showing up, you know, after what happened opening night."

"I'm sorry an unexpected death intruded on your otherwise glorious opening. I read in the paper that the police may suspect foul play. Surely that can't be true."

"I'm afraid so. And I'm also afraid I'm a favorite suspect at this point."

"That's ridiculous, you didn't even know the man."

"The cops think otherwise. Turns out he's the one who vandalized the theater ten days before we opened. If I'd known he was the one who had trashed the theater after all our hard work, I might have been tempted to kill him—but I didn't. Kill him, that is."

"Of course not," he said.

"Well, Kendra and I are making some discreet inquiries. I hope to find something—anything that will make the police lose interest in me as a suspect."

Marco stopped unpacking bottles, gently grasped my shoulders and turned me to face him.

"You be very careful, *cara*. If there is a killer at large, the last thing I want is for you to rattle his cage," he said, looking into my eyes with tenderness.

I gulped and looked away.

"Don't worry. I'm not the heroic type. In fact, I'm the chicken type. So nothing dangerous."

"Good. I'm glad to hear it. I wish I could stay for tonight's show. I've never seen *My Fair Lady* on the big screen," Marco said.

"I have once, but it's been ages. I wish I could slip into the theater for the show, but I have to mind the store," I said with an exaggerated sigh.

"It's tough being the boss," he said. "I'm afraid I'm booked up with obligations most of this weekend, but after I've dispensed with those and you've gotten through your Sunday matinee, would you come out to the vineyard for some wine and some of Maria's canapés? Dad would love to see you—and I might even be able to arrange a little surprise. Say around seven Sunday evening?"

I hesitated. Butterflies in my stomach and daydreams were one thing. But this sounded like an actual date.

"Please, Halley. I promise to be a complete gentleman."

That was both reassuring and slightly disappointing, but I accepted his invitation.

I rushed to get things ready for tonight's show. I opened the doors at six and was a little worried when the first customer didn't enter the lobby until about six fifteen. But by six thirty we had a decent crowd. I was hustling to serve coffee and wine, as well as selling tickets from behind the bar. And I was beginning to worry my projectionist wasn't going to show up. I'd tried to call her a couple of times. But Delores walked briskly through the front door at about five to seven. She was supposed to arrive at six to sell tickets.

"So sorry I'm late," Delores said, waving as she walked by and went straight up to the projection room. No gold lamé evening gown tonight, but she was wearing a hat as well as a pencil skirt and high heels.

Champagne was again popular during intermission, and I held my breath as Delores started the second half of the film, keeping my fingers crossed that no one would have to leave the theater on a gurney tonight. I heaved a sigh of relief after everyone had gone and I locked the doors behind them just after eleven.

Instead of finishing up with cleaning behind the bar, I rushed upstairs, kicked off my shoes and collapsed into the recliner, ready to put my feet up for a bit. I called Kendra and told her what Paula had told Trudy and me after yoga class today.

"I think we should go have a little chat with Edgar. He's clearly holding out on me. And he's cheating on Trudy."

"Hey, any flirtation between Edgar and Trudy is purely harmless fun," I said.

"Still, she'd feel foolish if she realized he pulls that act with just about everyone. Plus, I'm sure he wasn't telling me the whole story when I met him for coffee. I knew he was acting dodgy. That scoundrel. I think we should confront him. Maybe we can go over first thing in the morning."

"Right. Wait. I have to go over in the morning to pick up scones for the coffee bar anyway. You can go with me. That will give us the perfect opportunity to have a little chat with him."

After my call to Kendra, I wanted to go to bed. It had been a full day. But I had to get the coffee bar and the bathrooms cleaned before I could open for business in the morning. Cleaning the auditorium would have to wait until after morning coffee service.

First thing Friday morning I dressed and hurried downstairs to vacuum the lobby—the one necessary cleaning chore I had failed to accomplish before calling it a night. I felt my cell phone buzz and switched off the vacuum. It was Edgar, calling to tell me not to come by Tudor House to collect the scones for the coffee bar this morning. He said he'd deliver them personally.

"I'll be there at a quarter of eight. That way I can have you all to myself for a few minutes before customers distract you."

"Fine. I'll see you then." Since it was a phone call, he couldn't see me roll my eyes. I called Kendra to let her know Edgar would be coming to the theater to deliver the scones.

"Oh, good. It's always convenient when your quarry comes to you. We can ambush him without interference."

I was a bit taken back by Kendra's glee at getting the drop on Edgar. He had clearly stirred the ire of my normally congenial friend.

True to his word, Edgar arrived just before eight, delivering a variety of scones, along with jams and clotted cream.

"Oh what a beautiful morning, oh what a beautiful face," he said with an adoring gaze. I was worried he might burst into a Rodgers and Hammerstein song from *Oklahoma*.

As I pulled the espresso shot he'd ordered, Kendra walked in from the hallway.

"Good morning, Edgar," she said in a sing-song voice.

For a moment I thought he was going to choke on his coffee, but he quickly pulled himself together.

"Oh, my, I'm starting my day with two of the loveliest ladies in Utopia Springs. Be still my heart."

Kendra walked up to the corner of the bar and shot our prey a withering glare.

"Edgar, I'm so disappointed with you."

"My dear Kendra, it grieves me to hear you say so. What have I done?" he said, trying to look innocent.

"We know you're checking into the boot from Vince's cottage. And *I* know," she said moving her face closer to his, "that you haven't been telling me the truth about the true nature of your conversations with Vince Dalton."

A panicked look crossed Edgar's face briefly, but long enough for me to see real fear in his eyes. That gave me an idea.

"Edgar, Vince was blackmailing you, wasn't he? What was he holding over your head?" I asked.

Kendra gave me a quick nod before pressing Edgar further. "I'm sure the police would like to know all about Vince's blackmail against you. Of course, if you weren't involved in anything shady then you really don't have anything to fear. We're just trying to help the cops look in the right direction for suspects, since they've been mistakenly looking in Halley's direction. I'm sure you want to help Halley out. Why don't you just tell us the truth?"

"The truth is Vince had somehow come into possession of the boot, which I'm sure is a complete fake, by the way. And he also had an authentically period-looking map that suggested Jesse James had hidden some loot in a cavern near one of the original springs here in town. I don't for a minute believe that's true, but I have an acquaintance who has done a series of cable TV shows about treasure hunters. I wanted to arrange for him to look at Vince's boot, map, and anything else he had that might entice said acquaintance to shoot a treasure hunting episode in Utopia Springs."

"I thought you said you don't believe the map or boot are authentic." I said.

"Perhaps," Edgar said with a gleam in his eyes, "but they could lead to treasure in the form of increased tourism, which would benefit all of us—including you two. And I would naturally be willing to give the scouts and production crew a special rate to stay at the Tudor House Inn for the duration."

"Naturally," Kendra said. "Go on."

"Well, Vince got quite angry when he found out what my plans were. He was afraid if word got out, other treasure hunters would swoop in and steal the buried treasure away from him. The man was delusional."

"What was he blackmailing you about?" I asked.

"Is that really important?"

"A man's been killed, and Halley is a suspect. I think you better tell us what was going on."

"If I tell you, can I trust your discretion?"

Kendra and I looked to each other.

"I see no reason to tell the cops—if you haven't committed a crime and it's not related to Vince's murder. You didn't kill Vince, did you?" Kendra pressed.

"Of course not. I wasn't even at the theater the night he died. Dozens of people can testify I was at the restaurant until after midnight. And security footage will confirm I didn't leave the building, and Vince didn't come through our door."

"Fair enough," Kendra said.

I nodded in agreement.

"While I did live for a time in England—Basingstoke, Hampshire. I'm not exactly a native-born Englishman."

"Where, exactly, were you born?" I asked.

"Peoria. My friends and business associates would be devastated to learn I'm not English. It could hurt business and I'd be humiliated," he said, hanging his head and looking pitiful.

Reaching out and giving his hand a squeeze, Kendra said, "Everyone is entitled to a secret or two—as long as they're not hurting anyone."

He seemed relieved.

"How much money did Vince take you for?" I asked.

"He never pressured me for money, just my silence. He wanted me to use my contacts with the historical society to find an expert qualified to authenticate the boot. But he told me if word leaked out to the public or a TV crew about the treasure, my little secret would leak out, too.

Edgar looked pale.

"My wait staff will be run off their feet with breakfast customers by now, I really must be getting back."

I walked him to the door and locked it behind him, then I asked Kendra, "How many people in town do you think know Edgar's accent is phony?"

"I don't know, I'm sure some people at least suspect. But people here are pretty live and let live."

"Trudy is so dedicated to clearing my name, I don't feel right not telling her about Edgar," I said.

"We didn't promise Edgar we wouldn't tell anyone, we promised our discretion. I agree with you, I don't think it would be right not to tell Trudy about Vince's blackmail against Edgar. But we still have no evidence to take to the police. Anyway, I believed him when he said he didn't kill Vince."

"Me, too. Unfortunately, that doesn't bring us any closer to figuring out who might have killed him."

"Remember what Trudy said. We don't need to find the actual killer, just a suspect to make the cops lose interest in you," she said.

"Right. But there's still a killer on the loose. Don't you want to see whoever it is caught and brought to justice?"

"Of course I do. But I think Vince was probably killed for very personal reasons. Most likely blackmail. It's not like there's a serial killer on the prowl. I did a preliminary search in the library archives. I'm going to run back over there now and do a bit of digging before the escape rooms open. Alan, the reference librarian, said he'd help me. Hope you sell lots of coffee and scones today."

I walked Kendra to the door, unlocked it and turned over the open sign as she left. I had just made it back behind the counter when a nerdy-looking guy who was trying to camouflage a receding chin with a scruffy beard walked in holding a notebook and a pen.

"May I help you?"

"I sure hope so, Miss Greer," he said, taking a seat on one of the bar stools at the counter. "I'm Clifford Caldwell with the *Utopia Springs Sentinel.* I'd like to ask you a few questions for a follow-up article in the paper on last weekend's tragedy."

"So far no one else has died here, knock on wood," I said, tapping against the quartz counter. "And I've already talked to the police."

"Oh, I know. You've also talked to quite a few other people this week, including the victim's landlady and his pal, the saloon owner."

*So Vince was friends with Trey.*

Have you been stalking me, Mr. Caldwell? That sounds like a good reason for me to have another chat with Detective Stedman."

"No, ma'am. I'm not following you, just observant. And people talk. We may have a lot of tourists, but Utopia Springs is really just a small town at heart. So tell me, what did you learn from the victim's landlady?"

I had no intention of answering his questions. "I have a question for you," I said.

"Shoot."

"Are you going to order something, or are you just loitering?"

I was leaning against the counter. He stood and leaned across, bringing his unshaven face within inches of my nose.

"I don't think you really want an antagonistic relationship with the local media, Miss Greer, seeing as you are a person of interest in a murder investigation."

"What's so interesting about me? Some guy got himself killed and I just happened to be in the vicinity—along with a couple of hundred other people."

"Maybe. But according to the autopsy report the victim's stomach contents contained a brown slurry of coffee and Cracker Jacks, along with a lethal drug dose. And you *are* the barista here."

I was too stunned to reply.

He gave me a smug smile before he turned and headed for the door.

"I'll be seeing you around," he said, which sounded more like a threat than a farewell.

Clifford held the door open for two women who entered as he left. Their fanny packs and I-*heart*-Utopia-Springs t-shirts were like tattooing *tourist* on their foreheads. They both ordered lattes and scones and made themselves comfortable on one of the plump loveseats in the lobby. I pasted on a smile and tried to put what Clifford had said out of my head. A steady stream of customers came and went over the next couple of hours. Some of them inquired about the calendar of upcoming movies scheduled at the Star Movie Palace, and I realized I needed to get busy making one up. I took advantage of the opportunity to ask people what they would like to see and scribbled down the suggestions on a notepad.

After the last two customers in the place left, I was about to go lock the front doors when Susie Stoneface marched in. Her usual deadpan expression was animated by a scowl and punctuated with angry eyebrows.

"Business seems good. Noticed you had gentlemen callers beating a path to your door even before you opened today."

"Something I can help you with, Officer Stone?"

"No, actually I'm here to help you, Miss Greer. Do yourself a favor and accept some friendly advice. If you want to keep time with Nick Raiford or Trey Tilby, be my guest. Or if you and your pal Kendra want to tussle over Joe Chang, fine by me."

She walked toward the counter with her chest puffed out.

"But stay away from Clifford Caldwell. Trust me when I tell you he's not your type."

I should've just smiled and kept my mouth shut, but she

ticked me off.

"I haven't gone near Clifford. He came here, as you are obviously aware. He gave the pretext of seeking information about last week's tragedy, even though he printed in the newspaper that Vince Dalton had been murdered before the body was even cold. Certainly before the autopsy. He obviously already has a source who's in a better position to provide that kind of information than I am."

Her eyes narrowed and she put her hands on her hips. Clearly I'd touched a nerve.

"Well, he didn't hear it from me," she said, so mad her voice was quavering. "Clifford's a professional, a top-notch investigative reporter. But playing Nancy Drew and digging into people's private affairs when you don't know what you're doing can be hazardous to your health. You'd do well to remember that."

"Is that a threat, Officer Stone?"

"No, sweetie, just a little friendly advice, like I said."

She sauntered out and I hurried over to lock up before another unwanted visitor could appear.

# CHAPTER 18

I ate the last scone, which was delicious, before cleaning up the bar. I did a quick touch-up in the bathrooms. Then I bought a box of Raisinets and slipped them in my pocket to snack on as I vacuumed the lobby—for the second time today—and cleaned the auditorium. After taking last night's receipts out of the safe, I went to the bank to make a deposit. I couldn't get what Clifford had said about the autopsy report out of my head.

I was dying to talk to Kendra and thought about slipping over to see if I could have a quick word with her. But as soon as I stepped outside I could see she was slammed. I spotted a group of five or six people huddled on the sidewalk across the street in front of the escape rooms and noticed one of them was holding a pager. Kendra hands out pagers to groups the way they do at restaurants for parties waiting to be seated. Curiously the contingent with the pager were all redheads, which made me think family reunion, unless there was a ginger convention in town. In any case, the pager indicated all three escape rooms currently had groups in them trying to puzzle their way out, and at least one group was queued up waiting to go next.

"Good for her," I thought, hoping I'd have a line of customers waiting to get in the theater for tonight's show.

Since Kendra was tied up, I made the familiar trek down to Mayfield's Gallery instead, dodging my way through a pretty healthy crowd for a weekday. Now late September, it was a different crowd than when I'd arrived the first of August.

Families with younger children had disappeared with school back in session, replaced by couples of all ages and groups of friends celebrating weddings, reunions and girls' getaways.

Trudy was behind the counter when I entered. Upon closer inspection I could see she was threading beads onto wire to fashion an earring.

"How was the coffee business this morning?"

"Eventful," I said.

I briefly told her what I'd learned from Clifford about the autopsy report.

"That at least partially explains why the cops are so interested in me as a suspect," I said, feeling like I was carrying concrete blocks on my shoulders.

"Hon, all that really tells us is that someone slipped something in Vince's coffee at the theater on opening night. We were already pretty certain of that. You may have made the coffee, but anyone could've dropped something in his cup."

"Yeah, you're right," I said, the weight of impending doom suddenly feeling much lighter.

"Oh, and Kendra and I questioned Edgar about taking the boot from Paula and what had really gone on between him and Vince Dalton. He knew the boot was a fake, but hopes he can use it to entice some guy who does treasure hunting documentaries to come to Utopia Springs to film an episode. The treasure Edgar is after is increased tourism dollars."

"I wouldn't object to that myself," Trudy said.

"And there was something else. Turns out Vince was also plying a bit of blackmail against Edgar."

"Do tell," she said.

"According to Edgar, Vince didn't ask for money but wanted Edgar to get an expert to verify if the boot was authentic—and to keep his mouth shut about some Jesse James loot possibly being buried in Utopia Springs."

"Did he say what Vince was holding over his head?"

"Trudy, I hope you won't be disappointed, but...Edgar isn't exactly English. He's from Peoria. And his British accent is completely bogus."

I was concerned there might be tears. Instead, Trudy started laughing.

"Oh, Halley, I already knew that. But please don't tell George. I'd like him to go on feeling just a teensy bit jealous of me and Edgar, okay?"

"Far be it from me to meddle in your marriage," I said.

"There was one other thing of note that happened today. Officer Susie came by to warn me to keep my hands off Clifford Caldwell."

"Oh my, you did have an eventful day."

"Trust me, she's got no cause for worry on that front."

By the time I made it back to the theater, I had to hustle to get everything ready for the Friday night show. Delores was late, as usual. The crowd was okay, but not great. After I closed up I was so exhausted I could barely climb the stairs. I'd have to think long and hard before I ran another feature so long it requires an intermission, although it probably boosts the wine and coffee sales a bit.


Since the coffee bar wasn't open on Saturday mornings, at least for now, I cleaned up after last night's show then decided to catch up on the financials. I carried my laptop down to the office, which I'd mostly cleared out, storing old files in the basement. Uncle Leon had always used ledgers for bookkeeping—definitely not a computer guy. But I knew that system wasn't going to work for me. Fortunately, Bart had come to my rescue once again. He had set me up with some fairly simple accounting software that's a good fit for small businesses like mine. I got the books in order and had just made an online payment for the utilities when Kendra phoned a little before ten o'clock.

"Hey, girl, we're about to open so I can't talk long, I just wanted to let you know if you've been worried I was jealous of all the attention the detective has been showing you, no worries. He came by first thing this morning to shower some suspicion on me."

"Really? About what?"

"He seemed most interested that I'd been looking through the library archives for Jesse James and treasure stuff, which makes me think the cops must know something of what Vince was up to. More disturbing to me was that he knew what I had been looking at in the library. Maybe Alan, the reference librarian, told the cops, although I have a hard time believing it of him."

"What did you tell the intrepid detective?"

"That I'd started looking at local Jesse James lore almost two years ago, which is absolutely true. And that I'd decided to give it another look."

"I had my own up close and personal visit with the local cops yesterday. Susie stopped by to tell me to keep my hands off Clifford Caldwell."

Kendra laughed so hard, she started snorting. "Try to control yourself around Clifford, Halley. He's already taken," she said, still giggling.

"Any attention from me toward Clifford is purely in Susie's mind—or maybe his. But he did let something slip about the investigation."

I told her about the autopsy report.

"Wow," she said. "I'll ponder the implications of that while I deal with a rowdy group that's already lined up here. I'll talk to you later."

After I got off the phone with Kendra, I checked the mail and found the last fragments of my former life in Nashville boxed up and sealed with packing tape. I had mailed final rent to my landlord in Nashville, and asked my neighbor in the building, who had a spare key, to pack up and ship the rest of my clothes, my DVD collection of old movie and my French press to me. I told her to feel free to take or sell anything else in the apartment—which wasn't much—or to leave it for the landlord, who didn't return my security deposit.

More interested in thinking about my new life than dwelling on the past, I wasted a little time fantasy shopping online for stuff to decorate the apartment. I had painted the living room walls and trim with paint leftover from the theater renovations, which freshened things up. I'd bought a new shower curtain and rug for the bathroom. And I'd slipcovered the old sofa, thrown a bedspread over the decrepit loveseat, and hung a couple of pictures. Oh, and picked up a cute lamp at a local flea market. That was about all the decorating I could afford, so far. Other stuff, including buying a real mattress and box springs instead of sleeping in the recliner or on the sofa, would have to wait until I had some cash flow. But it was fun to daydream.

The attendance for the Saturday night show was disappointing, but I knew there was a folk rock concert—a reunion tour of some seventies band—at the outdoor amphitheater that was probably drawing away our clientele.

Marco phoned Sunday morning to make sure I hadn't forgotten about our date for Sunday evening. I hadn't. I was distracted all through coffee and wine service for the matinee, and changed clothes three times before heading to the winery. I drove up the winding mountain back roads, making my way to the winery up the long drive—private road really—past the terraced vineyard. Leaves on the vines were beginning to yellow, following the grape harvest last month, as we eased our way into fall. I'm not exactly the outdoorsy type, but I had been holed up indoors a lot the past several weeks, working to get the theater and coffee bar up and running. I rolled down my window a bit to enjoy the pleasant late-September breeze. The wind on my skin and the rush of fresh mountain air in my lungs felt good.

I pulled up in front of the large, glass-front contemporary home. I'd barely stepped out of the car when I was greeted by Rafe Carvello, who walked out to meet me.

"*Cara mia*, it's so good to see you again," he said, clasping my hands and giving me a light kiss on each cheek.

"I wanted to have you to myself for a moment before my son sweeps you away to the vineyard. He has good taste in women—like his papa," he said with a chuckle.

We walked arm in arm through the open living room with soaring ceilings and through sliding glass doors, which offered an expansive view of the vineyards, onto the generous patio where we'd enjoyed the wine tasting on my initial visit. Marco was standing at the table pouring sparkling wine into three flutes. He handed a glass to me and his dad before raising his own in a toast.

"*Cin Cin!* You are even lovelier than the view, my dear," Rafe Carvello said, turning toward me and chinking his glass against mine.

"Dad, I worry that flirting with beautiful young women could be bad for your heart condition."

"Ha! Beautiful women are what keep my heart beating. I'll leave you two to enjoy this glorious sunset. Sunrises are better timed for me these days. I start nodding off just after dinner. *Salve*," he said, throwing me a kiss before he turned and walked toward the house.

"Don't tell him I said so, but I think my dad has a little crush on you, Halley Greer."

"Don't tell him I said so, but I think I have a little crush on your dad."

"Ah, I only hope I can be as charming as my father."

He poured more sparkling wine in my glass and raised his just as the sun began to dip behind the horizon in gorgeous shades of red and orange.

"Let's toast the sunset, because it signals the time is nearly right for my little surprise," he said with a twinkle in his eye.

We sat at the table and enjoyed some crackers with goat cheese and bruschetta with tomato and basil. After about fifteen minutes, Marco stood and picked up a picnic basket from the end of the table.

"Follow me," he said as he walked toward the vineyard.

I followed. Once we had gone a little distance from the lights on the house, it began to get progressively darker as we made our way through rows of vines on the terraced hillside. Suddenly, I saw some soft light ahead. We entered a clearing, which had two candlelit lanterns atop a table, along with a projector. Beside it were two chairs with a small table between them. About twenty feet beyond, a large white canvas was strapped to the front of an arbor, lashed on top and along each side.

"An outdoor movie theater!" I exclaimed. "Oh, Marco, this is some set-up you have here."

"I'm so glad you approve."

"What's the feature?"

"*My Fair Lady*. Since neither of us got to enjoy the showing at the Star Movie Palace, I though a private al fresco screening was in order."

He set the picnic basket on the ground between us and opened it. He pulled out a covered bowl of popcorn and set it on the table, along with two wine glasses and a new bottle of wine.

"There are some homemade almond cookies and a thermos of hot chocolate for later. I wouldn't attempt to make coffee—that's your area of expertise. And in case you think I'm taking liberties by choosing such a long film. We don't have to finish it tonight. We can stop at intermission, if you like. It will give me an excuse to have you return for a viewing of Part Two. But if you're game for the whole show tonight, I won't object."

"We'll see," I said.

He opened the wine bottle, a Carvello special reserve, and I nibbled on some popcorn topped with parmesan.

"Even the popcorn at Carvello's is gourmet. I'm impressed."

Reaching into the oversized basket again, he pulled out a shawl and handed it to me.

"And this is in case it gets chilly."

I ran my fingers across the fine wool shawl in a blue green color.

"This is lovely."

"It belonged to my mother."

I touched the soft shawl to my face.

Marco was a charming movie companion, watching attentively and making occasional comments. During the scene in her bedroom where Audrey Hepburn sang "I Could Have Danced All Night," he suddenly stood and extended his hand. We danced under the stars and he even spun me around a couple of times.

The movie paused and an "intermission" sign popped up on the screen shortly after Eliza Doolittle's debut at the races.

"Halftime," Marco said, holding up his hands in a time-out gesture.

Marco reached into the basket and fished out a plastic container and a thermos. He poured some hot chocolate into a paper cup and handed it to me along with a cookie.

"*Mmm*, this chocolate is rich and the cookie is great, too," I said.

"Glad you like it. I like to take care of my guests—and my friends. I know we haven't known each other long, but I've been a little worried since you told me that you and Kendra were snooping into Vince Dalton's murder. If it really turns out to be murder, that obviously means there's a killer out there. And I don't want you, or Kendra, doing anything to upset him—or her."

"You're sweet, but trust me you've no reason to worry. All we've really done so far is look around his cottage. And that was after the cops had already cleared boxes full of stuff out of there."

"Find anything interesting?"

"Maybe. But you'll laugh at me if I tell you."

"I won't laugh. Scout's honor."

"Were you really a Boy Scout?"

"No, I have to admit that I wasn't a scout. But honor is a big deal in my family, so I'll keep my word."

"Okay, so we found this old boot..."

I proceeded to tell him what we found and what Kendra thought it could mean and how she was quietly trying to find out from the historical society if anyone had been researching the Jesse James gang or hidden treasure. Although, it wasn't as quietly as we had supposed since Detective Stedman had brought it up when he questioned her. I didn't mention the possible blackmail because I had promised I wouldn't.

True to his word, Marco didn't laugh but he did give me a big smile.

"Well, there are many underground tunnels in town, and I imagine people can get pretty crazy, and even dangerous, when they believe there's a fortune at stake. You and Kendra be discreet, and if you run up against anything or anyone that makes you feel uncomfortable please call me anytime—day or night."

"Thank you, but I think we'll be—"

"I'm serious. You two are the brains of this operation, but if you need a little brawn..." he said, curling his arm and flexing a pretty impressive bicep, "I'll bring out these guns."

"Thank you for the offer, and for the lovely evening." After a beat I added, "As much as I've enjoyed this, it's getting a bit late to finish the film. I think I'm going to have to say goodnight."

"Of course. It was all part of my devious plan anyway, choosing a very long movie so I'd have an excuse to turn one date into two. You will come back to watch the other half with me sometime soon, won't you?"

"I'd love to."

We strolled hand-in-hand to my car. I handed him the shawl wrapped around my shoulders as I opened the door, and he leaned over and gave me a soft kiss on the cheek.

# CHAPTER 19

I woke up early Monday—and in a good mood, humming tunes from *My Fair Lady* and twirling as I danced my way from the living room into the open kitchen. I took a few gulps from a bottle of orange juice as I surveyed the contents of the fridge and decided I'd once again have breakfast at The Muffin Man.

*I should get a volume discount.*

I walked briskly to the end of my block. Zeke called out to me as I entered.

"Mornin', Halley."

"Good morning, Zeke."

I got in line and stared up at the menu board on the wall behind the counter, even though I already knew what I was going to order.

I had just sat down at a table with my oversized cinnamon roll and large coffee when I saw Nick walk in. We exchanged waves before he stepped up to the counter.

Appearing next to my table holding coffee and a muffin he said, "May I join you?"

"Sure, I'd appreciate the company."

I felt I'd been a little unfair to Nick the night he walked me home from the Wooden Nickel, especially after he'd rescued me from an uncomfortable conversation with Trey. We'd only exchanged a couple of shy waves from across the street since then.

"You look awfully perky," he said. "Not saying that's a bad

thing. Just that I'm not a real morning person. I guess it would make sense that you are—a morning person, that is. Since coffee is your thing."

"I hadn't thought of it that way, but yeah, I guess I am kind of a morning person. I've been meaning to drop by your store to say hi," I said, followed by an awkward pause. "So, have any customers gotten stuck in a kayak lately?"

"No, fortunately. But I did lead a group on a kayaking trip on Porcupine Lake this weekend. The weather was perfect."

"That sounds lovely. Are there any porcupines around Porcupine Lake?"

"I've seen a few," he said before launching into a story about how the family dog when he was growing up ended up on the losing side of an encounter with a porcupine.

"Aw, poor fella," I said, envisioning a cocker spaniel with a muzzle full of quills.

Nick and I conversed comfortably and before I knew it, we'd been chatting for almost an hour.

"Wow, it's later than I thought. I guess I should get going," I said, thinking it would be nice to end our conversation before it hit a sour note—for once.

"Yeah, me, too. I need to work on some mountain bike repairs. It was good seeing you again," he said.

"Yeah, thanks for keeping me company over breakfast."

Nick opened the door for me as we left and we walked down the sidewalk in companionable silence, parting ways in front of the theater. Nick was just walking away as I unlocked the front door, when I heard a car pull up to the curb behind me.

"*Buongiorno.*"

I quickly turned to see Marco calling to me from his convertible.

"Good morning, Marco."

"I'm on the run this morning, but I just wanted to tell you

again what a wonderful time I had last night. Talk to you soon."

I returned his wave as he sped away and caught a glimpse of Nick giving me the side eye as he crossed the street. I walked in and sat down on a loveseat in the lobby, feeling flustered.

*There's absolutely no reason I should feel bad about Nick overhearing my exchange with Marco.*

I wished I could talk to Kendra about Nick—and about Marco. But the escape rooms were closed on Mondays and she was spending the day in Fayetteville. Simon's mother was in town for a visit and she and Kendra were going to have a spa day together, followed by a family dinner at Bart and Simon's house. I certainly wasn't going to call her and interrupt any of that.

I decided to banish any lingering thoughts about Nick by busying myself with work. Since there's no coffee service on Monday mornings, I did some deep cleaning in the auditorium. After a break, I put posters out front for the next movie we'd be showing. *My Fair Lady's* run had ended, and we had a new feature starting Thursday night.

I unlocked the access door and ascended the steep steps to the level above the lobby, one of those cool secret places in the theater that no one ever gets to see. I climbed through the access panel and stepped out onto the platform behind the marquee, then put on a safety harness and secured the line to the steel truss supporting the marquee. After carefully crawling under the reader board onto a two-foot platform, I removed the letters spelling out *My Fair Lady*. Then, letter by letter, I replaced them with the name of our next feature: *Charade*, starring Audrey Hepburn and Cary Grant. As I scanned the marquee, making sure everything was correct, I could see a small crowd gathered across the street, watching me. Some of them actually applauded as I slipped back behind the marquee. I wasn't sure if they were applauding my efforts or my choice of film. Either way, I'd take it.

I caught up on paperwork and by six o'clock decided to knock off work for the day.

A few minutes later I was standing in line at the takeout counter at Jade Garden waiting for my dinner order, trying to stave off starvation with a peppermint stick. I had grabbed the piece of candy from the counter after dropping a donation in the jar for the Lion's Club to help the sight- impaired.

I heard Clifford Caldwell's booming voice emanate from somewhere behind me. Glancing over my shoulder I saw him talking to a man I didn't recognize as they waited to be seated in the main dining room. I inclined my ear, and fortunately Clifford talks loudly enough to drown out the growling of my stomach.

"Later this week, we'll have an update in the paper on the murder investigation that will shed a new light on a few things."

I peered over my shoulder again, which seemed to make the woman in line behind me nervous.

The man Clifford was talking to looked nonplussed. But I was extremely interested in learning more about Clifford's exposé.


I got up a bit earlier than usual because this particular Tuesday morning was a special one. It would be my first day to feature breakfast fare from Our Daley Bread at the coffee bar. I guess Adam at Donut Dealer and Zeke had given Gisele a favorable report on me, because she had called on Friday and said she was in for Tuesday if I still had an opening.

I walked over to pick up the day's selections, entering the bakery wearing a big smile. Gisele's face wasn't wearing a smile, even a little one. I decided that must be her normal expression, and I wasn't going to let it get me down. She already had everything boxed up for me.

As I walked back to the theater, I spotted Nick outside his store, sweeping up. I smiled and waved. He looked right at me with a blank stare before retreating into the store with his broom. I crossed the street before I reached his place.

I got back to the theater, set the box on the counter and opened the lid to find still warm banana nut bread and coffee cake. But even the heavenly aroma emanating from the box didn't tempt my appetite.

*Darn that Nick Raiford. He's an acquaintance I've run into around the neighborhood and we've had a neighborly conversation a couple of times. Nothing more.*

I was still ruminating when Kendra dropped in for coffee, as she and Trudy were developing the habit of doing just before the coffee bar officially opens.

"Hey, what's up?" she asked as she walked to the bar.

"Mornin'," I said, apparently looking as down in the mouth as I felt.

"Whoa, what's wrong? You look, I don't know...glum, I guess."

"That's a good word for it. Glum. Or dumb. That would probably be an even better word."

"I'll take a wild guess that your mood is either about the murder investigation or about men. Which is it?" she asked as she climbed onto a barstool.

"I hate to be predictable, but you hit it head on when you said men."

I told her about my date with Marco. Or at least I told her a little about my date with Marco. I said we'd had a nice picnic in the vineyard. I didn't go into details about the outdoor movie and dancing and hand holding. She couldn't even acknowledge her feelings for Joe, so I wasn't going to admit I felt like a blushing schoolgirl every time I was around Marco.

"Okay, I must be the one who's dumb because I can't think

of any reason you should be depressed about last night. It sounds like a nice date. What am I missing?"

"It was a nice date, but I just met Marco. And then the whole thing this morning with Nick..."

"Nick? Wait, back up. I totally missed the part about Nick."

I told her about my nice breakfast with Nick and Marco's drive-by comment as Nick was walking away, followed by Nick's brush off this morning.

"There's absolutely no reason I should feel badly about Nick overhearing that I went out with Marco. In fact, breakfast this morning was the first time Nick and I have ever had a conversation that didn't end badly. But then, he did help out with the renovations and he did kind of rescue me from an uncomfortable conversation with Trey Tilby."

"Hold up. Why would you even talk to Trey Tilby? Scratch that. Unfortunately, I've got a bunch of stuff I need to do before I open up today. Come to my place tonight around eight thirty and we'll continue this conversation. Or start a new one if you prefer, okay?"

"Kendra, you really don't need to worry about me. I'm being maudlin for no good reason."

"I will not take no for an answer. I have no life. The least you can do is talk to me about yours. Gotta go," she said heading toward the door.

As she was leaving she repeated, "Eight thirty."

Business was brisk, which made the morning pass quickly. The coffee cake and banana bread were a hit. We sold out. That should please Gisele, I thought. Not that it would ever register on her face.

After cleaning up the coffee bar and running upstairs for a quick bite of lunch, I decided it was time I tried to foster a more amicable relationship with the local media. My less than brilliant plan was to go to the newspaper office and buy a subscription to the newspaper as a sign of good will. Then I'd try to casually make conversation with Clifford. The last time he came by the coffee bar he let some information slip about the autopsy report. I figured if I were lucky, he'd let some new information slip out. He definitely liked the sound of his own voice.

The *Utopia Sentinel*'s offices were located on the edge of the commercial district in a plain brick building identified by the paper's name in a script font on the front window. There was no bell or fanfare when I entered. In fact there was no one manning the reception counter and no one sitting behind the desk with a name plate that read "Heidi Howzer, advertising sales." Which was disappointing because I would've enjoyed saying "howdy" to her. I did, however, spot a sign that said "Newsroom" on a door in the back.

The door was open a crack and as I approached I heard smacking sounds, which I presumed were being made by someone noisily eating lunch. It turned out to be even less appetizing than that.

"Susie, behave. Someone could walk in and see us."

"Cliffie, you know I can't get through the day without a little sugar," she said, making smooching sounds.

"Well, I guess cops can't live on doughnuts alone."

I felt my stomach lurch.

"The sign on that door says 'utility,' so let's make use of it for a little smooching. But we have to hurry. I need to get back to work. The chief frowns on long lunches," she said.

"Come to Papa."

She giggled like a schoolgirl and I heard a door close. I peeked in tentatively before tiptoe running across the room to Clifford's desk. I tapped the space bar on his computer and a story in progress popped up on the screen. Unfortunately, it was a story about a new pet grooming business opening in town.

*I wonder if Eartha would abide a grooming session? Probably not.*

I scanned the desk hoping for a printout of the murder story to no avail, but then I hit the jackpot. His notebook was beside the keyboard with the computer mouse sitting on top of it. I picked it up and started flipping through pages. I thought about snapping photos with my phone, but his handwriting was barely legible and I was afraid Susie and Cliffie might hear the camera clicks.

I kept flipping pages and until I saw Dalton's name. I decided to just quickly scan through and see if I could get the gist of it. Vince had been working in Little Rock as a private investigator before he moved here. He had also had his P.I. license suspended, something about misrepresentation and possible misdemeanor. But his license had recently been reinstated.

That's as far as I got when I heard an eruption of giggles. I took that as my exit cue, fearing Susie and Clifford would emerge from the closet at any moment. I sucked in a deep breath before tiptoe racing out of the room. Fortunately, the front office was still empty, so I walked briskly out the front door, hoping no one had seen me. My subscription to The *Utopia Sentinel* would have to wait for another day.

# CHAPTER 20

George dropped by to deliver some leftovers at Trudy's behest. I texted Kendra to let her know I'd be bringing dinner for us. It was a safe bet Kendra wasn't planning to cook. She texted back with a jazz hands emoji. Or maybe it was supposed to be a hug.

At eight thirty sharp, I showed up at Kendra's door with an offering of homemade enchiladas and rice. Kendra heated the leftovers in the microwave, set out the nice plates—meaning not paper—and poured us some red wine.

I didn't want to spoil our appetites, so I decided not to mention the love scene I'd overheard between Clifford and Susie.

After supper, continuing our conversation from that morning I briefly recapped my first encounter with Trey, starting with his unwelcome attention and slobbery hand kiss. And how Nick had come to my aid by pretending he and I had prearranged to meet. Ending with Nick putting his foot in his mouth and putting *me* on the defensive, which seems to be a habit of his.

"Anyway, Marco and Nick, and even Trey, aren't really the problem. The men who are causing me real grief right now are Detective Stedman, who is still lingering on me as a suspect, and Vince Dalton, who I didn't even know."

Kendra shot to her feet and said, "*Aarrgh!* These guys are getting on my last nerve. Grab the wine glasses and follow me. We need some air."

Instead of heading downstairs and out the back door as I expected, she stepped onto a stool and pulled down access stairs from her ceiling. Once in the attic, she tugged on a cord, dimly illuminating the space with a single bare bulb. She continued to a wall and up a metal ladder where she pushed open a hatch to the roof. I wordlessly climbed up right behind her.

"Hold this, please," she said, handing me the wine bottle.

Kendra grabbed a couple of lawn chairs tucked under the eaves of a little utility shed, unfolded them and took a seat in one. I handed her the bottle and sat down in the chair beside hers. She poured wine into both our glasses.

The view was spectacular. Colorfully lighted shop signs up and down the streets, porch lights on houses dotting the hillside and stars twinkling overhead against a black sky.

"Let's stop thinking about mean old Detective Stedman and, for that matter, let's try not to think about the late, not-so-great, Vince Dalton. Let's talk about some men actually worth talking about for a change," Kendra said.

"If you're going to start matchmaking, forget it. I've told you—"

"Nope. No matchmaking. The men worthy of conversation I had in mind are Bart and Josh."

I smiled at the thought of Josh, but the very next instant a lump formed in my throat.

"For example," Kendra continued, "what's something you and your brother loved to do together? I'll start. Whenever Bart and I are in the car, we sing show tunes. He can really belt out 'Cabaret' along with Liza Minnelli on the stereo. But my favorite Broadway tune for us to sing together is 'Don't Rain on My Parade.' We don't sound anything like Barbra Streisand, of course, but I think we sound pretty good. We never sing when Simon's in the car, though. Sweet guy, but he can't carry a tune."

"Taking a car trip with you and Bart sounds fun."

"How about you and Josh, any favorite pastimes?"

"I'm sure this will come as a big surprise, but we enjoyed watching old movies together. Everything from old horror films with Bela Lugosi to Bogie and Bacall movies—and we both loved to rattle off snappy bits of dialogue. One of Josh's favorites to fire at me whenever I started dishing dirt on someone was that Joan Crawford character's line from *The Women*. 'There's a name for you women, but it isn't used in high society outside of a kennel.'"

"Ooh, great line. I don't think I've ever seen that movie. We'll have to watch it together sometime. My glass seems to be empty, how about yours?"

I nodded and held my glass out for a refill.

"My turn. What was the angriest Bart ever got at you?"

"That's easy. He still brings it up sometimes. My junior year in high school I took off to Florida with two senior girls for spring break. My parents never would've given me permission to go, so I lied and told them I was visiting Bart for a few days. Big brother was not in on my deception, by the way—he was even more protective than Mom and Dad. I thought I'd gotten away with it, but a few weeks later my mom happened to casually mention to Bart something about my spring break visit with him, the visit he knew never happened. Fortunately, he didn't give me up to Mom, but he gave me plenty of grief later. Wanted to know exactly where I went, with whom and what we got up to, and warned me I'd better never pull a stunt like that again. The truth is I had a miserable time on that trip. It rained half the time. I wanted to feel all grown up, but the older girls made me feel left out. I'd never admit to Bart, even now, that I had anything less than a fabulous time that spring break—not after the way he raked me over the coals about it. What about you? Did Josh ever rain fire and brimstone on you about anything?"

"Hmm, honestly the maddest I ever remember him was

back in school when I told a girl he had a crush on that he liked her. She was this cute little redhead and I could tell she liked him, too, so I thought I was helping him out, you know? After I told her, she started paying attention to him. He got so mad, he didn't speak to me for days."

"Why? If she liked him, too, it sounds like a good thing," Kendra said.

"I don't know. He was completely embarrassed. I could tell because his ears turned bright red. Of course, he was *only* in the third grade at the time."

"Oh, that's great," Kendra said, laughing. "Clearly, the little man wasn't ready for commitment, big sister."

Kendra and I both went quiet, taking in the view. I don't know if it was the wine or the sultry night air, but a warm feeling washed over me.

I slept well. Maybe it was the generous amount of wine I'd enjoyed at Kendra's the night before.

I walked down to the Donut Dealer and picked up a baker's dozen of cake, glazed and jelly-filled doughnuts. It took all of my less than considerable willpower to make it back to the theater before plucking one out to sample. I arranged six on one cake stand and six on another. I dispatched the extra doughnut to my mouth, telling myself an even number made for a more pleasing display.

I was beginning to think neither Kendra nor Trudy would show up this morning. I had just unlocked the door for coffee service when Kendra strolled in.

"Thought I'd check and see if you had a hangover this morning."

"No. But I didn't have any trouble sleeping."

"Same here," she said.

Trudy walked in and tossed her hands in the air.

"I dearly love George, but this morning he started tap dancing on my last nerve before I'd even had a cup of coffee."

"I'm not qualified to offer relationship advice. But how about some coffee? Would that help?"

"It can't hurt. Let me have the pretty kind with the design on top."

"Coming right up."

"What's up with George?" Kendra asked.

"Sometimes he just feels this need to release his inner curmudgeon. It's never a good sign when he puts on his cranky britches so early in the day. Please distract me by talking about anything else."

"Well," I started, "if you haven't eaten yet, please help yourselves to a doughnut. What I'm about to tell you may cause you to lose your appetite."

They looked at each other and then back to me.

"I had a granola bar," Trudy said.

"Bagel with cream cheese here. Go on," Kendra said.

"I went by the newspaper office midday yesterday to buy a subscription to the local rag and generally make nice with Clifford."

"Just how nice?" Kendra said with a Cheshire grin.

"Only nice enough that he might let some information slip about the murder investigation."

I explained how I'd overheard him talking at Jade Garden about a big update story.

"When I arrived no one was up front so I walked toward the room labeled 'newsroom.' As I approached I overheard Clifford and Susie talking all lovey dovey to each other."

"Do tell," Trudy said as she and Kendra both leaned forward slightly, eager for details.

"Susie wanted to make serious kissy face and Clifford

suggested they step into the utility closet for privacy."

Trudy said, "Oh, my" and Kendra added, "*Eeew.*"

"I quietly raced to Cliffie's computer hoping to see the story on his screen. Long story short, I flipped through his notebook quickly and caught a few details. Vince was a private investigator in Little Rock before he came here. His license had been suspended, but it had been reinstated shortly before he died. That was as far as I got before giggles from the closet made me think I should make my exit before they made theirs."

"His private investigator background would explain why Vince was so good at digging up dirt on people," Trudy offered. "Did Clifford's notes say why his license was suspended?"

"I ran out of time—and Clifford's penmanship could be better. But it's also possible that someone he dug up dirt on in Little Rock could've followed him here. In fact, maybe he came here to get away from trouble there."

"Perhaps the person or persons who reported him for whatever got his license suspended weren't happy to hear his license was going to be reinstated. Could be they considered him a problem that needed to be dealt with," Trudy said.

"You're being awful quiet," I said to Kendra, who had a perplexed expression.

"Was it just Clifford giggling or did you hear Susie giggle, too?" she asked.

"Believe me, it was a stomach-turning duet."

"I'm having a hard time imagining Susie giggling."

"Count yourself lucky."

"Hah," Trudy said. "Halley, I hope you sell lots of coffee and doughnuts today. Kendra, you should go lock people up in escape rooms. I'm going to check on my sourpuss."

# CHAPTER 21

It had been a good, but quiet day. Then, just after ten o'clock, Kendra called me, hysterical.

"Halley, I just locked up behind my last customers. I need to talk to you. Is it all right if I come over?"

"Of course, I'll come down and let you in the front—"

Before I could finish my sentence she had hung up. She was gently rattling the front door by the time I got to it. I locked the door behind her and when I turned around, she was nervously pacing back and forth in the lobby.

"What's wrong?"

When she stopped and looked at me, I could tell she'd been crying.

"Ling dashed down to the escape rooms a little while ago. You remember her, the hostess at Jade Garden? Anyway, she wanted me to know that the police had taken Joe in for questioning earlier this evening after arriving with a warrant and searching his car. And she had just overheard his mother say they were keeping Joe overnight at the jail."

Kendra broke down crying. I gave her a hug and suggested we go up to the apartment. I didn't want people passing by on the sidewalk to view her emotional state. Inside my apartment she collapsed onto the sofa sobbing. I grabbed us two beers from the fridge.

"Would you prefer if I made you some tea?" I asked as I started to hand her the beer.

"No, this is good."

"Did Ling know if Joe or his parents have called an attorney or if Joe has been charged with anything?"

Kendra wiped her face with her sleeve. I didn't have any Kleenex, so I grabbed a roll of toilet paper from the bathroom cabinet and sat it on the coffee table in front of her. After she'd blown her nose, she nodded.

"Yeah, I did ask her about the lawyer and she said yes. She didn't know if Joe had actually been charged with anything. But if they've locked him up, it can't be good."

Kendra paused and pressed a length of tissue over her eyes.

"Joe's parents are very private people. Ling hurried away, saying she had to get back to the restaurant and asked me not to let Joe's folks know she had told me about a personal family matter. I wanted to know more, of course, but Ling didn't feel it was her place to ask. I'm grateful she at least let me know what was going on. I'd been a little concerned because I hadn't heard from Joe today and had tried to call a few times. But he's constantly forgetting to charge his cell phone, so I wasn't too worried—until now."

"Oh, Kendra, I'm so sorry. Assuming this is about Vince's murder, we know Joe had nothing to do with that. The cops will figure that out, too. I think Detective Stedman is just grasping at straws at this point because he hasn't made much progress on this case."

"That's exactly what I'm afraid of. I'm worried the cops are feeling pressure to make an arrest. And somebody could be trying to frame Joe—maybe even the cops."

"I suppose someone could've put something in Joe's car, but I don't think it's the police. He may not have much experience investigating homicides, but I think Detective Stedman is a by-the-book, upright kind of guy. And as much as I dislike Susie Stoneface, I don't think she'd stoop to planting evidence," I said. "Hey, it looks like we could both use another beer, you want one? Or I could run downstairs and grab a bottle of wine."

"No, I'll stick to beer. It should give me less of a hangover. Line 'em up right here," she said, pointing to the coffee table.

"In that case, I think you'd better spend the night. You take the sofa and I'll sleep in the recliner. Derek can stand guard."

"I hope somebody up there," Kendra said rolling her eyes upward, "is watching over Joe tonight."

"Don't worry. I think Joe's perfectly safe in the Utopia Springs jail. He'll probably sleep better tonight than you or his parents. Anyway, let's hold good thoughts. I have a feeling they'll release him tomorrow morning. Here's to Joe," I said, raising my bottle and chinking it against Kendra's.

"I hope you're right. Bart is driving over in the morning to help me. I guess I was pretty emotional on the phone."

"Understandably so. I'm glad he's coming down."

"Me, too. Oh, by the way, I saw you'd changed the title on the marquee to the new old movie you're showing this week, the first one since *My Fair Lady*. I forgot the name?"

"*Charade*. It's another Aubrey Hepburn film, but not a musical and with a very different leading man—Cary Grant."

"Mmm, Cary Grant is my favorite old movie dude. He was dreamy," Kendra said.

"He still is—on the big screen. That's the magic of movies. Anyway, I just hope we have a good crowd, and more importantly, that they buy lots of wine and coffee. And that Delores shows up on time and handles ticket sales. She's a character. Do you know the deal with her? George didn't tell me much, and I haven't really had a chance to talk to her one-on-one."

"I don't know much. I know she's involved with one of the live theater groups in town. I think she mostly does seamstress work, but she's also done some acting. I saw her appear in a small role in one of their productions last year."

"What was her part?"

"She was basically the crazy cat lady neighbor. She didn't have a lot of lines, but she got a lot of laughs," Kendra said with a faint smile. She got up and grabbed two more beers from the refrigerator. Predictably, the conversation drifted back to Joe.

"I hope this crazy police mix-up doesn't cause trouble between Joe and his dad," Kendra said.

"Why would it, if Joe hasn't done anything wrong? And we know he hasn't."

"Mr. Chang is a very proud man. After he had a heart attack last year, he officially turned management of the restaurant over to Joe, but had a really hard time letting go. Joe had been pushing for a while to turn the restaurant into a buffet. His dad wouldn't hear of it, he still thought of the Jade Garden as serving fine Chinese cuisine, with prices to match. But in a place like Utopia Springs, the tourists want food served quickly, and there aren't enough locals to support it as a special occasion kind of place, more like their Fayetteville location.

"Joe changed the lunch hours to a buffet, which upset his dad. And it seemed to add insult to injury for his dad when profits soared. Joe and his mom tried to get his dad onboard with changing the dinner hours to a buffet as well, but he wouldn't budge. Six months later Joe made the change to dinner buffet as well, and his dad has been distant ever since. He tries not to show it, but it really bothers Joe. Both of them feel like they've lost respect in the other's eyes, you know?"

"Yeah. Family relationships can be complicated," I said, thinking about my own mother.

"Tell me. It took Dad a while to accept it when Bart came out, but fortunately he came around before...well, before the plane crash."

As the night wore on and our cold beer supply dwindled, Kendra said how much she cared about Joe—stopping just shy of actually admitting she loved him. And at some point during the night, past the point of tipsy, we both may have shared some personal details about things like first boyfriends.

It was all a bit blurry to me by the time sunlight assaulted my eyes, and I doubted Kendra would remember much about it either. I awoke with Eartha Kitty on my chest, gently pawing at my face. And Kendra was on the sofa, snoring loudly, with an empty beer bottle still in her hand.

I let her sleep while I made coffee in the French press, boiling water in a kettle and letting it cool briefly before pouring it over coarsely ground coffee beans and slowly pressing down the plunger. After steeping for five minutes, I decanted the aromatic brew into an insulated carafe. Kendra roused as I was pouring coffee into a couple of mugs.

"Ouch," she said as she sat up quickly and pressed her fingers against her apparently throbbing temples. In a moment she said, "Morning. Did you get the license plate number of the truck that hit me?"

"I think it was a brown bottle with a billboard on the side that said, 'one too many.' Here, have some coffee."

I handed her one of the mugs, hanging onto it until I was sure she had a firm grip.

"Oh, thanks. I may need a few of these. Do you have any aspirin?"

"Sure, just a sec." I retrieved a pill bottle out of the bathroom medicine cabinet for Kendra. "Here's some aspirin-type stuff. Do you want some water?"

"No, this is fine. Thanks."

I walked into the kitchen and dropped two slices of sourdough bread in the toaster and scrambled some eggs.

"I wonder if Joe is still in jail." Kendra said.

I plated up our breakfast and set Kendra's on the coffee table.

"I imagine so. It's only five after seven. Wait a minute. Let me call George and see if he can find out anything. He's buddies with most of the old guys in town, including some of the powers that be at city hall, I think. Although George never reveals his sources."

I phoned George and told him what little we knew. He said he'd call back in a bit. Then Kendra's phone buzzed. It was Bart saying he was about to hit the road and should be here by about 9:20.

"I should get cleaned up and pull myself together, but I don't want to leave until you hear back from George."

"You're welcome to use my shower and I can loan you a clean t-shirt."

From the sound of water I knew Kendra was still in the shower when George called back.

"I don't know about when Joe might be released. But he hasn't been charged with anything. And I don't know exactly what they found in his car, but a reliable source says the search warrant was for prescription drugs based on an anonymous tip."

"Thanks, George."

"No problem. Wait. Trudy wants to talk to you."

"Halley, how is Kendra holding up?"

"She was really upset last night. She ended up sleeping on my sofa. And we both might have had a little too much to drink. Fortunately, Bart is driving over to help her out today at work."

"Oh, good. I'm glad to hear it. You let us know if you hear anything and we'll do the same."

"Thanks, Trudy. You and George are the best."

In a few minutes Kendra emerged from the bathroom with a towel wrapped around her head and wearing my blue t-shirt. The shirt looked better on her. I told her what George had reported.

"An anonymous tip? That stinks like poo. I'm guessing those prescription drugs were used to kill Vince. Can't the cops see that someone is trying to frame Joe?"

She broke down crying again.

"You're right. It stinks. But George did say Joe hasn't been charged with anything. I'm guessing they'd need to find some way to tie him to the drugs. After all, you need a prescription to buy prescription drugs."

"You're right. I need to hold good thoughts. I've got to get things ready to open at my place, so I better be going."

She picked up the toast on her plate and took a bite.

"You want some coffee to go?"

"Yeah. It'd be a bad idea to drink beer this early, right?"

"Right."

I filled her cup and handed it to her. "Try not to worry too much."

"Thanks for everything. If you hear anything else from George call me right away, okay?"

# CHAPTER 22

I hurriedly got cleaned up and dressed and went downstairs to get the coffee bar ready to open at eight. A few customers came and went. A little before ten, I walked over to the sitting area in the lobby to collect some empty coffee cups left behind by customers, when I spotted Joe walking up the sidewalk to Hidden Clue Escape Rooms. I felt relieved knowing he'd been released. He must've called because before he even reached the door, Kendra shot out onto the sidewalk. She propelled herself into his arms, throwing her arms around his neck. Her feet left the ground as he swept her into a tight embrace. After a long moment, she pulled back and gave him a smile so bright it almost blinded me from across the street. She took his hand and led him inside. I was so happy for Kendra—and Joe.

In a bit, I had finished going over the carpet and was putting the vacuum cleaner away when I heard a loud rattle at the front door. I looked up to see Kendra and rushed over to let her in.

"Joe's been released," she said beaming.

"I know. I happened to catch a glimpse of him walking up the sidewalk to your place."

She blushed, presuming, I guessed, that I'd seen their emotional hello.

"We've got customers, so I should get back and help Bart. I just wanted to let you know."

"I'm glad you did. What did Joe tell you?"

"It was prescription drugs in the glove box, which of course Joe knew nothing about. It's some kind of strong heart medicine, but it's not the same drug they prescribed for Joe's dad after his heart attack last year—which should have immediately put Joe in the clear. But the cops tried to suggest Joe's sister, Jennifer, the one in pharmacy school, somehow got the drug for him, like it was this big family conspiracy he dragged his little sister into. Ridiculous," she said, shaking her head.

"They also asked him a hundred times about leaving the theater during the movie on opening night. Remember, he ran across the street to make sure everything was okay at the restaurant, even though Ling had promised to call him if anything came up. Anyway, his guess is the cops think he went to the restaurant or to his car to get the drugs when he saw Vince was here—which is also dumb."

"They released him, so that has to be good, right?"

"Yeah, they can only hold suspects like a day or two without charging them, so obviously they don't have anything on Joe that they could actually charge him with. Plus, there's zero motive. He didn't even know the guy. I think even the cops know the whole anonymous tip thing is pretty lame."

She turned to the door, then froze and turned back toward me.

"I almost forgot. Joe invited me to have dinner with him tonight just after closing to celebrate being out of jail. He invited you and Bart, too. But Bart's leaving as soon as we close to drive back to Fayetteville, since Simon's not traveling at the moment. Will you come with me?"

"No, I think that's a dinner you can handle all by yourself," I said, opening the door for her.

I did touch-up cleaning in the restrooms and caught up on paperwork. Midday, my thoughts were just turning toward lunch when I got call from Kendra.

"Hey, girl. Bart is shooing me out, telling me I should take advantage of his being here to take a real lunch break for a change. You want to grab a bite somewhere?"

"Sure, what are you in the mood for?"

"I thought we could eat at the pizza parlor. I know I eat that a lot, but it's always take-out. Dining in would make for a change."

"Sounds good to me. When?"

"Is now okay? I'm standing in front of the theater."

I met her outside and we started walking up the hill. We'd only walked a few steps when I spotted Detective Stedman cross the street and enter The Wooden Nickel Saloon.

"I wonder if he's going to question Trey," Kendra said.

"I don't think anybody goes to The Wooden Nickel for the food, and I can't imagine our straightlaced detective drinking in the middle of the day."

"Since the detective has accused both of us of following the cops around, why don't we?"

"Why don't we what?"

"Follow him into the saloon and see what he's up to," Kendra said. "I'd like to know he's pursuing suspects other than Joe."

When we walked in I spied Detective Stedman standing next to a booth, talking with a young couple.

Kendra and I took a seat at the end of the bar, where we had a good view of most of the room. Trey was punching keys on his cell phone, but glanced over to us with a lurid smile before calling out to Doofus, "Get these ladies a drink."

We each ordered a Red Stone. Trey's underling popped the tops off the beers and placed them in front of us. I handed him some cash.

"Just let me know if you ladies need anything else."

Detective Stedman stepped up beside me but didn't look my way.

"Mr. Tilby, could you spare a minute for me. I'd like to have a word." After giving Kendra and me the side eye he added, "In private."

Trey tried to put on a game face for the lawman, but he couldn't quite mask his annoyance. "Detective Stedman, can I get you a cold one?"

"No, I'm good. Is there somewhere we can talk privately?"

"Always happy to oblige the police. Let's go to my office." Trey dropped his phone on the back bar and exited at the far end of the bar with Detective Stedman following him around the corner.

"I wish we could eavesdrop on that conversation," Kendra said. "Wonder what he wants to talk to Trey about?"

"Whatever it is, I hope it leads to an arrest. What I'd really like is to get a look at Trey's cell phone to see if there are any texts between him and Vince."

Doofus was loading up a tray with cocktails. As soon as he turned his back to us to deliver the drinks, Kendra flung herself across the bar top and stretched her arm out, just barely able to retrieve the phone from the back bar. She quickly settled back onto her barstool and held Trey's phone against her thigh, shielded from sight by the bar.

"Dang. I should've figured it's locked." She sighed. "Looks like a six-number or letter password. "Maybe Nickel?"

She punched that in.

"Nope. Saloon?" she said as she typed. "Nope."

Thinking back to my first visit to the saloon, I had a sudden inspiration.

"Try 36-24-36."

"We're in," she said with a big smile. "How did you—"

"Long story. Hurry and check the text messages."

"We're in luck. Vince is one of the regulars in the text section, along with several female names."

I pulled my phone out of my pocket.

"You scroll through the messages and I'll take pics of the screen."

We were able to quickly get shots of five or six screen's worth, but Trey's assistant had made his way back behind the bar, mixing drinks just a few feet away from us.

"We need to put the phone back where we found it before Trey returns," I whispered.

It was a tense few minutes. Fortunately, an impatient customer started waving and calling out to the bartender, who left the bar and walked over to his table.

"I thought Curt would never leave," Kendra muttered.

*So Doofus has a name.*

Kendra leaned over and tossed the phone. It skittered across the counter and I feared it was going to slide right off the bar. But it came to a stop in roughly the same spot it had occupied earlier, just as Trey and Detective Stedman emerged from the hallway.

Kendra and I finished our drinks and left just after the detective, continuing on to the pizza parlor.

We sat next to each other in a booth and pulled up the text shots I'd taken. They were all texts from Trey to Vince with no replies from Vince.

*Miss Alcorn went my way. Sucks to be you. ha*

"Were they fighting over the same woman?" Kendra asked.

"Maybe. Hard to imagine any woman choosing Trey, the way he oozes sleaze. Here's the next text."

*You owe me. Pay up.*

And the one after that said, *Come by tonight or I'll come for you.*

The server came over and we ordered a large mushroom

pizza and two Cokes. Unfortunately, the detective had no intention of letting us eat lunch in peace.

"How's your investigation going?" he said as he slid into the booth across from us.

"How many times do we have to tell you, we're not investigating the murder," I said.

"If you say so. I still want to see what you got off Trey Tilby's phone."

I glanced over to Kendra and we shared a brief "busted" look.

"The guy I was talking to when you two walked in the bar was an off-duty police officer. Rookie mistake," he said. The corner of his mouth twitched upward briefly in what I assume passes as a smile for him.

I brought the text shots up on my phone and passed it to the detective. He pulled the notebook out of his pocket and wordlessly scrolled through as he took notes. He deleted the screen shots before handing the phone back to me.

"I'm sure you'll tell the Mayfields about the texts, but please don't mention them to anyone else—for your own safety. And, a word of advice, Trey Tilby is bad news. Don't tangle with him."

Our pizza arrived just as the detective left. I moved to the other side of the booth, facing Kendra. He'd really taken the wind out of our sails. I could barely work up the energy to suck soda through my straw.

"I think we had shots of seven texts and we only got a look at three of them before the detective deleted them," I said.

"Yeah, it seems unfair. What can we learn from the ones we did see?" Kendra asked.

"It seems pretty obvious Trey and Vince weren't getting along. They were fighting over some woman and over money. And Trey was getting impatient," I said.

"The detective could've been nicer to us. We gave him

information he couldn't have gotten a search warrant for. Wait. That means he can't even use the information, right?"

"I don't think he can use it directly as evidence. Maybe it will point the cops in the right direction—away from Joe. And me. We can hope.

"Anyway, I think his version of being nice to us was not putting us under arrest. And, Kendra, I thought you showed great restraint not plowing into him about holding Joe in jail overnight."

Her eyes flew open wide and her face flushed.

"I can't believe it. He had me so flustered I forgot all about Joe," she said, exhaling her pent-up frustration with a loud sigh. "He lucked out on that one."

We quickly finished our lunch. Kendra said she'd left Bart on his own for too long and hurried away up the hill. I turned in the opposite direction and walked down to the gallery to give George and Trudy an update. I felt they deserved one, since George had been nice enough to check on Joe's status first thing this morning.

When I entered Mayfield's Gallery, Trudy was in her usual spot behind the counter.

"Hi, hon. How is Kendra?"

I walked up to the counter and answered softly, "Much better now that Joe's been released. Are there any customers around?"

"No, and we'll hear the bell if someone comes in."

"First, I wanted to fill you in on what Kendra heard from Joe."

"Hang on a sec. George, come up front, will you? Halley's here with some news on Joe."

George came through from the studio, wiping his hands on a paint-smudged cloth.

"What's the news?" he asked.

I filled them in about the prescription drug, the lame idea that Joe's sister procured the drug for him and the detective's keen interest in Joe's comings and goings on opening night.

"I remember Joe's little sister, Jennifer. She was just a sweet-faced teenager when they moved here," Trudy said. "Have they lost interest in Joe as a suspect?"

"I hope so, but I'm afraid it could be more that they didn't have enough to hold him," I said. "I think the key question is, 'Who turned in that anonymous tip?'"

"The killer," George said, matter-of-factly.

"Right. But I think another good question is, 'Why would the killer want to frame Joe Chang?' and 'Why now?'" Trudy said.

"Good points. I had the feeling I was the detective's favorite suspect. But maybe I flatter myself. It appears something has happened to make the killer nervous, what with them turning in an anonymous tip."

"We can hope they've gotten careless and the police will catch whoever it is soon. But just in case they don't, from what little we know, who are our best suspects?" Trudy said.

"Well, we know Vince had blackmailed Linda and Edgar, and maybe Paula. And Trey was Vince's pal, and perhaps partner," I said. "In fact, Kendra and I have some new information on Trey and Vince."

I brought them up to speed on our procuring texts from Trey's phone—and getting caught by the detective.

"You and Kendra make a crack detective team," Trudy said. "I'm impressed you were able get at information like that."

"They got caught, Trudy, or did you miss that part? And I'm more worried than impressed. You two were lucky that you got caught by the detective instead of Trey," George said.

"As much as I'm loathe to agree with the grouch, you and Kendra need to be careful."

"Don't worry, we will. I promise. Vince and Trey seemed to have had a falling out over some woman." I told them about Miss Alcorn.

George smiled. "I think Miss Alcorn was likely a bet on the Mississippi College-Alcorn State football game."

"Oh." I said. "Maybe Vince owned him money on a bet, but Trey still seemed mad."

"The detective's interest in Joe coming in and out of the theater opening night brings up an interesting point. If Vince's drink was spiked at the theater, it was most likely by someone who knew he was coming to the show or by someone who saw him come in and then went and retrieved the drug. They wouldn't be just carrying drugs around with them. Most people keep their prescriptions in the medicine cabinet at home, don't they?" George said.

"Not necessarily. Someone with a heart condition might carry their medicine with them," Trudy said. "Among Linda, Edgar, Paula and Trey I'd guess Edgar as the one most likely to be taking heart medicine, wouldn't you think?"

"Maybe. But Edgar wasn't at the theater and has witnesses. Plus, he says video footage shows Vince didn't come by the restaurant that evening," I said.

"I don't think we can rule out Linda on the heart meds," George said. "She's over fifty and overweight."

"And she *was* at the theater on opening night by her own admission," I noted. "And it was packed. People were elbow-to-elbow in the lobby. She could've easily dropped something in his drink."

"Assuming she takes heart medicine and just happened to have it with her," Trudy said.

"Or maybe she spotted Vince walking past her store and saw him go in the theater. She could've retrieved the drug and followed him to the theater, seizing it as an opportunity to get rid of her blackmailer," I said.

"I suppose it's possible, but I still have a hard time imagining Linda as a killer. We know for certain Trey wasn't here. Saturday night is a busy night at the bar, plus he doesn't exactly blend in. Vince could have stopped by the bar right before he came to the theater, and Trey coulda slipped him a mickey in his drink," George offered.

"Trey looks pretty healthy. I can't imagine him having a heart condition," I said.

"I feel certain Trey Tilby is the kind of guy who could obtain any contraband he really wanted to, including prescription drugs," George said.

# CHAPTER 23

At about six, I opened the coffee and wine bar for the Thursday night show. It sweetened my mood when Delores actually showed up on time. And even better, we had a pretty good crowd.

After closing, I finished what little clean-up I had left to do behind the bar and did a quick clean-up in the restrooms, which I was relieved to find in pretty good shape. I decided to leave cleaning the auditorium and vacuuming the lobby for the morning, which was becoming my routine.

Once inside the apartment, I kicked off my shoes and fixed myself a bowl of cereal. It had been a long time since the pizza Kendra and I had for lunch. I finished my cereal, settled into the recliner and watched a few minutes of some random TV cop show when the building alarm sounded off. At first I was startled, then terrified. I heard the clang of metal in the alley and rushed over to the windows. I saw a figure sprinting away around the corner and could see my back door standing wide open.

I was confused that someone seemed to be breaking out, instead of breaking in. But I knew the police would respond to the alarm—the one George installed after Vince Dalton had broken in and vandalized the theater. It was kind of late, but I called George and Trudy. She picked up.

"Trudy, I'm sorry to call so late. But the alarm is going off and I just saw someone running off down the alley."

"Have the police arrived yet?"

"Not yet. Should I go downstairs to let them in?"

"No. You stay put. We'll be right there.

In a couple of minutes my phone buzzed. The dispatcher asked me what was going on. I told her and she said for me to remain in my apartment and that officers would be there soon.

Trudy called to say she was coming in the back and would tap on my door in just a minute. I let her in and locked the door behind her.

She responded to the panicked look on my face with a big hug.

"You're okay, hon."

"Where's George?"

"He went through to the front to meet the cops when they arrive. You and I will just wait here until then."

I had just started recounting to Trudy what I'd seen when her phone rang. George said the police were here and for us to come down. As we got the bottom of the stairs, George peeked in from the hallway and escorted us to the lobby.

I was less than thrilled to see the responding officer was Susie Stoneface, who greeted me with her usual charm.

"What time did you lock up tonight?" she asked, staring at her notebook with pen in hand.

"About ten thirty. An older couple staying at the hotel up the hill were the last to leave. I locked the door behind them."

"Did you do a walk-through downstairs before going up to your apartment?"

"I always take a peek in the auditorium. And I cleaned up in both restrooms. I didn't see anyone. But just after the alarm started blaring I heard a crash in the alley and ran to my window. I saw a figure running away around the corner and noticed my back door standing open."

"What did this figure look like? Male, female? Tall, short?"

"I'm pretty sure it was a man, wearing dark clothes. Beyond that, I have no idea. I only got a glimpse of him disappearing around the corner."

"What do you do with the ticket and concession monies collected?"

"I put the bank bag in a drop safe in the office."

"Have you checked the office?"

"No, I stayed in my apartment waiting for you to get here."

"Let's take a look."

The four of us walked past the bar and down the side hallway. The office door was locked. I opened it with my keys, but nothing looked disturbed.

George said, "It looks like the basement door is open a crack. Have you been down there today, Halley?"

I shook my head.

Officer Stone shone her flashlight down the stairs before flipping on the light switch.

"Y'all wait here for a minute."

She descended the stairs slowly as the three of us huddled in the doorway. I could see the beam of her flashlight dart about the room before she told me to come on down.

"Can you tell if anything has been taken or disturbed?"

"I don't know if anything's been taken. I don't think there's anything really valuable down here. But those boxes," I said, pointing to a stack, "have been moved. They were against the wall and now they're out in the center."

"Are you sure? It's kind of a jumble down here."

"Yeah, I'm sure. I just recently brought those boxes down. It's some of Uncle Leon's..." I started to say junk, but stopped myself, "belongings that I packed up from the apartment."

Officer Stone said nothing and walked back up the stairs.

"Let's take a look at the back door."

We walked through and the door was still wide open.

"I came through when I arrived, but didn't touch the door," Trudy said. "George walked through to the lobby to wait for you."

A couple of buckets that had been hanging on a rail were lying next to the dumpster.

"I guess this is what made the clatter I heard," I said.

She looked closely at the door.

"No sign of forced entry. Plus, you saw someone running away. It would seem someone hid in the theater until after you closed."

"Why would they break into the basement? I'm sure that door was locked," I said.

"Hmph," she said as if she doubted me. "Even if it were, someone could make quick work picking the flimsy lock on the basement door. Maybe they had planned to look in the office for cash. But that heavy door and deadbolt deterred them, so they went downstairs hoping to score something for their trouble."

She turned to leave and spoke over her shoulder. "If you discover anything missing, or any more messages telling you to go home, give us a call."

George's face was red and he started to say something, but Trudy patted his arm and shook her head.

"Halley, I'd feel better if you stayed with us tonight."

"I'll be fine, I—"

Kendra suddenly appeared from around the end of the building.

"Hey, what's up? I just saw the cops leaving."

Trudy suggested we all go upstairs. I locked the back door and we went up to the apartment, where everyone but Trudy accepted my offer of a beer. I pulled over a dining chair as Kendra and Trudy sat down on the sofa. George claimed the recliner.

"Okay, tell Kendra what happened. And as you go through

it again, try to remember every detail," Trudy said.

I went through everything from locking up after the last customer onward.

"Do you remember anyone acting oddly? Like some guy wandering the wrong direction to the men's room? Or a man who had been hanging around while you were chatting with customers?" George asked.

I tried to rummage through my memories of the evening.

"Nope. Truth is, when I'm busy making lattes, I could miss someone slipping down the hall. And I did clean the ladies' room first, so if a guy was hiding out in the men's room, or even in the auditorium, he could have slipped out without my seeing. The question is, who would want to?"

"What about Trey Tilby?" Kendra said. "The texts on his phone indicated he and Vince had a falling out. If they were partners in a treasure hunt, maybe Trey was following up on information Vince had dug up about a possible old tunnel entrance in the theater basement."

We exchanged glances, mulling over Trey as a suspect.

"I know you only got a brief look at the intruder, but could it have been Trey?" George said. "And if so, maybe in the morning you could call and tell Susie that you're not absolutely certain, but you think the guy you saw running away was Trey. Then they can rattle his cage a bit." George said.

"George, I'm not sure that's a good idea. That guy is creepy. I don't think we want to do anything to put Halley in his crosshairs," Trudy said.

I sat staring off into space, replaying the scene of the guy running away over in my mind as they talked about my next move.

"Halley, what is it?" Kendra asked, reaching over and nudging me.

"The thing is...while I can't make a positive I.D., and as

much as I'd like it to be Trey, I really don't think it was him. He has more of an athletic build with long strides and, I don't know, more confident movements. The man I saw seemed more like he was running scared and definitely didn't have smooth or athletic moves. If I scan through the list of possible suspects in Vince's murder, the person who springs to mind as the best fit for the person running away is Edgar."

"I'd like to go rattle that guy's cage," George said, doing that thing he does with his eyebrows when he's riled up.

"No, honey. I think we'd have more luck getting information from Edgar if Halley and I go by and have a quiet chat with him."

# CHAPTER 24

The next morning when I awoke, Eartha was curled up on the arm of the recliner. I must have slept soundly because I didn't remember her arrival. She was pretty stealthy. I had finally shooed everyone out of the apartment last night after Trudy again made a plea for me to spend the night at their place and Kendra offered to stay and bunk on my sofa. Perhaps surprisingly, I felt perfectly safe in the apartment. Maybe it was knowing the alarm system worked just fine. Or maybe it was latching onto the notion that last night's intruder was Edgar, rather than someone much scarier like Trey. Trudy called around seven thirty and we discussed strategy about confronting Edgar. She said she'd meet me at the theater at two thirty.

At straight up eight o'clock I flipped the sign on the front door to open. My first customer walked in a couple of minutes later. It was an older man with a sweet smile, who was becoming a regular. He wasn't that chatty, but he always nodded and tipped his hat to me when he said, "Good morning," and I thought he was cute. He ordered his usual Americano to go. The thought that my little morning coffee service was already developing regulars made me happy. I hoped one day he'd take a seat and stay a while so I'd have a chance to learn his story.

I got the theater cleaned up and ready for tonight's show, then headed upstairs to change clothes before Trudy and I went to talk to Edgar. I considered putting on a Girl Power t-shirt to get myself pumped up for a confrontation. After some thought, I decided to wear a navy blue skirt and pink ruffled top to throw Edgar off his game. While I was getting dressed my cell phone buzzed. It was George, which concerned me a bit since he almost never phoned me.

"Hi, George, what's up?"

"I just want to warn you not to get sucked in by Edgar Wentworth's charm—the way *some* people have."

I could almost hear his eyes roll.

"You can't trust that guy as far as you can throw him. He's a complete phony—even his hoity-toity British accent is phony. But don't tell Trudy. She thinks he's made of tea and scones and in line to the throne. I don't want to shatter her illusions. Just be sure you don't get taken in by his act, that's all I'm saying."

"Don't worry, George. I'll be on my guard."

After I got off the phone, I couldn't help but laugh.

Trudy arrived on the dot and we walked over to the Tudor House Restaurant. It was teatime, but surprisingly the dining room was sparsely populated. Edgar rushed over to greet us just as he had before. Maybe it was my imagination, but he seemed a bit nervous. He pointed to a back corner booth, but Trudy suggested it would be better if we talked in his office. He was definitely acting nervous now, and it wasn't my imagination.

After Edgar ushered us into his well-appointed office outfitted with a huge mahogany desk and antique desk set with blotter and inkwell, Trudy and I took seats in vintage leather side chairs. He sat down behind his desk.

"Now, what can I do for you ladies?"

"I think it's more a question of what we can do for you, Edgar—like sparing you a visit from the police," Trudy said in a very businesslike tone.

"I, I, I don't know, wha, wha—"

I interrupted him mid-stutter.

"Edgar, I know it was you running out of my alley last

night. After the benefit of some sleep, and replaying the scene in my head, I feel confident enough to tell the police I'm almost certain it was you. If you tell me why you were in my basement, and tell me the truth," I said leaning forward to give him the full weight of my stare, "I may not need to bother the police with this."

He fell silent and looked back and forth between Trudy and me.

"Edgar, breaking into Halley's basement was behavior unbecoming for a gentleman like you," Trudy said, shaking her head. "I think you better tell us what this is all about."

He heaved a heavy sigh.

"I was in the theater basement, but you have my word I didn't take or damage anything."

"Why? What were you doing down there?" I asked.

"Well, as I told you and Kendra previously, I was trying to gather enough plausible evidence to suggest Jesse James and his gang spent time in Utopia Springs and stashed some loot here. I was looking for some markings on the basement wall on the street side..."

"If you thought there was evidence in the theater basement why didn't you mention it to Kendra and me earlier? And why didn't you just ask me if you could look around?"

"I was afraid you were still upset with me. Besides, I didn't know about it then. Honestly. I've been digging through the library archives with help from the reference librarian, and I happened across some papers that claimed there were markings on that wall in your basement. I couldn't believe it, but running my hands across the back wall—I found them. If you look very closely some of them are visible."

He jumped up excitedly, unlocked the credenza behind the desk and pulled out a sheet of white copy paper folded in half.

"I tried to shoot some photographs with my phone camera,

but the markings didn't show up, so I did an old-fashioned pencil rubbing. It's faint, but you can see it here. Notice the anchor-shaped facing 'Js'—like the ones on the notorious boot."

He placed the paper on the desk and switched on a banker's lamp beside it. Trudy and I leaned forward to take a closer look.

"You believe these markings were made by Jesse James?" I asked, doubtfully.

"No, they definitely were *not* made by Jesse James. But they could've been made by some treasure hunters, probably in the 1930s, who believed that wall adjoined a collapsed tunnel which may connect to the original springs cavern. As I told you before, I'm trying to come up with evidence that would entice my cable documentary friend to shoot an episode here in town. And this could help."

"Wait a minute. Halley, wasn't it the reference librarian who squealed on Kendra when she looked through the archives about the buried treasure?" Trudy asked.

"Yeah. How come the reference librarian ran to the detective, who grilled Kendra—but he didn't tell the cops about you?"

"I had no idea Kendra had been questioned. But I can assure you it wasn't Alan who told the police about Kendra's research. He'd never do that."

"Who else would've known?"

"My guess would be the assistant librarian, Elaine Stedman."

"Stedman, as in Detective Stedman?" I asked.

"Yes, his wife. She likes to talk and tell all she knows. Especially to her husband."

"Hold on, I thought Elaine was the school librarian," Trudy said.

"She was. But when school started back they had hired a new school librarian and Elaine was quickly brought on with the public library. No one seems to know why, or at least no one's talking," Edgar said.

After we left Tudor House, Trudy said she'd better get back to the gallery and check on George.

I started ambling back to the theater under a cloudy sky, taking a circuitous route, lost in my thoughts. I couldn't stop wondering who framed Joe, and the bigger but related question of who killed Vince. George and Trudy seemed convinced of Linda's innocence, which was understandable since she was a long-time friend of theirs, and I admit, she seemed pretty innocuous on the surface. But she had been blackmailed by Vince more than once. She had told Trudy and me that when she refused to sell the shop he tried to make some other blackmail arrangements. We only had her word for it that she had refused, and blackmailers were generally insistent. Plus, she was the only one of our favorite suspects that we knew for sure was at the theater on opening night. And she could be taking heart medicine—or she could've stolen the drug from a friend's medicine cabinet for all we know. One thing I knew, I wasn't ready to write her off as a suspect just yet.

I decided it was time I went shopping for some windchimes—and maybe a bit of a fishing expedition while I was at it.

I strolled into Bell, Bath and Candle. Windchimes tinkled as I entered, and Linda walked toward me in her signature flowing fabrics that fluttered when she moved as though she were walking into a light breeze.

"Greetings, gentle spirit," she said.

"Hi, Linda, nice to see you again. I'm shopping for a birthday gift for my grandmother. I'm thinking windchimes."

"Lovely. Appearance matters, of course. But I tend to choose windchimes for myself based on their sound," she said, reaching out and lightly brushing her hand across one of the myriad windchimes hanging throughout the store. It jingled melodically. "Feel free to check out the tune, if you will, on as many chimes as you like."

"Thanks. Are any of them made locally? I thought it would be nice to send her something from Utopia Springs, since it's my new home."

"Yes, many of them are made by local craftspeople. The chimes in this whole section," she pointed out a grouping, "are made by Maddy Macon, a local artist and real mountain woman."

"Perfect." I checked out the "tune" on a couple of the chimes, which were beautiful.

I was the only customer in the store, so I took advantage of the privacy.

"Paula Turpin said Vince had rented the cottage from her for almost a year, but hadn't renewed his lease, even though she mentioned it to him. Did Vince ever mention to you that he had any plans to move? It seems that he hadn't really put down roots here," I said.

"Actually, he had expressed an interest in moving into the carriage house behind my house. I gathered he was tired of Paula's accommodations."

That's an odd way to phrase it, I thought.

"Did he try to blackmail you for free rent?"

"We never talked about a rent amount. The carriage house had been vacant since my mother passed away. I'd never gotten around to sprucing it up for a tenant. We really just talked about it in generalities."

*Hmm, she seemed to have quite a bit of idle chitchat with her blackmailer.*

"I heard recently that Vince had been a private investigator in Little Rock, although he wasn't practicing his trade here—at least not officially. Did you know he was a P.I.?"

"Yes, I did. And he gave me the impression he planned to set up shop here at some point." She suddenly changed the subject. "How about these chimes for your grandmother. They're lovely and have a lovely tune, as well," she said as she lightly strummed her fingers across them.

"I do like those," I said, stepping over to get a closer look at them—and the price tag. "I'll take them."

"Excellent choice. I think I have a box just the right size for them," she said, breezing off and retrieving a box from a shelf beneath the cash register.

My bag jangled as I walked home thinking about the conversation I'd just had with Linda. She appeared to have a more nuanced relationship with her blackmailer than one would expect. But what did it mean?

As I neared the theater I noticed the newspaper stand and bought a copy to see if Clifford's murder update had finally made it into print. It had. The clever headline below the fold read, "Murder Investigation Update."

Back at the apartment I placed my noisy purchase on the dining table, heated water and made myself a cup of chamomile tea. Leaning back in the recliner, I scanned through Clifford's article. Not much was in it I didn't already know from his notes and my visit to Linda. Vince's private eye license had been reinstated, he planned to set up shop in Utopia Springs. And the cops here knew he was a former private investigator, which along with his relatively young age, had made them immediately suspect his death might be foul play. I sipped tea as I replayed the weird conversation with Linda in my head. I had some time before I had to get the theater ready for tonight's show and it was almost closing time for Mayfield's Gallery, so I decided to walk down and have a quick chat with Trudy and George.

"Hi, Trudy. Hi, George," I called out toward the studio as I walked to the counter. I gathered business was slow since Trudy was painting her fingernails.

"I like that color," I said, referring to the deep raspberry polish.

"Thanks, hon. Me, too," she said, holding her hand out to admire her manicure. "It's been a slow day."

"I'm sorry to hear that."

"Oh, not to worry, hon. Some days are busy, some are slow. It all evens out somehow," Trudy said.

George walked into the store, ringing the bell as he entered, and we exchanged hellos.

"Halley, I'm glad you're here. I'm afraid I have some disappointing news about Trey Tilby. He finally rented the excavating equipment."

"Wait, what? That makes it even more likely that he was in cahoots with Vince on some treasure hunting scheme. That's wonderful," I gushed.

"I'm afraid it's not so wonderful. The excavating equipment is at his house, not the saloon. His home basement has a low ceiling and he wants to dig it out to increase the overhead clearance. Sorry."

"That is disappointing," Trudy said.

"Yeah, I really liked the idea of Trey getting locked up."

I struggled with whether I should say anything about Linda to George and Trudy since she was a friend. But after my somewhat puzzling conversation with her, I decided to just throw it out there and see what they thought.

"I went to Bell, Bath and Candle this afternoon to shop for some windchimes for my grandmother. Her birthday's coming up. Anyway, I took another shot at talking to Linda about Vince and she said something kind of odd."

"What did she have to say?" Trudy asked.

"She knew Vince had worked as a private investigator and said he'd led her to believe he planned to set up shop here in Utopia Springs. She also said they had talked about Vince moving into the carriage house behind her house. It just struck me that she seemed to chitchat with her blackmailer more than one would normally expect. And she seemed almost, I don't know, pleased at the prospect of Vince moving out of Paula's place and into her guest house. Doesn't that seem a little odd?"

"Hmm," Trudy said, looking pensive. "You're right. It would've been a good move for Vince. The carriage house behind Linda's old Victorian is two-story, at least twice as big as the cottage he rented from Paula. And nice, too. I visited there a couple of times before Linda's mom died. I'd kind of wondered why Linda never rented it out after her mother passed."

"She said she needed to paint and spruce it up a bit," I said.

"What do you think, hon?" she said, looking over to her husband.

George tilted his head to one side and then the next, seeming to weigh his thoughts.

"Remember when she first talked to us about the blackmail? How she said the blackmailer tried to make alternate arrangements after she refused to sell the shop?"

"Yeah, she did," Trudy said, haltingly.

"Maybe Vince looked around her basement enough to decide there was nothing of interest there. Maybe he decided free rent in a bigger, nicer place would be a fair exchange for his silence."

"That makes sense. I mean, it had been sitting empty for at least a year. Linda wasn't collecting rent on it anyway," Trudy said.

"And remember, about three or four years ago, she had that break-in at her house. They stole some silver and electronics, I believe. Anyway, Linda is just looney tunes enough to think having a man—even a blackmailer—living in the carriage house might deter burglars," George said.

They both looked to me.

"If that's true then it makes it even more unlikely that Linda is Vince's killer," I said, exhaling a long sigh.

It was annoying me that every time I'd settled on a favorite suspect, we came up with information that cast doubt on their guilt.

# CHAPTER 25

When the customers had all gone Friday night, I did a careful walk-through, including checking the office and basement doors and the men's room. After last night's break-in I wanted to ensure I was alone. I'd just started cleaning the ladies' room when my phone buzzed. Kendra was at the front door.

"I just locked up and was dying to hear how your talk went with Edgar," Kendra said as I let her in the lobby.

"We'll go downstairs and I'll show you what Edgar was looking for. But first, I wanted to let you know you should be careful what you say in front of that assistant librarian, Elaine. Turns out she's Detective Stedman's wife, and apparently thinks she's on a stakeout for the police."

"Wow, that's good to know. I think she only works part-time, so I'll try to do research when she's not on the clock."

"Or on the case," I said.

"And here I was thinking Alan must have snitched on me, even though that doesn't seem like him at all. By the way, Alan raved about the theater renovations and how wonderful everything looks. He called the theater a local treasure. And that's high praise coming from Alan, he's very serious about the preservation and conservation of historic sites."

"Did he come to see *Charade*?"

"Not yet, but he plans to. Actually he attended the showing of *My Fair Lady* on opening night. I was kind of surprised to hear that because I didn't remember seeing him and I was really trying to work the room, encouraging people to have more refreshments," Kendra said with a laugh.

"All sales appreciated."

"Anyway, he said he bought a ticket and then had to run home. He remembered he hadn't fed his cat, Luna. He has a picture of that cat on his desk. By the time he got back to the theater the movie was about to start. I told him when he comes to the theater again to be sure to introduce himself to you. He's a little shy."

"I'd love to meet him. Let me grab my keys and we'll go down to the basement," I said, slipping behind the bar to collect my key ring and a flashlight from under the counter.

"By the way, turns out George has known all along that Edgar's accent is phony. But, get this, he asked me not to tell Trudy because he doesn't want her to be disappointed."

"Aw, they're too cute. And as secrets go, Edgar's phony accent is pretty harmless. We all seek to reinvent ourselves at times. For some people it's a new hair color. For others it's a new accent," she said with a smile.

We went downstairs to the basement and a moved couple of boxes out of the way to make a clear path to the wall on the street side. I pulled up the photo on my phone of Edgar's pencil rubbing of the wall markings and handed it to Kendra.

"Here's what we're looking for—and what Edgar was looking for when he broke into the basement last night."

"He admitted it?"

"Trudy had to apply a little pressure, but he caved pretty quickly," I said.

"What are we looking at? No, wait, I think I spot an interlocked 'J.' Does Edgar actually believe these marks were made by the James Gang?"

"No. He speculates that some treasure hunters in the 1930s made the markings, believing that this wall adjoined a tunnel, which possibly connects to the original springs cavern."

I looked closely as I ran my hand along the wall.

"I definitely feel some carved marks along here," I said, running my fingers over the grooves.

Kendra ran her hand over the spot.

"As evidence goes, this is pretty sketchy," she said.

"Edgar admitted as much. It's just one more thing to add to his stack of so-called evidence to present to his documentary pal."

Scanning with my flashlight I spotted a loose brick on the adjoining wall. I poked at it with one of the larger keys on my key ring and the brick fell out. Something shiny tumbled to the floor after it. It glinted as I shone the flashlight on the floor beside the brick. I looked to Kendra, barely able to contain my excitement as I knelt down to retrieve the object.

It was a gold coin. An old-looking one.

I handed it to Kendra, who examined it as I directed the beam of my flashlight into the void where the brick had been. Behind the old bricks was a solid wall.

"Does that coin mean there really could be treasure somewhere beyond this wall?"

"This is an old coin, but I'm pretty sure it's not *that* old. My guess is early twentieth century, but I can't make out the date," she said, eyeing it closely. "I could ask someone to look at it. In fact, Alan at the library is a pretty knowledgeable coin collector."

"How did it get here?" I asked.

"At one time it was common practice for people to place coins in walls and under floors for good luck. I think that's probably what we've got here."

"This is just fool's gold," I said, feeling like a kid whose shiny red balloon had just been popped.

Kendra smiled and laid a hand on my shoulder.

"Not at all. I think this is an omen of good things to come. I agree with Edgar that a TV show being filmed here could boost tourism. That's treasure. And this theater is real treasure; it's your future. If you don't mind me hanging onto the coin for a few days, I'll see what Alan thinks."

"Sounds good. Just make sure Elaine Stedman isn't lurking when you do."

Saturday morning I woke up thinking about my exploration of the basement with Kendra the night before.

*It would be nice if that gold coin we found was worth a mint.*

I was also thinking it would be nice to have one of Zeke's mammoth cinnamon rolls for breakfast, so I dressed and headed out the door to The Muffin Man. I'd only taken a few steps when a familiar figure fell in step beside me.

"Mornin', Ms. Greer," Detective Stedman said.

"Good morning, Detective," I said without looking over or breaking my stride. "I assume you'd like a word, so why don't you join me for breakfast at The Muffin Man. I'm starved and I'm really not much for talking before I've had my morning coffee."

He didn't reply but kept pace with me. When we arrived at the muffin shop he opened the door for me."

"The usual, Halley?" Zeke said as I stepped up to the counter.

*The usual? I should probably cut back on my cinnamon roll intake.*

The detective asked for black coffee. We collected our orders and sat at the corner table farthest from the door.

"I'm surprised a coffee aficionado like you would condescend to drink regular coffee in a place like this."

"This happens to be a nice place. When it comes to coffee I

prefer a French press or the forced hot water method of an espresso machine, but I'm not a snob about it."

Truth is I'm a caffeine addict and I'll take it any way I can get it in a pinch, but I didn't say so.

I savored a bite of the cinnamon roll and a sip of coffee before meeting the gaze of the lawman sitting opposite me. I waited for him to speak.

"I understand you had some excitement at your place Thursday night."

"I assume you're referring to the break-in. I wouldn't describe it as excitement. It was unsettling to say the least."

"According to the report it was more of a break-out than a break-in, wasn't it? Supposedly, someone hid in the theater after closing time and left through the alley door, setting off your alarm."

"Someone broke *into* my basement before leaving through the back door and setting off the alarm."

"Right. Did you ever ascertain if anything was missing?"

"No. There's a lot of junk in the basement. I don't think anything was taken. Nothing of value, anyway."

"Seems odd, doesn't it, that someone would go to the trouble to hide in the theater and break into your basement and not take anything?"

"You're right, Detective, it seems odd, creepy even. But that's exactly what happened."

"You know something else that seems odd to me, Ms. Greer, how with the alarm going off, signaling that there was an intruder in the theater, you ran to look out the window."

"I don't know what it says in the report, of course. But as I explained to Officer Stone, just after the alarm sounded I heard a metal clatter in the alley. I assumed someone was breaking in, not out, and I looked to see what was going on. I saw someone running away and the back door to the theater standing open.

When we looked later, with Officer Stone, there were some metal pails overturned near the back door, which is probably what made the racket."

He leveled his gaze at me, and I tried to remain calm.

"Ms. Greer, I do hope you're not wasting police time with a false report by staging a break-in."

"A false...Staging a...That's a ridiculous accusation, Detective Stedman. What could I possibly hope to gain by setting off my own alarm?"

"Perhaps you believed if it appeared as though someone were after you, that you were in some kind of danger, the police would be less likely to consider you a suspect in our murder investigation."

"I was under the impression the police had moved on to considering Joe Chang as a suspect in your murder investigation based on an anonymous tip by someone obviously trying to frame him. And just for the record, I didn't turn in the anonymous tip any more than I filed a false report."

I noticed people at other tables looking our way and realized I'd been talking louder than I meant to and lowered my voice.

"Besides, if Kendra and I weren't trying to find the real killer, we wouldn't have retrieved evidence of Vince's relationship with Trey on Trey Tilby's phone—evidence you could not have gotten otherwise."

"You only shared that information with me because you got caught. And for all I know, your main goal could've been to go into Mr. Tilby's phone and delete texts that could implicate you. The other texts you found may have just been a bonus."

I'd had about as much of the detective as I could stomach, so dropped my cinnamon roll back in its white paper bag and grabbed my coffee cup.

"If you'd like to chat with me further, you know where I

live—and work," I said, getting up and storming out.

I walked slowly, expecting the detective to fall in step beside me again at any moment. But as I reached the theater, unlocked the front door and glanced back up the hill toward the muffin shop, there was no sign of him.

"Oh, that, that...policeman!" I muttered as I stomped up the steps to my apartment.

I was so mad at Detective Stedman I wished I had a voodoo doll to stick pins in.

*Wonder if they sell those at the doll shop near the depot?*

I took a sip of the coffee in my to-go cup and found it had gone cold. I poured it into a ceramic mug and reheated it in the microwave, then sat at the dining table. I took a sip of the coffee, which tasted foul, but I needed the caffeine to ease the headache pounding at my temples. I pulled the cinnamon roll out of the bag. Its sweetness comforted me somewhat and countered the bitterness of the coffee.

I wanted to rush down to George and Trudy's place to tell them what the mean old detective had said to me, but I was slightly paranoid at this point that I was under surveillance. I thought for a moment about calling Trudy before deciding I was being ridiculous. I washed the sticky residue of the cinnamon roll off my hands and left by the alley door, walking to Mayfield's Gallery.

A couple of customers were in the store. One lady was looking at some of Trudy's handmade earrings, while another woman seemed to be studying one of George's larger paintings. That looked like a big sale, and I certainly wasn't going to interrupt. I waved to Trudy and pointed to the studio as I walked back. George was standing in front of an easel, stabbing paint onto a canvas. This painting was obviously in the early stages. I couldn't tell yet what it was going to be, but the laser focus in George's eyes told me the picture was already clear in his mind.

After a couple of minutes, he noticed I was standing a couple of feet away.

"Oh, hi, Halley. Can I do something for you?"

I felt a little guilty. George and Trudy were always doing something for me. They were so generous, I felt like a moocher. At that moment I quietly resolved to think up something nice I could do for them.

"There's a woman in the store seriously looking over one of your large paintings," I whispered. "Should you go talk to her as the artist to help facilitate a sale?"

"No. I always let the work speak for itself," he said, dabbing another splotch of paint onto the canvas in front of him. I was impressed by his focus—and artistic integrity.

"Do you mind if I watch you paint for a bit. I don't want to unnerve you. It's just cool to watch you create art."

"Sure. If you think it's exciting to watch paint dry," George said with his typical charm.

From the unformed background a landscape of rocks and trees began to emerge. I was mesmerized by the process and lost track of time. Trudy laid a hand on my arm, interrupting my focus on the painting and bringing me back to the present moment.

"Hey, hon. Good to see you. George, could you carry a painting out to the car for a customer," she said in a normal voice before rubbing her husband's back and whispering, "I just rang up a big sale."

She looked at me and flashed a broad smile. If George was excited, he didn't show it, but he complied with her request.

"Trudy, you guys are busy. I'll come back later."

"Don't be silly, you're always welcome. Besides, there's no one in the store as soon as George dispatches the lady with the painting."

Trudy perched on a worktable and pointed to a stool next to the easel.

"Pull up a chair and tell me what's shaking."

"My fists were shaking earlier. Detective Stedman makes me so mad I can't stand it."

"What's he done now?"

George rejoined us, leaning against the table Trudy was sitting on, just as I started recounting my conversation with the detective.

"Well, I never," Trudy said, shaking her head.

George turned red, the flush on his face rising up like mercury through a thermometer.

"I oughta go down to the station and tell the detective a thing or two."

"George, please don't. While I think he was out of line, the truth is we do know who the intruder was. And I didn't tell the detective. If he finds out, it probably won't go well for me."

"Halley has a point, hon. We just have to hope the cops don't question Edgar about the break-in. That man folds like an accordion under pressure."

# CHAPTER 26

Saturday night the Star Movie Palace had its biggest crowd to date. People arrived and started ordering coffee and wine early. Even Delores arrived early, and she was in rare form, chatting up and entertaining the customers as she manned the ticket booth. I was beginning to believe Kendra was right about the gold coin being a harbinger of good luck.

A few minutes after the movie began, Father Ben emerged from the auditorium and walked to the counter.

"Hi, Father Ben, I didn't see you come in."

"Business was booming with wine sales when I arrived. I didn't want to interrupt you. I also didn't want to stand in line," he said with a grin. "I'll have a glass of red wine, please. As much as I like your coffee, I'm afraid it might keep me awake. And I have to be at work early tomorrow, you know."

"I'm glad you're here, padre. Have you seen *Charade* before?"

"Yes, many times, in fact. It's a favorite of mine, but I've never seen it on the big screen. This is a real treat."

I served him his wine and he handed me his payment.

"Halley, I don't mean to nag, but maybe you should call your grandmother. I talked to Evelyn briefly yesterday. She's worried that you're mixed up in this murder investigation and fears bad guys are after you."

"What? Oh no, I'm afraid that's my fault. In my last e-mail I think I mentioned that Kendra and I had done a little research on the victim. Gram's imagination can go all kinds of places from there. I'm sorry she keeps pestering you."

"Not at all. And I believe I put her mind at ease. I told her Kendra has a good head on her shoulders and is just the kind of friend she'd want you to have. I also told her that Leon's dear friends, George and Trudy, have developed a parental, or grandparental, affection for you. But I think she'd still feel better if she heard from you."

"I'll e-mail her tomorrow. I promise."

"You and Kendra will be careful?"

"I promise that, too," I said.

"I should get back to the film. My favorite part is when they figure out where the treasure is hidden and realize the fortune they've been frantically searching for has been right in front of them the whole time. Thanks for the wine," Father Ben said with a smile before disappearing beyond the auditorium doors.


Sunday morning I hurried through the bell tower and into the church just after Father Ben and the altar servers started processing to the front. I bobbed down and briefly touched one knee to the tile floor, making the sign of the cross as I slipped into the next to the last pew. I felt showing up for Mass now and again was the least I could do, since my grandmother kept calling the pastor. Plus, I'd been meaning to light a candle for Uncle Leon.

I looked around the nave as I pretended to sing along with the opening hymn. It was a lovely church with carved pews, kneeling angel statues that veiled their faces with their wings on either side of the back altar and multi-hued light pouring in through stained glass windows.

Father Ben gave a nice homily about turning the water into wine, or something about wine I'm pretty sure. My mind kind of wandered. He gave me a discreet little wave as he walked past me during the recessional.

I waited a moment for the aisle to clear out before I went against the stream flowing outward and walked up near the front of the church. A niche featuring a statue of Mary had rows of votive candles in front of it, about half of them flickering. I lit a candle and closed my eyes.

"Please take care of Uncle Leon and Josh. And watch over my Gram," I whispered.

Father Ben was greeting everyone as they exited. I joined the line, along with the last few stragglers.

"Hi, Halley, so nice to see you," he said.

"Thanks. It won't be an every Sunday kind of thing," I mumbled by way of apology.

"I understand," he said. "We're always open."

I walked the several blocks from the church to Mayfield's Gallery. Trudy had called and invited me for brunch.

"Hi, hon, you're right on time," Trudy said as I let myself in through the unlocked door. "I'm just about to dish up everything."

She stepped away from the stove and gave me a quick hug.

"Pour yourself some coffee," she said, before hollering for George to come to the table. He turned off the TV and stepped in from the living room.

Trudy usually served bread from the bakery, but today she'd made homemade biscuits. She served them buttered, alongside scrambled eggs with sausage, and cheesy hash browns.

She put generous helpings of everything onto three plates and we gathered at the table.

"I went to Mass this morning. It had been quite a while, but Father Ben's been really nice. He even puts up with calls from my grandmother. She worries."

"He is a nice man. I'm not much of a churchgoer and George is a heathen. But St. Cecilia's is beautiful. We attend the occasional funeral there," Trudy said. "Feel free to give your grandmother our number."

"You should probably give us your grandmother's number, you know, for if you have an appendix attack or something like that and end up in the hospital," George said.

"That's a good point. Assuming your grandmother is the person you'd want us to call."

"Yeah, she'd be the one to call," I said.

"Kendra and I took a look at that basement wall Edgar was all fired up about. If you run your hand over it you can feel some minor indentations, but I doubt that documentary guy would get excited over it, or if it would even show up on camera."

"Maybe they could spray it with something that glows in the dark," George suggested.

"That's a brilliant idea," Trudy said with a surprised look. "Where did you come up with it?"

"I have brilliant ideas sometimes," George said. "And I watch cable."

"These biscuits are melt-in-your-mouth good. And thanks for feeding me—again. I'm afraid I take advantage of your hospitality."

"Don't be silly. We enjoy having you around. You're the grandchild I'll never have. My son is married to his job," Trudy said.

"Wait. How did I not know you and George have a son?"

"I was well past having kids by the time George and I got married. Tony is the product of my first marriage, and frankly the only good thing to come out of that union. But Tony's a good boy, calls at least once a month, visits at the holidays. He's just not interested in marriage or family. He won't even commit to a cat."

"I'm committed to a cat, but it's a one-way street. Eartha Kitty comes and goes as she pleases. That's the arrangement she had with Uncle Leon, so I have to respect it."

"As long as you keep filling her bowl, she'll keep coming back," Trudy said.

"Like me. You keep cooking wonderful meals and I'll keep showing up at your table," I said.

"We certainly hope so," Trudy said with a laugh.

"Well, I hate to eat and run, but I have a matinee today and I'd better get ready for it. Last night we had our biggest crowd yet. I'm hoping that we have good attendance again today—and that they're all thirsty."

The crowd for the two o'clock showing of *Charade* was decent for a matinee.

Shortly before the movie began a bespectacled man with graying hair and a neatly-trimmed goatee, came up to the counter and ordered a latte.

"Hi, Halley," he said shyly. "Kendra told me I should say hi. I'm Alan, by the way."

"From the library, right?"

"Yes. I'm the reference librarian. I work mostly with old books and archives, and on my days off I enjoy watching old films."

"Me, too."

Alan paid and I handed him his order. He started walking away but paused and turned back toward me.

"I just wanted to say I think you did an excellent job with the renovations. And I'm really glad because this theater is truly a local treasure," he said.

"Thank you, Alan. I'm pretty proud of it."

He nodded, casting his eyes down, and gave me a nervous

little wave before going into the auditorium.

The bad thing about early afternoon shows is, people generally don't order as much wine, which cuts into revenue. A consolation today was that near the end of the almost two-hour film, Marco dropped in.

"Hello, *cara*," he said as he approached the bar. "I had some errands in town and couldn't resist stopping by to see the lovely theater owner."

"Aw, you flatter me—but I don't mind it. Could I offer you some coffee? Or, if it's not too early for you, we serve some of the very finest wine here."

"Now you flatter me—but I don't mind," he said with a broad smile. "I wondered how you were doing and if you and Kendra were behaving. I worry."

"Kendra and I are behaving fine. But the local police have lost their minds. Did you hear about them holding Joe Chang at the jail overnight based on some lame anonymous tip? Kendra was beside herself."

"No, I hadn't heard. The police let him go? That must mean they've cleared him as a suspect."

"I don't know about that. It means they didn't have enough evidence to arrest him, but I worry the police are eager to make an arrest. I can tell you one thing: Kendra and I are more determined than ever to look for who really killed Vince Dalton, even though from everything I've heard he wasn't a very nice man."

"He was, as you say, not a very nice man. You and Kendra are much too nice to put yourselves in harm's way over him. Whoever killed that blackmailer is obviously willing to kill in order to keep their secrets safe. Please promise me you won't do anything foolish—or else," he said, trying to put on a stern face, but the unintended smile turning up the corners of his mouth and the tenderness in his eyes gave him away.

"Or else what, Mr. Carvello?"

"Or else I'll have to spend more time with you to make sure you stay safe."

"If that's a threat, you're going about it the wrong way," I said, reaching over and gently touching his sleeve.

He slid his hands across the counter and I placed my hands in his. At that exact moment, the auditorium doors flung open and people started pouring out as the credits rolled. Marco gave me a smile and walked over to the seating area.

A few customers lined up at the counter to get coffee and candies to go. Out of the corner of my eye I saw Marco lingering in the lobby, occasionally glancing my way.

A group of four were the last ones in line. They all ordered glasses of wine.

"I know the movie is over, but we have some time to kill until our dinner reservation. Would you mind if we called some other friends to join us here? We promise to buy lots of wine," one of the gentlemen said. "And don't worry, we're not driving. We're on foot and having dinner later at the hotel on the hill."

"Of course," I said, looking over to Marco. I couldn't afford to turn away paying customers.

Marco shrugged and waved before heading out.

My paying customers were true to their word. Three more friends joined them and they kept coming back for wine, and bought a few boxes of candy, as well. They were in a really good mood as they told me goodbye, promising they'd make a return visit sometime. I got busy cleaning. In a bit, I realized I'd forgotten to lock up. When I walked to the front door, I noticed Kendra pacing in front of Hidden Clue Escape Rooms, so I stepped onto the sidewalk and waved to her. She waved and jogged across the street.

"Is everything okay?" I asked. "Difficult customers?"

"The customers are fine. It's big brother who's getting on

my nerves. Bart encouraged me to get out for a while. I guess I was getting on his nerves, too," she said with shrug.

"You should take a break while Bart's around to mind the store. The weather's beautiful and we've both been cooped up inside all day, why don't we talk a walk?"

"You're right. It's too pretty not to soak up some sunshine."

I locked the door and we started strolling.

"Where should we go?" I asked.

"Let's head up toward the hotel. That way we'll be walking downhill on our way back."

"Sounds like a plan."

We pointed to a few things in shop windows, but didn't talk much as we weaved through the tourists. We reached the top of the hill, arrived at the beautifully landscaped hotel grounds and sat down together on a park bench.

"I didn't know Bart was going to be here today."

"He drove down on a whim. Simon won't be home until late tonight. How's business at the Star Movie Palace? I saw some people coming out of your establishment laughing. Looked like they were having a good time."

"Yeah, the wine was flowing pretty freely today, especially for a matinee. A bunch of people also told me they were excited to finally see *Charade* on the big screen."

"Audrey Hepburn films in general are probably a safe bet and I'm not knocking *Charade*, or anything with Cary Grant, but I lean more toward musicals or a screwball comedies. Musicals would be enough to bring Bart down for a show, too. Be sure to let me know when one of those is coming up."

"I'll do you one better. You and Bart make a list of some of your favorites. I have a bit of pull with the theater owner."

"Excellent. I'll e-mail you a *long* list."

My mind had wandered somewhere else. Suddenly I was aware of Kendra waving a hand in front of my face.

"Hello, Halley? Anybody home?"

"Sorry for spacing out. Your librarian friend, Alan, was at the show today. I see what you mean about him being a little shy. But something else about him just occurred to me."

"What's that?"

"He was privy to all the research at the library into Jesse James and buried treasure lore by Vince, Edward and you. Maybe he was Vince's partner," I proposed.

"You think Alan could be the killer? I'm having a hard time envisioning that."

"Remember how you said Alan had referred to the theater as a local treasure? He used those same words again today when he was talking to me. Maybe there is a connection to some tunnel or cavern through the theater basement. If Vince knew about it, Alan could've killed him to stake a claim for himself."

"If that's true, that could mean Edgar's life is in danger, as well," Kendra said. "I still don't see Alan as a killer, but I guess we should add him to the list of suspects."

"And in the meantime, you need to be careful what you say around him, as well as Elaine Stedman."

We stood up and wandered around the grounds, stopping by a trickling fountain near the entrance to the hotel. Once again my mind wandered.

"Halley, I've lost you again. Do you need to take a nap?"

"Oh, I'm sorry. I was just thinking about something Father Ben said to me last night about why he likes the movie *Charade* so much. He said he loved how the thing they were frantically searching for turned out to be right in front of them the whole time."

"You're wondering if there's something we know about Vince's murder that we just haven't put together?"

"Yeah, something like that."

My mind was wandering again—to a place I really didn't

want to go. I had a growing uneasiness and a terrible sense that I might know who the murderer was.

"Kendra, it's beautiful here, but I better head back. I just remembered I left laundry in the washer that I need to move over," I said, making up an excuse to leave.

"That's okay. I really should get back and check on Bart. It's been pretty busy today. I probably shouldn't leave him on his own for too long."

We walked back and parted ways at the escape rooms. Just as the streetlights came on I crossed the side street and took a seat on the bench in the pocket park, trying to gather my thoughts, pull all the jumbled pieces of the puzzle together. What was it Father Ben had said? *It was right there in front of them the whole time.*

Only now, it was right in front of *me*.

# CHAPTER 27

When I talked to Marco earlier he had referred to Vince as a blackmailer. But I was absolutely certain I'd never mentioned anything about blackmail to him—I'd promised George and Trudy I wouldn't. And I knew it hadn't been in the newspaper, either. I wasn't even sure if the police knew about it. How could he know?

Something else was there, too. What was it?

On opening night, Marco was behind the bar. He was in a perfect position to slip something into a drink without being seen. And I had been writing the customers' names on the coffee cups as I made them and set them out for pick up on the side bar, making it easy to identify his target.

The autopsy report had shown evidence of Cracker Jacks and coffee, along with a lethal dose of some prescription heart medicine in Vince's stomach contents. And Marco's dad has a heart condition. Marco mentioned it at the winery when his dad was pouring on the charm for me.

Why would he want to kill Vince? It didn't make sense.

I kept running it over in my head. I needed to be sure before I mentioned it to anyone. The whole idea was crazy, wasn't it? There had to be a perfectly reasonable explanation.

I let myself in through the front of the theater and walked to the back. I needed to vacuum, but that could wait. I ran up the stairs and entered my apartment, half-dazed.

I looked up and gasped.

"Marco," I said, struggling to breathe. I could feel myself trembling.

There he was standing in my kitchen next to a board of chopped onions and tomatoes, holding a large knife. He lay the knife down and took a step toward me.

I jumped back a step.

"Halley, I'm sorry. I wanted to surprise you, but I certainly didn't mean to startle you."

I tried to steady my breathing and act normal.

"Well, you did. I'm used to coming home to an empty apartment, except when my cat decides to visit."

Eartha slinked over and rubbed against my leg before leaping onto the recliner and curling up on top of the headrest.

"How did you get in?"

"Trudy gave me the key. Please don't be upset with her. I talked her into it. I wanted to surprise you by making a spaghetti dinner for us. I'm a pretty good cook by the way."

When he took a couple of steps in my direction I nearly jumped out of my skin. I forced a smile, but the fear in my eyes had betrayed me.

"I slipped up earlier today, didn't I?"

"What are you talking about?"

"Don't try to play coy, *cara*. You have a lovely face, but it's not a poker face. Please understand that Vince Dalton left me no choice."

"He had been blackmailing some people into selling their businesses. He wasn't trying to buy the winery, was he?"

"No, but once he saw how lucrative his little blackmail sideline could be, he didn't mind expanding his circle of terror. My father isn't perfect, but he is a good man. His family, and his reputation, mean everything to him. I wasn't about to let the likes of Vince Dalton drag my family's good name through the gutter.

"My dad wasn't born Rafe Carvello. He grew up as Ralph Carver in Brooklyn. He'd learned some Italian, spending a lot of time at his Italian neighbor's home while his mom worked. He worked hard to climb his way out of a poor neighborhood, married my mom, had me. But then he had some tough breaks financially. Finally, through a series of fortunate events, you might say, he won some money at the casinos and had a chance to reinvent himself. He spent a bit of time in Italy and eventually ended up here as respected winemaker Rafe Carvello, living his dream life. And Dalton thought he could take that all away. My dad had already paid that scumbag, and he came back for more money. I knew he'd never stop coming back, unless someone stopped him."

My heart was pounding so violently I felt bruised from the inside. Marco had killed Vince—and I was his next victim.

*Stall, Halley. Stay calm. Keep him talking.*

"Why did you decide to kill him at the theater? Were you trying to frame me by putting the drug in the coffee?" I choked the words out, my throat as dry as dust.

"You may not believe this, but I didn't plan it. I'd entertained plenty of murderous thoughts about Dalton, but I had no plan as to how or when. The night of the opening, an opportunity just presented itself, as if it were predestined.

"I had picked up my dad's heart medicine at the pharmacy before coming to the theater because I knew they'd be closed after the show. I told the guy at the drug store I didn't need a bag and just stuck the pill bottle in my pocket. Did you know cardiovascular drugs are the second most common cause of all fatal overdoses?

"I knew that too much of the medicine could be deadly. The doctor had cautioned us, and I read up about it online so I'd understand more about the prescription and how it might affect my dad.

"I had no idea Dalton would be at the theater. Then suddenly there he was, standing in line at the counter. I stepped to the side and quickly crushed up the pills. I worried they might not dissolve in the wine. Then I heard him order coffee, a hot liquid to dissolve the pills. I saw his name written in marker on the side of the cup. I walked over to get more wineglasses from beneath the counter and dumped the powder formed by the crushed pills into his cup as I leaned over. It was almost too easy."

Marco had slowly made his way from the kitchen area into the living room.

"We could've been good together, Halley. Dad really liked you. He's never liked any of the women I've gone out with before. But you just wouldn't let go, even after I gave the cops another suspect to get you off the hook."

"You put the prescription pills in Joe's car?"

Marco didn't reply. Instead he pulled a scarf out of his pocket and wound a length of it around each of his hands, pulling the fabric taut. He inched toward me and I stepped behind the recliner, as if that would provide protection. I could scream, but who would hear me? My eyes darted around looking for a weapon, but there was nothing within reach. Eartha Kitty, catnapping on the top of the recliner, must have sensed my fear. She suddenly leapt at Marco with a ferocious growl and dug her skillful mouse-hunting claws into his face.

I bolted out the door that hadn't completely closed when I came in, scrambled down the stairs to the back door and hit the alley in a dead run. My legs instinctively started running to George and Trudy's, although it probably would've been smarter to round the building in the other direction and flee into the lighted, well-populated main street.

I never heard Marco's footsteps behind me and never turned around to look for him, but a chill down my spine told me he was in pursuit. When I made it to the cross street, suddenly a man's hand grabbed my arm and pulled me toward the side of the building. I twisted against his stronghold, struggling to escape.

"Halley, it's Joe."

I spun around to face him as he quietly said, "What's wrong?"

Relief and terror coursed through me in equal parts.

"Joe, hurry inside the restaurant," I said in a panicked whisper. I grasped his hand and he followed along as I ran down the side of the block, across the street and into Jade Garden. Once inside, he led me down the hallway and into the office.

"What's going on? Who are you running from?" he asked as he closed the door. I reached past him and turned the lock before taking a deep breath and collapsing into the desk chair.

"Marco. He admitted to me that he killed Vince. Now he wants to shut me up for keeps."

"We have to call the cops."

I picked up the receiver on the desk phone.

"The line's dead," I said, holding the phone to my ear. I patted my pocket. "And my cell phone is under the counter at the theater."

"My cell's dead. I forgot to charge it—again," Joe said.

The lights went out and a cacophony of voices speaking English and Chinese rang out in the restaurant, and a few seconds later the crash of breaking glass as a fist punched through the glass panel in the office door just behind Joe.

Dimly illuminated by emergency lights in the hallway, I could see Marco's hulking figure. He wrapped his arm around Joe's neck. Joe freed himself, dropping down to a squat and stabbing his elbow upward into Marco's stomach as he shot up from the kneeling position. Marco doubled over briefly then lunged at Joe. I grabbed the desk phone and slammed it into the side of Marco's head as hard as I could.

He reached out and grabbed my leg as he fell to his knees before collapsing forward.

Bright flashlights blinded my eyes as a familiar and humorless voice said, "Okay, everybody, hands up where I can see them," just as the house lights came back on.

In a moment, Detective Stedman came lumbering up behind Officer Stone.

"What's going on here, Mr. Chang?"

I jumped in. It might've been Joe's restaurant, but this was my party.

"Marco Carvello killed Vince Dalton. He told me so just before he tried to strangle me."

"That so," the detective said doubtfully. "Did he happen to say why he killed him?"

"Yes, he did," I said, trying not to show how ticked off I was at the moment. "He said Vince was blackmailing his dad. And after his father had already paid him, Vince demanded more money."

"I see," Detective Stedman said, pulling his notepad out of his pocket and jotting down a note as if he were making a grocery list, completely ignoring the semi-conscious man at his feet. We could tell he was alive from the moaning, but there was a possibility he needed medical treatment. Not that I was all that concerned about his health, since he'd planned to kill me. But it seemed to me the cops should have expressed some interest. Officer Stone finally put away her sidearm and knelt down to take a closer look at Marco. She talked into the microphone clipped to her collar and said, "Send an ambulance to Jade Garden."

I was in disbelief as Detective Stedman stood silent, staring at his notebook. Joe jumped in.

"Detective, I bumped into Halley as she was running out of

the alley, terrified. She said Marco was chasing her and we hurried in here and locked the office door. The lights went out, Marco broke the glass in the door, came in and jumped me. I punched him in the gut and Halley clocked him in the head with the desk phone. Then you showed up. By the way, how did you know to show up? When we went to call the police, the phones were dead."

"Officer Stone was in line at the takeout counter when the lights went out. She heard breaking glass and then overheard an employee tell Mrs. Chang there might be a robbery in progress. I was waiting in the car when the officer radioed me about the situation," he said in his droning monotone voice.

Only Detective Stedman could make the takedown of a murderer sound boring. I bet his ghost stories around the campfire have the scare factor of a bed sheet flapping on a clothesline.

"Um, hello, Detective? Here's the guy who killed Vince Dalton, tried to kill me and just attacked Joe. And you're standing there like you're waiting to be seated for dinner."

He glanced up at me briefly before scribbling something in his little notebook.

It was a long few minutes before the EMTs arrived and loaded a still addled Marco onto a stretcher. Officer Stone handcuffed him to the gurney and accompanied him as the EMTs wheeled him out.

# CHAPTER 28

Joe and I went down to the police station to give statements. It was late by the time I emerged from the interview room. George was waiting for me in the area by the front desk.

"Trudy insists you're staying at our place tonight. Told me not to come home without you, so don't get me in trouble with the missus by saying no. By the way, I think she's right."

I'd held it together pretty well until then, mostly because I was in shock, I think. But hot tears began to roll down my cheeks. I leaned into George's shoulder as he wrapped an arm around me.

"Okay, kiddo, let's get out of this joint."

We got into George's car and drove the few blocks to their place. I thought about having him stop by the apartment to pick up a few things, but I just couldn't face the specter of the spaghetti sauce Marco had been preparing. And the raw emotions of everything else that had happened tonight.

"By the way, Joe was waiting for you when I arrived. He didn't think you should be on your own. I told him Trudy and I would take care of that."

Trudy was waiting for us in the kitchen when we arrived. After a tearful hug, she said, "Let me heat up some meatloaf for you, hon. You'll sleep better with something in your stomach."

"Thank you, but I'm too tired to eat."

"I understand. I'll fix you a big breakfast in the morning."

Trudy had made up the sofa bed for me. An oversized t-shirt was lying on my pillow.

"There's a fresh towel and washcloth laid out for you in the bathroom, and an unopened toothbrush courtesy of George's dentist."

I crawled into bed and quickly drifted into a dreamless sleep. I awoke to the smell of bacon and coffee, and the sound of George complaining.

"Did you see this? Those blood-sucking leeches on the city board are proposing a tax hike—again."

"George, shush. You'll wake up Halley."

Hearing them squabble was somehow comforting. The aroma of bacon might have had something to do with it, too.

I dressed and went in the kitchen. George brought me coffee and orange juice. And Trudy served me a plate of pancakes arranged in the shape of a bunny, with a medium pancake for the head, a larger pancake for the chubby body, smaller ovals for the feet and elongated ovals for the ears, with a scoop of butter where the tail should be. Of course, she served it with syrup and a side of bacon. I gave them both an appreciative smile.

"Y'all are so good to me. Thanks for letting me stay over. I just wasn't quite ready to face the apartment last night."

"Hon, you've been through a lot and you're welcome to sleep on our sofa for as many nights as you need," Trudy said.

"What she said. Plus if you're on the sofa, Trudy can't kick me out of bed and make me sleep there."

"Oh, when have I ever?" Trudy said, swatting at George with her napkin.

We ate in silence for a few minutes. George jumped up to refill my coffee before my cup was empty.

"As he was leaving the station, Joe told me the gist of what happened last night leading up to Marco's arrest, but said he didn't know the details of what happened before you ran into him in the alley. Do you want to tell us what happened?"

"If you're not up to talking about it, it's okay, hon," Trudy said.

I hesitated a moment.

"I was so scared," I said, my voice quavering. "I'd just worked it out that Marco must be the killer, and I was struggling to wrap my head around that when I walked into the apartment and found him standing in my kitchen making spaghetti."

"So, he's the one who made that mess—which I cleaned up, by the way. After Mrs. Chang called us, I sent George down to the police station to wait for you and I ran up to check on the apartment."

"Marco said he wanted to cook dinner for me, and that you had let him in so he could surprise me."

"He said *I* had let him in? I would never let anyone into your apartment without your permission."

"I figured as much. He was really there because he knew he'd made a slip of the tongue earlier during the matinee when he referred to Vince as a blackmailer. I had told Marco about Kendra's buried treasure theory and the boot, but I never once mentioned blackmail. What he had said didn't hit me until later. Then other pieces started falling into place, like Marco being behind the bar on opening night. And the autopsy finding evidence of some heart medicine mixed in with the coffee in Vince's stomach contents. I also remembered Marco mentioning that his dad has a heart condition.

"When I saw him in my apartment, I tried to play it cool. But, as he pointed out, I don't have a poker face. I practically jumped out of my skin when he took a step toward me. He admitted to me that he killed Vince. Told me Vince had blackmailed his dad and had even come back for more money after his dad paid him off. As he was telling me everything, I knew he intended to kill me."

"Oh, Halley. I've got a knot in my stomach just thinking about it. Did he come at you with that big knife he was using to chop vegetables?"

"No. That's what I assumed he was planning to do. But then he reached in his pocket and pulled out a scarf and started winding it around his hands. He was going to strangle me.

"Eartha was lying on the top of the recliner in front of me. She must have, I don't know, sensed my fear. She suddenly leapt claws first at Marco's face, and I took off running for my life."

My breathing was labored just remembering how terrified I'd been. Trudy got up and stood beside my chair, wrapping her arms around me and cradling my head against her chest. I leaned into her embrace, both our bodies shaking as we sobbed. I caught a glimpse of George dabbing a napkin to the corner of his eye.

The tears subsided and Trudy gave my shoulders a final squeeze before letting go. The three of us lingered over another cup of coffee before I decided it was time to go home. They offered to go with me.

"I'm happy to spend the night on your sofa tonight, if you'd like," Trudy said.

"Thank you, but honestly I'm not afraid to be in the apartment, knowing Marco is locked up. Plus, I have an attack cat, you know."

"All right, hon. If you change your mind all you have to do is call. And don't worry about the hour. Oh, and be sure your windows are locked. I noticed one of them was open when I went by last night, so I closed it. That's probably how Marco got in—up the fire escape and through the window," Trudy said.

After walking the few blocks home, I entered through the alley door, but headed straight to the lobby, remembering I had left my cell phone under the counter. It was almost dead and showed two missed calls from Kendra. I needed a little time to myself before I went through the details of the previous night again, so I went upstairs.

Despite my brave front with Trudy and George, I hesitated before turning the doorknob to the apartment. I was grateful Trudy had cleared away everything and washed up the dishes. But the vision of Marco standing in the kitchen and the glint off the large knife were still sharp in my mind. I took a deep breath, walked to the kitchen and grabbed a Red Stone beer from the fridge as a way of reclaiming this territory for myself. This was my home, and I wasn't going to let Marco rob me of that. I sat down and leaned back in the recliner, raising my bottle to Derek before taking a big swig. I pulled my nearly drained cell phone from my pocket, reached over and plugged it into the charger on the side table. Then I closed my eyes and tears began to roll down my face again.

I didn't know why I was crying. I truly wasn't afraid anymore. After puzzling over it for a few minutes I realized I was grieving. Grieving the loss of the relationship I had thought was beginning to blossom with Marco. Grieving that I never had a chance to know Uncle Leon. And grieving that I couldn't talk about everything I was feeling with Josh. I guess coming up against your own mortality stirs a lot of emotions. After a good cry I gave Kendra a call.

"I talked to Joe. I'm really glad you spent the night at George and Trudy's. How are you?"

"I'm going to be okay, but I'm really tired. Do you mind if we don't talk about last night? I told it all to the cops. And I went through it all again with George and Trudy. If you want the scoop you can talk to Trudy."

"I understand. Do you want some company? We can talk about anything you like, or about nothing. I suck at gin rummy, so we can play cards and you can win," she said.

"I appreciate the offer—and I'll remember that if we're ever playing for money—but if you don't mind I think I just want to be alone for a while. I'm going to curl up and watch some old movies."

"Sounds good. Call me later if you want."

After thumbing through a box of DVDs and ruling out *Dial M for Murder* and *Roman Holiday*, I flipped on the TV. The old movie channel was running a marathon of The Three Stooges and I decided that would be perfect.

# CHAPTER 29

I had taken Monday off as a day of recuperation—and bereavement. But I resolved that today the pity party was over. I had a new life in Utopia Springs and a business to run. I washed my face, tamed my hair and even slapped on a bit of makeup. After dressing in a black top and black jeans, I gave myself a once-over in the full-length mirror on the bathroom door.

Not bad, I thought.

As I jogged down the stairs and out to the lobby, it occurred to me I should come up with a logo—and a proper name—for the coffee bar and print it on t-shirts, like Kendra had done with the Hidden Clue Escape Rooms logo.

While I got things ready for service behind the counter I mulled over names for the coffee bar.

*Star Palace Coffee Bar? Too long. Palace Coffee Bar? Maybe. Café Cinema? Hmm, I like the sound of that.*

At about five till eight I was still weighing name options when someone tapped against the glass on the front door. I hurried over, ready to greet customers. I was a little let down, and frankly annoyed, to see Detective Stedman peering at me from the other side of the glass. I unlocked the door anyway.

"Good morning, Detective," I said, turning and walking back to the bar as soon as I'd let him in.

"Good morning, Ms. Greer. I know I'm probably not your favorite person due to the somewhat adversarial nature of our conversations since you arrived."

*Somewhat?*

"But I'm hoping we can make a fresh start now, if you're open to that. Utopia Springs is a small town, after all. We're bound to run into each other. I hope we can be...neighborly."

The stern-faced detective was actually smiling. That was a first. So I returned the favor.

"Okay, Detective. I understand you were just doing your job. And with the stress of the murder investigation I wasn't exactly at my best or most neighborly either. What kind of coffee would you like? It's on the house."

"No, no, I'll pay. I don't know that much about coffee. I like it strong, so maybe an espresso?"

"An espresso shot coming right up."

I made and handed him his coffee and he paid for it.

"This tastes good."

"Thanks, it's what I know. I don't want to spoil our fresh start, Detective, but maybe you could tell me one thing I don't know that's been bothering me."

"If I can," he said noncommittally.

"Marco indicated that he tried to frame Joe to take me off the radar for the police and, let's face it, to help himself, too. But why did he pick on Joe?"

"Joe was in the perfect position to get set up. Marco, of course, knew Joe was here opening night, and that he left the theater a couple of times. He knew Joe's dad had a heart attack last year, and he likely knew Joe's sister is in pharmacy school."

"Ah, of course."

"But anonymous tips always give me indigestion. Plus, we couldn't come up with any motive for Joe to kill Vince. And the pills were in Joe's glove compartment, but his fingerprints weren't on the baggie. In fact, there weren't any fingerprints on it. Why would he wipe off the fingerprints then leave the pills in his glove box? It would've been easy to just toss the pills in a drain or flush them down the toilet. The whole thing seemed a little too convenient."

I started to ask why they locked Joe up overnight when it seemed so bogus, but I decided not to tarnish our new good neighbor policy.

"Thanks, Detective."

"There are some things I could ask you. Some things I'm pretty sure you knew but didn't tell me that could've saved us both some trouble."

I started to speak, but he cut me off, holding his hand up like a traffic cop stopping traffic.

"Don't worry, I'm not going to ask. I get that you were new in town and in a difficult situation. I hope we can foster the kind of neighborly relationship that will make you feel you can talk to me next time."

"Next time? The murder rate in Utopia Springs is super low, right?"

"No, no, I don't mean murder," he said with a laugh. "Just little problems that sometimes arise."

The door opened and some tourists, easily identified by their fanny packs and souvenir t-shirts, walked in. Detective Stedman finished off his coffee and rose from the barstool.

"I'll see you around, Ms. Greer," he said as he turned to leave.

"Call me Halley," I said to his back and he shot me a little wave over his shoulder.

After morning coffee service was over, I felt a need to stay busy, and I truly wanted to show appreciation to my new friends. I wasn't sure if a party was exactly appropriate, but I certainly wasn't going to hold a wake for Vince—or Marco. I did want to thank the dear, wonderful people who had been there for me during a tough time, so I decided to call it a gathering instead of a party. To accommodate Kendra's schedule, I set it for eight thirty Wednesday night.

I quickly made up some cute theater-themed invitations on the computer and printed them out on cardstock. I hand-delivered invitations to Kendra, Joe, and the Mayfields and e-mailed one to Bart.

I walked over to Ozark Trail and Stream to invite Nick. He politely declined the invitation, mumbling some excuse about needing to catch up on things.

"If you finish up work in time, please come on over." I said, leaving his invitation on the counter.

I spent the rest of the afternoon making arrangements for my not-really-a-party party.

The lobby of the Star Movie Palace is a fabulous entertaining space.

*Maybe I could rent it out for private parties on non-movie nights.*

Wednesday morning after closing up the coffee bar, I went shopping and bought party supplies along with some beer— Uncle Leon's favorite brand—and a variety of liquors for cocktails. No Carvello wine. Mr. Carvello's assistant had called to inform me they would be discontinuing our arrangement— which was probably for the best. I planned to approach one of the other wineries to see if we could come to a similar agreement.

I ordered several appetizers from Jade Garden, including their delicious spring rolls and crab Rangoon. I argued with Ling when she refused to accept payment for the order, but she said I'd have to take it up with her boss. Joe had told her it was on the house.

Joe was the first to arrive for out little get-together just before eight thirty and I gave him grief about not accepting my money.

"Hey, Joe, you should let me support my favorite local

restaurant. It's the least I can do after luring a killer into your office," I said.

"Are you kidding me? I'm getting so much mileage out of this. My mom and dad are bragging to everyone that their son is a hero who captured a dangerous killer twice his size by wrestling the villain to the floor and holding him until the police arrived."

"All that is true," I said.

"Yeah, it kind of leaves out the part where you knocked Marco semi-conscious and the cops arrived like a minute later," he said with a laugh.

"Joe," I said, touching his arm, "you are a hero. I was terrified, running for my life, and you were there for me. Thank you."

"By the way, the phone company finally got the landline working again today," Joe said, eager to change the subject from any talk of him as a hero. "Cutting the phone line to the restaurant wasn't the worst crime Marco committed by any means, but it was still inconvenient."

"I'm glad everything is in working order again."

Within minutes the whole gang had gathered, minus Nick. I had set up the alcohol on one side of the counter and a buffet along the other side of the theater's L-shaped bar.

"Bart, would you do the honors of mixing some fancy cocktails? Kendra tells me you're a master bartender," I said.

"I should be. I worked my way through college tending bar."

"In that case, I'll have a have a martini—very dry," Trudy said, affecting an aristocratic tone.

"The rest of us placed our drink orders.

"Eat up, everyone, there's plenty of food, courtesy of Jade Garden," I said.

"Yeah, but remember you'll probably be hungry again in an

hour," Joe said with a mischievous grin.

Kendra groaned. "I've never found that old joke about Chinese food to be true."

"George is always hungry again in an hour no matter what kind of food he eats," Trudy said as George piled food onto his plate.

After we'd settled comfortably in the lounge area with drinks on nearby tables and plates balanced on our laps, I turned to George.

"Other than what I experienced first-hand, all I know about the case is what I read in the newspaper. Have you heard any details from your friends in high places?"

"Word is when the cops searched Marco's rooms at 'the villa,'" George said, rolling his eyes as he made air quotes around the word "villa," "they discovered evidence Vince had been using to blackmail people, which I assume included Edgar and Linda and probably some other folks. But there was zilch about Marco or his dad. Apparently, Marco had already destroyed that evidence."

"I'm happy that Edgar's and Linda's blackmail secrets seem to be safe. There was nothing about it in the *Utopia Springs Sentinel*," I said.

"We may never know the whole story, but the police have a solid case against Marco for Dalton's murder, as well as attempted murder against you. Losing it and going after you and Joe like that at the restaurant sealed the case against him," George said.

"A toast to Halley, Uncle Leon—and to that ferocious feline, Eartha Kitty," Bart said, raising his glass.

"Here, here," Trudy said.

"Believe me, Eartha will be getting lots of treats and attention. Maybe I can even persuade her to be more of a house kitty," I said.

"Trust me, a leopard—or a calico—isn't likely to change its spots, so don't waste your time trying to change someone. I learned that a *long* time ago," Trudy said, looking at George.

"What could you possibly want to change about me," he said, eliciting a big smile from his wife as he batted his eyelashes and waggled his out-of-control eyebrows.

"You lovebirds remind me that I need to get home to Simon. He should be back from Tulsa by now."

"How much have you had to drink? Are you okay to drive?" Kendra asked.

"I just had one small drink and plenty of food. It's only an hour's drive, little sister. It's not like I'm driving all the way to *Florida*."

I caught the reference to Kendra's taboo spring break trip, and she and I shared a knowing smile.

"Wait. Bart, before you go, there's something I wanted to say to all of you. I can never thank y'all enough for the way you rallied to help me through all the craziness after the vandalism, and especially after the murder. When I inherited the theater I thought I was moving here to start a new business. I never expected to find a family. But that's exactly how I feel about each of you."

I went misty and the group closed in and crushed me with hugs.

# CHAPTER 30

After everyone else had said their goodnights, Kendra helped me carry some leftovers and serving platters upstairs.

"I'm too hyped up to sleep. Can I hang out here for a while?"

"Kendra, I don't know why I couldn't bring myself to tell George that Rafe Carvello isn't from Italy. I guess it's like what you and I had talked about before. How everyone is entitled to a bit of reinvention. Like Edgar and his British persona."

"And Eliza Doolittle's transformation," Kendra said.

"Exactly. And me as a theater owner."

"No, not like you. You're still who you are. You've just moved into the next chapter of your life. But speaking of the theater and your next chapter, there's something I'd like to give you."

Kendra pulled a little velvet pouch from her pocket and shook a shiny pile of something into her palm.

"By the way, that gold coin you found in the basement is an early twentieth century Indian Head Quarter Eagle, currently worth about three hundred bucks. I hope you don't mind that I took the liberty of having Trudy polish it up and make the gold piece into a necklace," she said holding it up. "The chain belonged to my mom."

"Oh, Kendra, it's beautiful. I'll get another chain for it. I can't possibly accept—"

"No, no. I have lots of my mom's jewelry. I want you to have this. Here, let me put it on you."

She placed it around my neck and fastened the clasp. I ran over and admired it in the bathroom mirror.

"It's gorgeous," I said, touching the coin that lay against my skin.

"It's part of the theater—and a legacy from your uncle. I think you should wear it as a good luck charm."

"I will. And it's a good luck charm because I'm lucky enough to have a friend like you."

I gave her a little hug then tried to move on before we both started bawling. I'd shed more than enough tears in the past few days.

"I'm going to have a beer chaser to follow those fancy drinks Bart made at the party. You want one?" I asked.

"Might as well."

We sat down on the sofa and took a drink of our beers.

"You know I'm actually getting used to your uncle's skunky beer. Not sure what that says about me?"

"It says you have a sophisticated palate," I said.

"That must be it."

"Looking back, I see now that Marco only asked me out after I mentioned that you and I were investigating the murder. He just wanted to keep tabs on what we found out and make sure it wouldn't point the cops in his direction. I have absolutely no judgment when it comes to men. First the plantation owner's son, and then the vineyard owner's son. I guess what that says about me is that I'm a complete idiot."

"You are not an idiot. Sounds like you just need to avoid men involved in agriculture."

We both started laughing and I leaned my head back with a sigh. Looking up I said, "My love life may be out of control, but one male I do have control over is Derek. While you're here would you help me take him down?

"I thought you'd decided to keep him."

"Oh, I'm keeping him all right. I just thought he might look better positioned somewhere else on the wall. It seems kind of odd having him up over the door frame like that."

"I see what you mean," Kendra said, gazing up at the deer trophy mounted above the bedroom door. She moved a chair from the dining table and set it in front of the doorway.

"I'll take Derek down and hold him in different spots on the wall and you can decide where you like him best."

"Sounds like a plan. We can re-hang him and worry about patching the holes later."

She stepped onto the chair, reached up and grabbed Derek by both sides of his neck. Suddenly his head swung out from the board it was mounted to.

We both gasped.

"That's strange," Kendra said, peering into the back of the head. "This looks old school."

"What does that mean?" I asked.

"There's a wire frame and paper maché inside. The more modern method would be to have polyurethane foam inside the mount. Wait a minute...this is just a reproduction."

"Are you saying Derek's a fake?"

"As fake as Edgar's accent. Actually, he's a safe," Kendra said, pulling an envelope from the inside of the head and holding it up.

"You mean, there's a hidden compartment in there?"

"Yep." Kendra stepped down from her perch, walked over and held the envelope out to me.

My hands trembled as I took the envelope and sat down in one of the dining chairs as Kendra joined me at the table. I shook a stack of photographs out of the envelope and fanned them out on the table.

There was a picture of eight-year-old me standing in front

of a television holding my Pokémon Pikachu doll, and one of my brother Josh and me playing in our backyard around that same time. Then there were a series of pictures, recent pictures of me walking down the sidewalk in Nashville, and other candid shots of me behind the counter at the coffee bar where I'd worked there.

After a quiet moment of disbelief I turned to Kendra.

"What do you think these photos mean? Do you think Uncle Leon hired Vince, or some other private investigator to locate me?"

Kendra picked up and leafed through the pictures.

"We'll probably never know the whole story. But one thing's for sure. You may not have thought much about your Uncle Leon since you were eight years old. But it seems he never forgot you."

# AUTHOR'S NOTE

Jesse James is as much a legend as a historical figure. He and his gang reportedly hid stolen loot at various times and places in the Ozark Mountains. Cryptic carved symbols discovered on cave and cliff walls have been attributed to the James gang. Jesse and Frank James were known to have visited step-grandparents who lived about fifteen miles from Eureka Springs. The house is still standing and was used as a location in the 1994 movie, *Frank and Jesse*, starring Rob Lowe.

Café Cinema's Utopia Springs is a fictional town inspired by the charming tourist town of Eureka Springs, Arkansas. My husband and I have traveled to Eureka Springs a few times and thoroughly enjoyed our visits. I hope I've captured a bit of its true charm in this book. (Learn more about this inspirational city at: www.eurekasprings.org).

Book Clubs and Sisters in Crime Chapters may contact Vickie about scheduling an event via FaceTime, Skype, or Facebook Live at: vickie@vickiefee.com.

— Vickie Fee

# READER'S DISCUSSION GUIDE

Halley's life takes an unexpected turn when she inherits a movie theater from a great uncle she met only once as a child. She refers to becoming the owner of a movie theater as a dream that she never remembered having—that was coming true, nonetheless. Has what could be called serendipity or fate ever played a role in your life? How would you describe it?

*My Fair Latte* is a blend of mystery, humor and a little romance. Do you feel the book achieves the right balance of those elements?

Utopia Springs is a small Southern town, population-wise (about 2,200). But as a tourist town with a half-million visitors a year, it has many more and varied kinds of businesses than the typical small town. What did you think of the setting and do you think it works well for the story and characters in the book?

Which character did you like/relate to the most?

Making friends in a new place can sometimes be difficult. Halley had the advantage that her late uncle's friends were keen to help her, prompted by their affection for Uncle Leon. Have you ever moved to a place where you didn't know anyone? What helped you make friends/feel that you belonged? Does a pet help a new space feel like home for you?

The cast in *My Fair Latte* is inter-generational. Kendra is about Halley's age, but George and Trudy are old enough to be her grandparents. (One of my dearest friends is twenty years older than me.) Have you had friends much older or younger than you? What do you think the age difference brings to the friendship? Why do you think Halley may have been especially drawn to these older friends?

Reinvention is a theme in the book. Some of it is a matter of organic change and personal growth and some is calculated. What do you think of someone reinventing themselves and their image? Do you approve of someone reinventing themselves in the way Edgar did?

If you were casting a movie version of the book, which actors would you choose to play these characters?

Did you have a favorite scene in the book? If so, why was it your favorite?

It's Halley's personal quest to find out more about Uncle Leon. She feels a connection to him, despite the fact she never had a chance to know him. Have you ever wished you could find out more or tried to learn more about your family or ancestors? What made you want to seek out that information, and how did you feel once you found it?

*Vickie Fee*

A decade ago, author Vickie Fee moved from Memphis on the banks of the muddy Mississippi River to Marquette on the shores of chilly Lake Superior, taking her accent, her sense of humor, and her recipe for Jack Daniels whiskey balls with her. She pens fun cozy mysteries with sassy Southern heroines. *My Fair Latte* is the first book in her new Café Cinema series. When she's not dawdling on social media and swilling coffee, you can find Vickie at www.vickiefee.com and in the coop at www.chicksonthecase.com.

**The Café Cinema Mystery Series
by Vickie Fee**

MY FAIR LATTE (#1)

**Henery Press Mystery Books**

And finally, before you go...
Here are a few other mysteries
you might enjoy:

# A MUDDIED MURDER

Wendy Tyson

## A Greenhouse Mystery (#1)

When Megan Sawyer gives up her big-city law career to care for her grandmother and run the family's organic farm and café, she expects to find peace and tranquility in her scenic hometown of Winsome, Pennsylvania. Instead, her goat goes missing, rain muddies her fields, the town denies her business permits, and her family's Colonial-era farm sucks up the remains of her savings.

Just when she thinks she's reached the bottom of the rain barrel, Megan and the town's hunky veterinarian discover the local zoning commissioner's battered body in her barn. Now Megan's thrust into the middle of a murder investigation—and she's the chief suspect. Can Megan dig through small-town secrets, local politics, and old grievances in time to find a killer before that killer strikes again?

Available at booksellers nationwide and online

Visit www.henerypress.com for details

# MURDER AT THE PALACE

Margaret Dumas

## A Movie Palace Mystery (#1)

Welcome to the Palace movie theater! Now Showing: Philandering husbands, ghostly sidekicks, and a murder or two.

When Nora Paige's movie-star husband leaves her for his latest co-star, she flees Hollywood to take refuge in San Francisco at the Palace, a historic movie theater that shows the classic films she loves. There she finds a band of misfit film buffs who care about movies (almost) as much as she does.

She also finds some shady financial dealings and the body of a murdered stranger. Oh, and then there's Trixie, the lively ghost of a 1930's usherette who appears only to Nora and has a lot to catch up on. With the help of her new ghostly friend, can Nora catch the killer before there's another murder at the Palace?

Available at booksellers nationwide and online

Visit www.henerypress.com for details

# MURDER ON A SILVER PLATTER

Shawn Reilly Simmons

## A Red Carpet Catering Mystery (#1)

Penelope Sutherland and her Red Carpet Catering company just got their big break as the on-set caterer for an upcoming blockbuster. But when she discovers a dead body outside her house, Penelope finds herself in hot water. Things start to boil over when serious accidents threaten the lives of the cast and crew. And when the film's star, who happens to be Penelope's best friend, is poisoned, the entire production is nearly shut down.

Threats and accusations send Penelope out of the frying pan and into the fire as she struggles to keep her company afloat. Before Penelope can dish up dessert, she must find the killer or she'll be the one served up on a silver platter.

Available at booksellers nationwide and online

Visit www.henerypress.com for details

# PILLOW STALK

Diane Vallere

## A Madison Night Mystery (#1)

Interior Decorator Madison Night might look like a throwback to the sixties, but as business owner and landlord, she proves that independent women can have it all. But when a killer targets women dressed in her signature style—estate sale vintage to play up her resemblance to fave actress Doris Day—what makes her unique might make her dead.

The local detective connects the new crime to a twenty-year old cold case, and Madison's long-trusted contractor emerges as the leading suspect. As the body count piles up, Madison uncovers a Soviet spy, a campaign to destroy all Doris Day movies, and six minutes of film that will change her life forever.

Available at booksellers nationwide and online

Visit www.henerypress.com for details

CPSIA information can be obtained
at www.ICGtesting.com
Printed in the USA
LVHW011630240220
648020LV00015B/1038

9 781635 115796